DO WAH DIDDY DIE

PAULINE BAIRD JONES

ABOUT THE BOOK

She came home for a wedding. She found bullets, secrets, and a detective who was not prepared for her.

Luci Seymour returns to New Orleans hoping to uncover the one truth her unconventional family refuses to reveal: the identity of her father.

But her aunts aren't talking.

Detective Mickey Ross likes order, routine, and cases that make sense. Picking up his future in-law from the airport should have been simple.

Then someone starts shooting.

Suddenly, Mickey and Luci are pulled into a dangerous search for answers, where every clue leads deeper into Luci's hidden past—and closer to whoever wants that past buried for good.

As danger escalates and sparks fly, Luci and Mickey

must survive family secrets, lethal attacks, and the unpredictable rhythm of the Big Easy.

Do Wah Diddy Die blends romantic suspense, mystery, humor, and New Orleans chaos into a fast-paced story where love, laughter, and danger collide.

1

An ancient radio was scratching out a Sousa march when Fern Smith unlocked the door of the seedy hotel room and found Donald posing in front of the cracked mirror with an AK-47 held at a military angle across his chest and a bandanna knotted around his mostly bald head. His long thin neck merged into plump jowls, making his head an uncertain rectangle, with the wispy remains of his hair trailing around three sides. A hang-dog expression adorned the fourth side. His puny shoulders were jaunty and self-satisfaction gleamed from close-set eyes as he regarded the speckled image in the substandard mirror. Donald was neither tall nor short—though he could appear either, depending on where he belted his pants across his beer belly—so his attempt at Rambo fell sadly short of the mark.

Fern pushed the door closed with her shoulder and

dumped the sacks she carried onto the lumpy surface of the less-than-double bed. When she snapped off the radio, her voice broke flatly into the sudden silence. "I still think we should have bought the Uzi."

Donald froze like a deer in headlights, then spun to face her. He grabbed the bandanna and stuffed it in his back pocket, then produced a wide, hopeful smile as he peered up at her, exposing the gap where his plates didn't meet his gums.

Fern was a tall woman, narrow everywhere but the hips, with stooped shoulders and long arms that made her look like a caricatured bird of prey. Her muddy gray hair, as wispy as Donald's, was drawn up in an off-center bun. Her narrow mouth, having long ago given in to the force of gravity, sagged on either side of her pointed chin.

"Teddy said—"

"I'm sure what Teddy said had nothing to do with the price." Fern's expression gave no quarter. "If you hadn't let Artie lay out the hit—"

Donald tenderly deposited the AK-47 on the dresser top, retrieved the bandanna from his pocket and rubbed his fingerprints off the AK. "His tab, his call."

Fern's sigh was silent, but it ruffled the back of what was left of Donald's hair as she reached around him to pick up the photograph of the target. She studied the face. There was something about her eyes, something deep in the mysterious green slits barely visible beneath drooping lids, that made Fern nervous. She tossed the picture down beside the gun.

"His way overdue tab, don't you mean?"

With a triumphant look, Donald pointed at something behind her. She turned and examined the beat up shoebox sitting on the table, its mailing label directing it to Reggie Seymour at a New Orleans address. With some reluctance she lifted the lid and found neat rows of envelopes also addressed to this Reggie. Inside one envelope was—

"A dollar bill?" She picked up the box, checked out other envelopes and found each contained a single dollar bill. "This is his down payment? A shoebox full of ones?"

Donald shifted his feet. "Ones or twenties, what does it matter as long as it's real?"

"No way there's half here—"

"He's good for it," Donald cut in, adding, "He's lucked into the perfect scam this time, Fernie. You should see him. Dressed to the nines, even has a Rolex watch. Said he'd cut us in on it. We pull this off and we can go to Disneyland in Japan if we want to! And that's just for starters."

"I thought marriage was his scam?" Fern tossed down the box with a snort of disgust. She'd never been able to see what all those women saw in Artie. "If he's willing to cut us in, there's more at stake than his new wife finding out about his other wives."

She wasn't surprised when Donald's gaze slid away from hers, though he tried to cover it by using his bandanna to rub the stock of the AK-47.

"He's just had a spot of bad luck, that's all. He needs to move something before the wedding but won't be able to if she comes—I don't know. It's complicated."

"With Artie it always is." Fern frowned. "Let's just forget the cut and take our fee—"

Donald twitched. Only once, but it told the rest of the story.

"He doesn't have it, does he?"

"He will. If we do the job." She raised a skeptical brow. He tried to trump her raise with a whine. "He's good for it," but his voice lacked the conviction. They'd both known Arthur Maxwell for too long. Of course, only an idiot stiffed a bopper. The fact that Artie was the biggest idiot she'd ever known, she tried to suppress.

A stray bit of sun found its way through a spot on the dirty window and fell across the polished AK-47. Fern gave another soundless sigh. A pity he'd fallen so hard for it. There was no persuading him to take the cute little Uzi once he'd made up his mind. He was the hit man, so he got to choose the gun. It was even possible he knew what he was doing. It hadn't been that long since their retirement. She watched him hitch his pants up over his sagging belly, then swagger to the bruised cooler stashed in the corner of the room, his knee joints popping with each step.

Then again...

"And when we're doing time—" she began.

"We done time before." He extracted a cold one, popped the top and took a noisy swig. At least he hadn't used his teeth. With their financial hopes riding on an AK-47, they couldn't afford to replace his plates.

Fern crossed her arms. "Not in this state."

He had to think about that for a moment as he ran down the list of places where they had done time. "Do you good to make new friends."

He sank into a sagging armchair and gave her a hopeful look.

"We got enough trouble with your old friends."

Donald scowled. "Don't start on Artie again—"

"I ain't stopped—" She shook her head. "You shoulda popped him the first time he poked his face in the door."

Why did Donald put up with him? What was the deal with men and their crib mates? Just because they pissed in the same pot, they had to be friends for life? Only bright spot, Artie didn't pop up that often because he was usually in stir making new friends. She'd feel more comfortable about the whole hit if she could just figure out why Artie wanted the Seymour woman out of the way so bad that he was willing to pay them to do it—if he paid them.

"I don't like it. Too much that can go wrong."

"It's not what I'd choose," Donald admitted. "But there's logic to it. Really," he insisted when she arched her brows again. "Drive-by isn't what I'd choose myself. But then, I've always liked the high ground." He took another noisy drink before adding, "I've had time to think and it's not as bad as it seems. First place, there's your element of surprise. Look how good the St. Valentine's Day massacre worked." He directed a triumphant look at Fern. "Taking someone out with a bang is a fine, old tradition."

He had to be joking, but a cursory examination proved her wrong.

"Come on, Fern. We can do this. You drive the car. I'll point the gun. It's what we do—"

"It's what we did—"

"When it's over, we're rolling in scratch."

She was familiar with the look in his eyes. A mixture of calculated entreaty and seedy charm, mixed with greed. She was too old to stop giving in to him—or to stop trusting his well-honed survival instinct. She sighed, trailing her finger the length of the AK-47. It was cool and smooth—like she used to be.

Hadn't she always done everything she could to avoid the dreary anonymity of her parents lives? Their walk-up apartment in Dayton wasn't a mirror of her parents' suburban hell in Jersey, but there were similarities when she let herself see them. Bingo at McDonald's instead of bridge at the country club. The occasional bus tour with other down-and-out senior citizens instead of summers at the seaside. Her parents had never lived wild or gone somewhere exotic. They had always been content with the mainland U.S.

"Enough to go to Disneyland."

Her parents had never been to Disneyland. Damn the boy, he knew she wanted to go to Disneyland more than anything. She wanted her picture taken with Mickey

Mouse in front of that castle more than she wanted to quit taking stupid hormones.

"Ain't she a beauty, Fernie?" Donald asked.

She sighed. If they had to shoot some woman to do it—

"It's not an Uzi, but I suppose it'll get the job done," she conceded.

"And then some." He mimed rapid firing.

She turned, pushing her worries to the back burner. From one of the sacks she'd dumped on the bed, she extracted two pairs of joke glasses—the Groucho Marx kind with dark frames, large noses, and mustaches attached. One pair she handed to Donald, the other she put on, adjusting the fit. Then she took a large muffelatta out of another sack.

"Get me a beer, will you?" she asked.

Donald put his glasses on, also adjusted their fit, and bent over the cooler, his pants sliding down to display his hairy butt crack. Fern did a quick right turn from the sight and spread their lunch out on the rickety table. Donald sat down in front of his half of the sandwich.

"What's this?" He handed her the beer and examined the offering: a huge half-round of crusty bread layered with spicy meats and cheeses, and topped with a tangy olive dressing.

"Muffelatta." Her mouth formed the unfamiliar words with the satisfaction of knowing this was another thing her parents had probably never done.

"Smells good." He took a huge bite, chewed a couple of times, then said through the remains of the bite, "Is good."

Fern studied her sandwich with satisfaction.

"What about wheels?" she asked before biting down.

"We'll pick a car up right before we head for the airport."

It was a peculiarity of Donald's, this waiting for the last minute to pick up a car. The three times he'd secured wheels early, he'd done jail time. He also had a pair of black thong underwear he wore, but Fern tried not to think about that. There were some parts of her middle-class upbringing she couldn't shed, no matter how far she got from it.

She watched him chew for a moment, then asked, "Do you think we could steal something foreign this time?"

Donald had strong feelings about driving American cars, but he got to pick the gun. Time for turn-about.

He looked up. She looked at the AK-47. It lay on the dresser, still gleaming in that stray bit of sun. His struggle at the thought of even a minor adjustment in his MO was written on his face in large block letters. With timing honed through long years together, she raised one brow. He grinned.

"Sure, Fernie, whatever you want." He bit into his almost decimated sandwich. His gaze strayed to her half of the sandwich. With only a moment's hesitation, she shoved it towards him. His appetite was always keen before a kill.

ARTHUR MAXWELL STUDIED the new shoes in the mirror. The shine was satisfactory, though it could be a touch brighter. The fit—he wiggled his toes—was good, though he wouldn't know for sure until he walked in them. He backed up, then walked toward the mirror. No pressure points. He backed up again to get the whole picture. Did the shoes fit with his suit? He stroked the fabric, enjoying the feel of expensive fabric. Silk was still too new for him to take for granted.

Prosperity suited him, he decided, smoothing an errant bit of hair back into the smooth line of his expensive hair cut. It suited him down to his toes.

"I'll take them," he said, turning to the sales clerk who was giving him a look with which he was all too familiar. Awe, admiration, a touch of lust. Women of a...certain age...had been reacting to him the same way since his hormones kicked in. It hadn't taken him long to realize there were benefits to be had from reacting back. Now it was second nature to smile with just a hint of shy to temper the charm. His eyes twinkled on schedule and her jaw went slack. She'd have been his, he knew, if he bumped up the stakes a bit, but he didn't need to anymore. He had money and he had Helen. "Let's box up my old ones, shall we?"

Well, he'd have money if Artie and Fern took care of Luci Seymour before she could get to her aunts. Which they would. He'd dangled a lot of money in front of his old cellmate, enough to get him to defy his ball and chain. Fern was the only woman alive of that certain age who was immune to Artie's particular brand of charm. Odd, unexpected, but overcome with cash, like most of life's problems. He might even pay them like he'd promised. He didn't have many friends and, well, Artie was a bopper. One didn't stiff a killer for hire unless...

It was a dangerous business and accidents did happen.

He smiled at the clerk, slackened her jaw again, as he counted out the exact number of bills needed to make the shoes his.

Outside, he unlocked his car and slid in. It didn't go with his suit, but it didn't matter. He had a nicer one waiting at home with Helen. He pulled his old shoes out, pausing long enough to sadly rub the scratch on the glowing surface before tossing them in the back seat with his other rejected shoes.

When he pulled out into traffic, he was only somewhat aware of the flurry of irritated honks and screeching tires. With any luck, it would be finished tonight. He could get his money and go home to Helen a free man. He should stop off and check his post office box. He made the turn without signaling and got another flurry of honked objections.

2

Mickey Ross was not a happy man.

He'd just come off a two-day stakeout and had the rumpled suit and unshaven chin to prove it. He was tired. He was cranky. And he wasn't home in bed having that dream where the cover girl for Sports Illustrated was rubbing sun tan lotion onto his back.

He looked at where he didn't want to be, but the waiting area of the New Orleans International Airport didn't fade to something more pleasing. Nor did the stuffed pig dangling at the end of his arm vanish into the nightmare realm where it belonged.

Mickey glared down at it. Bad enough for a cop to be keeping company with any pig, but this pig, well, if it's lurid pink and purple surface was any indication, it had never been a beauty. Time had rubbed away the fluff from its surface and left one sorry black eye hanging by a single thread over the patchy remains of a black grin on its square snout. Its tattered ensemble began and ended with a limp ribbon knotted around a fat neck.

In an effort to distance himself from his ratty companion, Mickey held it by the tatty end of the ribbon and twirled it with more than a hint of vindictiveness.

In between twirls, he pondered the unkind fate that had landed him in this fix. If Eddie hadn't decided to end sixty years of bachelorhood, he wouldn't be waiting for a damn flower girl for the damn wedding, with only a stuffed pig for an introduction. Who flew in a little girl for a geriatric wedding anyway? New Orleans was full of little girls who'd probably love tossing petals. But no, they had to import one, then pick a total stranger to collect her—with an obnoxious pig as the icebreaker. Convenient that Eddie had discovered pressing business in Mandeville tonight.

The least he could have done was warn him about the old ladies. How could his own uncle send him into battle, into that minefield of weirdness, without even a warning? A minefield that had kept going off in his face no matter what he did, a horror—except for the one small oasis of sanity known as Miss Gracie, who had saved him from the stuffed dragon, but not the pig.

He just wished he knew where Eddie's Unabelle—was that a name to make a guy flinch—fit in with the Seymours. She didn't seem to be a relative. She was just...there, like a black hole. He sure hoped the lights were on in her upper story for Eddie or he'd learn there were worse things than a lonely retirement.

A stir at the gate quickly became arrival as passengers filtered off the plane. With the end in sight, Mickey straightened in hope.

That's when it occurred to his weary brain that a stuffed pig might be a less than adequate introduction to the kid. What had possessed the parents to entrust their kid to the uncertain care of three batty old ladies? He studied each small, whining arrival, wondering which one was his. A security guard loomed up on one side and he had to produce his badge.

The case against Eddie just kept building.

A woman emerged from the breezeway and paused to get her bearings. Mickey straightened in an utter and complete moment-of-silence respect for the best legs he'd ever been privileged to lay eyes upon. The cop part of him was vaguely aware she was in her late twenties, maybe early thirties, almost of a height with him and the possessor of a slender build. Her hair was dark and cut short around a face made interesting by its square jaw and straight dark brows. Mouth was nice, too. Full and lush and lined in red.

He left off admiring her legs to contemplate her mouth, but his attention was drawn lower again when the legs went into motion. Brief appearances by her thighs, between the slash of her dark skirt, had him tugging at a too-tight tie. It took him a few seconds to realize that she'd stopped right in front of him.

With extreme reluctance, he dragged his gaze back to eye level. Her head was angled, her gaze directed toward the pig with a seriousness it didn't deserve. Just for a moment, something in the angle of her jaw had him wondering if he'd met her, but he dismissed the notion. A guy couldn't forget those legs.

His gaze drifted down again, but he flashed back to attention when she stepped closer, her nose bare inches from his, her lashes lifting with lust-building slowness to reveal emerald green depths.

His tie tightened to near strangulation level, but he couldn't move, let alone do something about it. Green eyes were always trouble for him. Too bad proximity and hormones took the edge off caution. If his partner, Delaney, were here, he'd recognize the signs of Mickey on the verge of falling in lust again. But Delaney wasn't here. The lucky bastard was in bed.

Carpe diem. Mickey knew his smile was his best opening gambit and produced it with practiced ease. "Hello."

Luci studied the smile, recognized the confidence and the intent behind it. She'd met smiles like this one. Smiles that were confident of their charm. Smiles that expected weak knees and a cessation of rational thought. It was fortunate she had a built-in immune system to charming smiles and didn't ever do rational thought. It went with being a Seymour, though her knees, just for a moment, signaled a willingness to depart from the norm. She reminded herself she was the result of a departure from the norm and said, "That's my pig."

This deviation from the opening pass widened his admittedly wonderful blue eyes and erased the smile. Luci took a moment to admire those eyes while the struggle to understand played in them.

"Your—pig?" he managed.

His voice was also wonderful, despite a certain strangled quality. Husky, it had a nice mix of bass and baritone. Confusion gave him a little boy aura to which even a Seymour couldn't be immune. Perhaps it was a side effect of her non-Seymour parentage. According to her mother —when her mother could be persuaded to talk about Luci's paternity—there were several annoying things she'd picked up from her father. It was, in fact, a moment of rare, though limited, openness about that paternity that had prompted her visit to New Orleans. The wedding was the perfect excuse, since she wasn't ready to admit to her family that she was father hunting.

The telegram from Boudreaux, her aunts' handyman, had provided assurance that they did understand she was coming, but no surprise it had been sparse on details, which explained the pig. Only her aunts would have kept it, remembered it and produced it in lieu of identification. She studied it with remembered fondness, noted the tightening ribbon, and looked up to tell him, "You're choking it."

Mickey gave this comment the lack of attention it deserved. "I don't think—"

Her straight brows rose in surprise. "Then it's time you started."

"But—" He shook his head, trying to punch through tired to comprehension. "This can't be your pig. You're not a little girl!"

"I used to be. But I grew up."

Her punctuating smile invited him to move on. The slow widening of her straight red mouth launched a feeling not unlike the plunge of a roller coaster. He wanted to move on. He did, but—

"Your aunts—" Mickey tried again, faint but pursuing.

"—probably liked the way the pig looked with your gun."

He clapped his hand over his weapon. "I'm a cop."

Luci had already figured that out, but she attempted to look enlightened. It wouldn't do to drive him to violence when he had the hardware to do something about it. She smiled. "A cop. Who's not afraid to pack a pig. I like that." She held out her hand. "I promise I am Luci Seymour."

Mickey took her hand. He didn't shake it. He couldn't. All he could do was stare into her green gaze as want did a quick crawl up his midsection. "Ross. Mickey Ross."

"Ross. That would put you on the bridegroom's side of the church." Her smile was pleased-to-meet-him, but the fluorescent lighting and her drooping lids turned her eyes bedroom soft.

"Eddie's my uncle," Mickey admitted through a dry throat.

Assessment entered her gaze, which then did an unnerving up and down.

"What?" he asked, trying not to sound as defensive as he felt, since it wasn't exactly PC to object to something he routinely did.

"Ever since I got the invitation, I've been wondering what kind of man would marry Unabelle. Are you and Eddie—"

"No! We're not at all alike. In any way. Except we're both cops. But that's it." Unbidden, the image of his uncle's fiancée rose in his mind. Faint. Indistinct, but somehow there.

"I guess that answers my next question."

"What?"

"Has Unabelle changed?" Her eyes sparked with amusement. "I can't wait to see her again."

Mickey shuddered. "Yes," he said positively, "you can."

Her smile was insistent. Mickey had to smile back. It was almost a moral imperative.

A PA announcement crackled. She stepped back at the same time he did. Mickey gestured down the terminal. "Uh, we need to go this way."

"Sure." With an agreeable air, she turned. As she passed, men turned to stare. Some ran into pillars.

Mickey loosened his tie, gave a silent whistle of appreciation, then started after her, the pig bouncing unnoticed against his leg.

FERN WAS tense as the Yugo they'd lifted passed at the legal speed limit through the arrival underpass of the airport. It was a grim place. Way too many cops around, and the thick humid air stank of gasoline fumes and something Fern couldn't identify but made her think of lingering death. She just wished it didn't make her think of her own.

"Pull in there," Donald directed.

He pointed to an empty space against the curb. She did as he asked with a sigh of relief at the respite from driving the unfamiliar car. It might have been a mistake to steal foreign, she admitted to herself, though she wasn't ready to admit it to Donald. Not only was the interior of the Yugo cramped, but the pedals were so small she was having trouble hitting them with her orthopedic shoes. The controls were opposite what she was used to and labeled with tiny, blurred symbols.

She reviewed her gear shift changes, in between keeping an uneasy eye on the two police officers aiding an attractive blonde who had locked her keys in her car. Only a shuttle bus and a couple of cabs loitered in the area. They were exposed, she noted, but Donald was too busy getting his rocks off on his new toy to notice.

She had a bad feeling about this.

"So, how are you related to Unabelle?" Mickey asked, breaking a silence that had ruled for most of the length of the terminal.

Luci looked at him, brows lifting in surprise. "I'm not. She's one of the aunts' debs."

"Debs?" Mickey looked, a puzzled frown putting tiny lines between his well-defined brows.

"Debutantes." She waited a moment, but understanding still didn't make an appearance. "Didn't you know they're matchmakers?"

"Matchmakers?" He stopped. "For real?"

"For real. For years." Luci grinned. "They specialize in the...hard-to-launch young ladies. And back it up with a guarantee."

"Guarantee?" Comprehension was beginning to break in his eyes, like little blue sparks. Very attractive blue sparks.

"They don't quit until the deb is walking down the aisle. No matter how long it takes." She hesitated, to smooth the giggles out of her voice. "Unabelle's been...a challenge. That's why she's the last debutante."

Mickey didn't try to hold back his chuckle. "How long—"

"Long as I can remember. That's one reason I had to

come and see who—" Her laughter-rich voice made his pulse thunder and the quick flash of her mischievous gaze was a minor lightning strike to his already eager libido.

Mickey tugged at his tie again, this time undoing the knot and the top button of his white shirt. It didn't help. He lengthened his stride, forcing Luci to recalibrate hers to keep up. That didn't help either. What he needed was a cold shower. A long cold shower—which just plain wasn't possible in the doggiest of the dog days of August.

"And," he said as he swallowed dryly. "Your other reason?"

"Reason?"

Luci's eyes widened in surprise and a hint of alarm, activating Mickey's cop instincts. It was almost as good as a cold shower. If gasoline could almost put out a fire.

"You came to the wedding?" he prompted.

Luci's lashes swept down like a lady's fan. "It's been a long time and I was feeling nostalgic."

He wasn't buying but was too polite to do more than look skeptical as he turned her toward the baggage claim sign.

As they descended via escalator, Luci studied Mickey. Pretty enough to be a calendar pin-up, he was lean, with shoulders just the right amount of broad, and a body just the right height to create symmetry. His cleanly-honed face was both reassuring and dangerous. The shadow of beard was sexy on his obviously stubborn chin, though she suspected the growth wasn't a calculated effect but a temporary setback. The crisp cut of his light brown hair hinted at a clean-cut personality, and his tired blue eyes suggested he'd just come off a long stint of something—which probably explained the touch of irritability. Though even the strong and the well rested had tough going in the Seymour zone.

She stole another peek and got caught. He tugged at his now wildly askew tie.

"What?" Another flare of irritation erased the weary in his eyes.

"Excuse me?" She arched one brow, punctuating the question with another admiring perusal of his assets. Red crept out from under his chin and up his face. Dang, the boy was cute.

"Nothing." He stopped by the luggage carousel and looked at the jumble of people and bags. He was too tired to do the bellboy thing if she had more than one bag. "Here comes the bags. Should I get a cart-"

"Why don't we wait until we see if my stuff made it. My luggage likes to take side trips to Raratonga or Katmandu."

"Okay." He watched a bag circle, then said, "If it does come—"

"Well, will you look at that. There they are!"

Mickey was starting to suspect that she didn't react to things the way normal people did. Her sincere delight at the sight of her luggage attracted almost as much attention as the pig and her legs. And did she have to bend over the luggage like it was lost children just found?

An unease filtered through tired and lust with distant words of caution. Green eyes, great legs and, a very nice ass —she was presenting it, so he took a good look before going to get a cart—were a temptation with a capital "T." But trouble started with a "T," too. If he had any doubts about the wisdom of steering clear, he had only to think of her aunts.

Insanity did run in families. No question it was running amok in hers.

"Donald." Fern grabbed Donald's arm and pointed as Luci Seymour came out the doors, walking next to a luggage cart. Perched on the two suitcases was a large pig, made lurid by the artificial light. She shuddered. "Someone should put that thing out of its misery."

Donald compared reality to the photo Artie gave them. "Someone is going to."

3

The hot air hit Luci in the face like a wet towel. She caught her breath, but it wasn't catchable with air that thick. Memories stirred. Old, happy memories of long slow days under shaded trees with...Stu? She examined the name from all sides. It seemed to fit within the memory, which returned in a sudden rush. Stu, like Seymour males large and small, had been an utter weenie, but he'd also been someone to play with who took orders well. He got a dragon when she got the pig. Yeah. Luci gave the pig a fond pat, tried out another breath and found it was a little easier, as if her lungs were already adapting to the slower pace and water level in the air.

"Luci, you're not in Wyoming anymore," she murmured.

"Wyoming?" Mickey looked at her. "I know someone from Wyoming."

Everyone, Luci found, knew someone from Wyoming. And expected you to know them, too. Granted it wasn't an over-populated state, but Wyoming people liked a large area of personal space. Miles large.

"What—"

"Butt Had," Luci said. No one ever knew anyone from Butt Had. If they did, they wouldn't admit it.

"Butt...Had?" Mickey blinked, getting that shell-shocked look again.

"I'm afraid so." Luci sighed. "You see, when they filed for incorporation, there was this broken "e" key on the typewriter—"

The white around the blue got larger, not smaller, and she decided to give it up as a bad job. "My mother won't live there, which is far more important to my piece of mind than a few missing 'e's'."

"Uh...huh." Despite his words, he kept looking at her like she was from Mars instead of a small town in Wyoming that should have been called Butte Head. Out of the corner of her eye, she saw the pig start to slip. She reached for it at the same moment as Mickey and ended up almost lip-to-lip with him.

He had nice lips.

She reined in her errant lips before they could take a taste. While he dealt with the pig, she stuffed her unruly libido firmly back in the box marked *don't open* and slammed down the lid. This was not the time to find she had something in common with her mother besides a last name.

Mickey settled the pig and tried to keep his gaze away from Luci, but it kept straying back. Questions about her bubbled across the surface of his mind. He happened across one he could ask without being rude.

"What do you do in Butt—there?"

She stopped. He did, too. The underpass didn't make the best backdrop for her, but it didn't seem to matter. There was something so...so...he didn't know—siren. That was it. She was like those mythical siren girls that called to men to crash on the—

"I'm a Do Wah," she said.

—rocks. He felt the impact, but the pity in her eyes blunted the pain. He choked a couple of times, then managed to croak out, "A what?"

She licked her red lips, the tip of her tongue pink and moist as it traced the curve. Lucky tongue—

"I'm a Do Wah."

Another crash against the rocks, but it didn't hurt as much as it should have.

"What the—" he struggled for a moment, managed to snap almost politely, "exactly what is a do wat?"

"Do Wah, not do wat."

"What is a do wah?" He squeezed it out through gritted teeth.

"A hummer with a bit of vocal thrown in." He swallowed three times and his eyes bugged just a bit from the sockets, but he didn't lose it. She was impressed. When she did "Seymour," men cried for their mothers.

"A—is that in a dictionary?"

"No, a club."

To aid in his understanding, she sang the first chorus of "Do Wah Diddy." His eyes widened in horror. They didn't narrow when she stopped, so she added, "I don't actually sing that, you understand? I hum until the do wah diddies."

She opened her mouth to sing some do wah diddies for him but he cut in, "Don't—I get the picture. You sing backup."

She gave him a pleased smile. He stared at her, and she counted four heartbeats before he said, "My car is over there."

FERN DONNED HER JOKE GLASSES, the smell of plastic filling her nostrils with cloying force as she helped Donald with his. They perched crookedly on the thick end of his real nose. She sat back, wiped a sweat-wet hand on her dress, then reached for the key and fired the engine.

Donald rolled down the window, his shoulder bumping hers at the end of each rotation. Humid gas-fumed air oozed inside, increasing, rather than decreasing, her rising claustrophobia.

"You ready?"

"Yeah," she lied through dry lips. She rested her hand on the gearshift. The seat belt that had attacked her when she closed the door now rubbed against her neck. She looped it behind her back and flexed her arms, trying to ease the tension in her shoulders. A river of sweat ran down between her sagging breasts and pooled in the clump of polyester fabric at her waist.

"Hit the gas and the brights at the same time, Fern," he directed, like she didn't know. He wiped his hands down the sides of his pants, then dabbed at the silver circlet of sweat that beaded around the edges of his hair. "And try to swerve in as close as you can get to the curb so's they can't see the gun 'til too late."

The man trundled the pig-laden cart closer, pulling their target—the Seymour woman—into their line of fire. Fern eased the car from the curb, and let it set its own pace toward the man bending to fit his key into the trunk. The woman walked behind him, looking around her as interestedly as if she were looking at a New Orleans tourist spot instead of a gritty underpass.

For one long unnerving moment, it seemed the woman looked right at her, the expression on her face so like the photo Fern had studied this afternoon it sent a chill that didn't cool down her back. She sucked the thick air in a hiss through the gap in her front teeth and opened her mouth to beg Donald to call it off, but he spoke first.

"Hit it, Fernie!"

Old instincts took over. She stamped on the gas. The

engine revved, but they didn't speed up. She took her foot off the clutch. It popped, bobbing both their heads and killing the engine.

"Damn it, Fern—"

She didn't try to talk, just cranked the engine over and tried again. The car jerked, but this time it went forward.

"Headlights!" Donald ordered. "You want they should see us?"

She reached for a knob. Wipers scraped dryly across her view. She hit another button and Waylon Jennings poured out the speakers.

"What you doing? Give me some damn light!"

Fern used her free hand to pull every knob she could find on the dash, biting back a muffled cry as Donald lifted the AK-47 free of the blanket, jabbing her in the ribs in the process.

Icy air blasted her face. The trunk popped open, cutting off her rear view. A soapy jet of water blanked out her forward vision. Then, when she'd almost given up hope, the lights came on at the same moment the car lurched up the curb.

She heard the rifle clatter against the metal frame of the window as the right side tires went up, a clunk as they came down. Donald howled. Fern joined him when the butt came down on her hand on the gearshift. Donald's joke glasses sailed off his nose and landed in her lap.

Fern stepped up the pressure on the gas, adjusted the clutch and shifted up. The butt of the rifle pulverized her fingers again. The wipers cleared her front view. They were weaving, but going toward their prey—who was already disappearing from sight, just bare seconds before Donald found the trigger and depressed it, releasing a deadly hail of lead outside the car and a painful rain of hot spent casings inside the car.

They might still have been able to do the job if Donald had been able to control the gun, but Teddy's AK-47 had its own agenda.

It bucked in Donald's grip, first tracing a line of fire up across the concrete roof of the underpass. Then it moved down to explode the pig into a pile of fluff. Donald cursed, wrestled the gun down, over-corrected and narrowly missed shooting out their tires. An erratic pattern of bullet holes appeared in the tarmac.

The AK-47's distinctive sound in the enclosed space of the car was something Fern would never forget. Her driving, already below standard, worsened with the unending pelting by the casings and her attempts to dodge the gun butt as Donald struggled to regain control.

She scraped past a parked car and almost crashed into a concrete support. Gritting her teeth, she managed to thread the wavering Yugo through cars and people the full length of the underpass, taking the final turn with a near flourish from sheer relief.

Behind them she heard the thunder clap of an exploding gas tank. In her side mirror, she saw a belch of black smoke surge out, clutching at them with vast dark hands, then the road curved to the left, carrying them out of sight.

Unbelievably, they were driving towards the freeway. Neither spoke until the car, now smoothly obedient, made the run onto the freeway entrance ramp.

After a long silence, Donald said, "I think we should have bought the Uzi."

It was a generous admission. Fern offered her own, "I think we should've stole American."

4

When he'd caught sight of the careening car and the gun sticking out its passenger window, Mickey's instincts had kicked in. A step, a leap, and he'd caught Luci mid-body, knocking her flat as bullets filled the air above them. His fumble for his gun netted him a handful of skirt—and thigh. He'd had to settle for uttering his choicest swear words as the Yugo swept past, giving him a tantalizing glimpse of a large-nosed-profile and a Groucho Marx behind the wheel before the car disappeared around the curving roadway.

The underpass filled with smoke from a burning something. Mickey's eyes watered as he did a quick visual survey, noting that the downed figures were, like him, beginning to look around.

No obvious casualties. That was good. He remembered Luci and looked down. "You all right?"

Her voice, slightly compressed, came from somewhere under his chin. "I think so." A pause, then she added, "Thank you for knocking me down and jumping on me."

Mickey shifted enough to get them eye-to-eye, just shy of lip-to-lip. He opened his mouth to say something, but what was there to say? You feel good? I want to kiss you?

"A lot," she said, the red mouth's opening and closing acting like a jump for his heart. "Uh, do you think you could get off me now?"

"Oh. Sorry."

The wail of approaching sirens played accompaniment as he made to roll off her. The sound of tearing fabric stopped him in mid-roll.

"I think I'm caught—or you are."

"I think you're right." Her hands moved down the sides of his thighs. "My skirt seems to be caught on your gun."

She looked far too calm for the situation. Only the speeded-up pace of her heart indicated agitation, that and a tiny frown creasing her forehead as she tried to unhook his gun from her clothes.

"If you could just shift a little—that's good—very good —yes—almost got it—"

Was that a smile tugging the edges of her straight mouth as she uttered breathy, suggestive things? He tried to focus on higher things, cooler things, but it wasn't easy in the heated underpass with her hands moving lower, and lower again, straying far too close to the area he was trying not to think of—

He jerked.

"Sorry." This time there was no question her lips twitched. He heard a short sharp tearing sound, and she said, "I think that's it. Try it now."

Slowly at first, then faster, Mickey rolled off her and got up. He paused only to brush his grimed hands down the sides of his pants before holding them out to Luci.

She gripped them, came up, then staggered slightly, as if her knees weren't as steady as her voice. Whatever the reason, she ended up in his arms and he found he wasn't averse to offering support for as long as she might need it. She tipped her head back, her smile a grateful one. Adrenaline screamed through his veins. He'd been a cop long enough to know the effects it could have on the sex drive, and he wasn't as relieved as he should be when she eased away from him and looked around. Discretion was the better part of lust, so he looked away.

There was a lot to see. It needed only a gun-toting Stallone to complete the mess as official-looking figures began to filter through the debris. A fire engine roared up, disgorging slicker-coated figures and adding to the noise. It was followed by every Jefferson Parish patrol car in the area, their police lights sending flickering blue flashes bouncing off the billowing smoke.

They had, he decided, been damn lucky...

The thought died when he saw the remains of his car, glassless, pocked with bullet holes, and sagging into the remains of what had been new tires. He bit back the expletives that crowded in his throat, heard Luci gasp and turned to find her studying a trail of tiny white puffs of cotton floating across the pavement.

Cotton?

Mickey followed the trail to the source. Her pig.

Or what was left of it. He grinned, feeling somewhat better about his own loss.

The pig wasn't the only casualty. Shots had ripped through Luci's luggage with ruthless disregard. One suitcase sagged half off, half on the cart. Mortally wounded, the rips in one long side bled frothy bits of white underwear and other feminine items. Jagged tears that dripped pieces of brightly colored clothing onto the pavement below scored the other. With the slow beat of his heart counting the seconds, Mickey waited and watched for her to finally react, to erupt, and to vent.

She drew a long shaky breath, then turned towards him, her eyes incredibly wide in her pale, smoke-smudged face.

"Someone must be really pissed at you."

"Me? What makes you think this was meant for me?"

Luci arched her brows. "The evil half of the universe wants cops dead, but who'd want to kill a waitress from Butt Had, Wyoming?"

"Waitress? But you said—"

"There's not," Luci pointed out, "a lot of money in do-wahing so I have to moonlight."

THE FAMILIAR MECHANISM of law enforcement soothed Mickey's frustrations. At least there was hope that the wheels of justice would, in time, crush the aging jerks that trashed his car. With martyred mourning in his heart, he watched a uniform speak into a radio, then turn to say, "They found the Yugo abandoned outside Lakeside Mall. Same place it was stolen from. It's possible they picked up their own car—or stole another one."

"They dust it?" asked another officer.

"Yeah, but it looks wiped."

"Can't shoot straight enough to hit the side of a barn but know enough to wipe away their prints," snorted a deputy from the Sheriff's Department. "What's crime coming to, anyways?"

"Oh, I dunno," drawled another deputy. "Did a fair enough job of shooting up this here underpass."

They all examined the erratic line of scoring in the cement over their heads.

"Can't believe no one was killed!" exclaimed a young officer, his Adam's apple rebounding with each word.

Mickey faced Luci and got the full force of her reproachful look over the shoulder of the EMT applying first aid to her scratches. In her lap was a fragment of pig snout. That's when he knew for sure that twinge behind his eyes was a headache in the making.

"The press boys are asking if it's a terrorist attack," the young deputy added.

"It would be a mistake for any of us to jump to conclusions," Mickey said, speaking with pain-induced passion. He rubbed his temples and scowled at the media hounds hovering avidly on the fringes of their much-too-public crime scene.

Somewhere just out of his reach, he knew something was bothering him about the attack. He groped towards it, but his subconscious refused to cough it up.

"Well, whatever the motive was, you were all damn lucky," the cop said.

"So were they," Mickey pointed out, looking down this time—at the jagged line of bullets scores in the roadway, marks that traced a path perilously close to the Yugo's tire skid marks.

AN AIRLINE OFFICIAL provided Luci with several plastic sacks that urged her to "fly with us" and a couple of large gray bins used to contain luggage that couldn't maintain structural integrity through the loading and unloading process. She felt Mickey watching her as she examined each item of clothing for damage, then assigned it a bin or bag. He was frowning again. She sighed. It was possible she'd never see his smile again, which was a pity but not a surprise. Being a Seymour did have its serious downside.

Which brought her mother to mind. One of the family peculiarities—among a host of them—was that Seymour women didn't marry. Luci's mother hadn't married, but she did get knocked up. It was a curious fact that when spineless, uninteresting Seymour men married their sturdy, plain, no nonsense—except in their choice of husband—wives, the coupling failed to dilute the family peculiarities by even a jot. There was no family history on female couplings, since Lila was the first to try it out, so Luci pretty much had to wing it in the theory department of her own peculiarities. She did know she was the only Seymour who seemed to be aware that the world couldn't see through Seymour eyes. It was as if her mother's genes had been unable to wholly combine with her father's, leaving Luci forever fractured inside.

Until this week, Luci hadn't given much thought to the man who had fathered her. Why should she when he was never mentioned? In some dim recess of her mind, she'd just assumed she was the result of a semi-immaculate conception and got on with her life. It was hard for non-Seymours to imagine their parents having sex, so she didn't feel she'd been unreasonable to avoid pondering the question for most of her twenty-seven years. Yes, other people had two parents, but Seymours weren't other people. There were times when she wasn't sure they even were people.

She'd probably have gone on not thinking about her sperm donor if Lila hadn't brought it up. When Lila made her twice-yearly call, Luci had mentioned the wedding invitation. With an uncharacteristic intensity, Lila had urged her not to attend, sounding almost motherly in her concern. Luci had probed this strange behavior further, causing Lila to make a fatal slip of the tongue and admit, "Your father is there and he doesn't know about you."

Since she refused to slip further details, including a name, for fear of what said father would do if he found out Lila had kept something as important as a daughter from him, Luci was forced to proceed to New Orleans without passing "Go" or collecting any more information.

Her aunts had to know who the sperm donor was and if approached right might spill what they knew. Getting useful information out of Seymour women was not like squeezing blood out of rock—it was harder. Useless information spilled forth in an endless fountain that couldn't be turned off. Luci hadn't counted on the non-Seymour Mickey being sent to collect her, though she wasn't surprised her aunts had lost track of a few years of her life and assigned her the role of flower girl. Attention to detail was not a Seymour trait.

Now, Mickey paced towards her, his expression as wary as if he approached a bomb. He learned fast. She watched through her lashes as she thrust her fingers through several bullet holes in a pair of jeans and waggled her fingers at him.

"How do you suppose the airline knew this was the perfect moment not to lose my luggage?"

Mickey grinned. "It's a gift, like knowing when to park in the garage instead of a no parking zone."

Luci basked in the unexpected approval of the grin. "Too bad about your car."

"Too bad about your luggage."

She sighed. "Yeah, I'm afraid Blossom's a goner."

"Blossom?" Mickey reached for his tie, but it was gone. "You name your luggage?"

Luci nodded. "Though he—"

"Blossom's a he?"

"Yes—though he didn't start out as a he or I wouldn't have called him Blossom. A few years ago I took him, or rather her, to visit my cousin George. He used to be a she, too. And when I got home, well, I could tell he wasn't a she anymore." She gave an elegant shrug. "This is the nineties. Her sexual orientation is his business, not mine."

Mickey opened his mouth, closed it, opened it again and asked, "And—your other piece of luggage?"

Luci arched her brows. "Samsonite."

"Oh." It seemed inadequate, but a woman in a short, sexy dress passed by, providing a well-needed distraction.

Luci followed his appreciative gaze, noting the quick smile he exchanged with the woman. It passed a lot of voltage in a very short time, its warmth touching her as it brushed past. Mickey turned back to Luci, the voltage fading as fast as it had arrived. It was a good thing. The world was unstable enough without another Seymour joining the battle of the sexes.

He pulled a notebook from one pocket, a pencil from another. "I have to get a statement from you about the attack."

"Okay." She gave him her attention. It seemed to disconcert him. "What do you want to know...officer?"

"I'm a detective. But—" He struggled, but good manners beat out personal desire. "You can call me Mick. If you want."

"Mick?" Luci said it doubtfully.

"What?"

"Well." She shrugged. "It sounds like a name for a gerbil."

He stared at her, producing then discarding several replies to this. Perhaps if he just ignored the things that didn't make sense he could get through this, deliver her to her aunts and then run for his sanity. It seemed like a good plan, so he went with it.

"Ross, then. Or Mickey—if it doesn't remind you too much of a mouse?"

She smiled. His toes curled in his shoes in time with the slow curling of the edges of her mouth and sent his plan drifting up into the smoke that still hugged the cement rafters overhead.

"I always thought Mickey was kind of cute."

He felt himself grin. Could tell it was the stupid one, but he didn't seem to care. It was enough to look into her eyes while she looked into his. It was enough to wonder how a mouth so straight could curve like that and would it taste as good as it looked?

A clang of machinery made them both jump.

"Yes, well." He shook himself, then said, "I just have a few questions for you, Miss Seymour—"

She twitched. If he hadn't been watching her closely he would have missed it. "What?"

Her mouth pursed in distaste. "It's just, being called that makes me feel like my mother."

"Miss Seymour reminds you of your mother?"

"I'm afraid so." Her sigh was just shy of dramatic.

He opened his mouth, remembered his plan and jumped right over this little bit of quicksand. He asked his questions, resisting her efforts to digress, until he got to his last question.

"Can you think of anyone who might want to kill you?"

She looked startled, then thoughtful, as if the question interested her in some distant, academic way. "I suppose anyone can have enemies and I am a Seymour, which means I bring out the homicidal in people."

Mickey opened his mouth to ask, then realized what he was about to do and stopped himself.

"I also know a lot of excitable gun-toting types, you understand, but none of them drive a Yugo. They drive off-road vehicles with gun racks, wear orange hunting vests and never wear joke glasses." She folded a blouse and tossed it in after the jeans, then picked up a silky scrap of white and lace. "Did you say you were in homicide?"

"Yes." Mickey felt the hairs on the back of his neck rise in warning.

"Oh."

"Despite the many TV plots," he said, "most perps try to avoid shooting a cop. It just gets them more trouble than it's worth."

"So someone wasn't trying to personally kill you?" The quantity of bullets fired at them seemed awfully personal to her, but she wasn't a homicide cop.

"I can't know for sure, of course, but I don't think so." He looked at her with a lot of wary in his eyes. "Why?"

"I was sort of hoping this—" she held up the white scrap to show him a bra with two blown cups, "would be covered under your insurance?"

No one came to the tiny French Quarter club for the drinks, though buying them at an exorbitant rate was required for sitting at ringside. Its claim to fame was its female mud wrestlers. Patrons had another good reason for buying liberally. They needed to get really drunk to get past their natural fear of getting down and dirty with said wrestlers, especially the one kicking patron ass at the moment. Even the dullest wit had to know she hadn't lost her front teeth just because of poor dental hygiene.

Fern watched the woman toss the over-confident college student clear across the ring. It wasn't possible for her to get drunk enough to crawl in there and get her ass tossed, but it was cathartic to watch someone else get tossed after their very public defeat. It didn't help to have an prosperous looking Artie sitting across from them laughing his ass off about their failure at the airport.

Donald let Artie pay for their drinks, which wiped the grin off his face. He'd always been a tight bastard. When the waitress was about two steps out of earshot, Fern said, "A guy who keeps all his dollars in one place—"

Artie pulled his feet in to keep a passing patron from stepping on his new shoes. "Hey, it's not easy to launder dollars. No one wants to bother with small bills anymore."

"No kidding," Fern said. "Let's see, I wonder why that could be?"

"Gets me." Artie leaned closer to confide, "Think about it. People freak if they lose five bucks in a scam. Have the postal inspector all over you. But for a buck? Not a peep. Just not worth their time to complain."

It made enough sense to be scary. Fern wasn't used to Artie making sense. She put down her drink. Maybe the cheap beer was affecting her more than she realized.

"Tell you what," Donald said. "I won't tell you how to scam if you won't tell me how to kill."

"Okay, okay." Artie threw his hands up. "The AK-47 was a bad idea. You do your thing and when you're done, let me know so I can do mine. Agreed?"

He pulled out a handkerchief and bent to wipe a speck of mud off his shoes.

Fern looked at Donald. He grinned. "What say we get ourselves an Uzi?"

A rare smile lit Fern's face. She should have been looking at the ring instead of at him. She just had time to register his look of horror before the wall of mud hit all three of them.

5

I t was late by the time Mickey found a car to take them to Luci's aunts' house. That it was a Yugo didn't help his headache.

"Did you get a chance to call your aunts and let them know—"

"You don't call my aunts," Luci said. "They have this aversion to technology."

"Uh huh." Mickey stowed her blasted belongings, then opened the door for her. "I could have sent someone—"

Her smile cut him off. It was too close, too charm-intensive with only the car door between them.

"They lost track of the last twenty years of my life. I don't think they'll notice I'm a few hours late."

She slid in, giving him a generous glimpse of her thighs as her skirt rode high. When her hands smoothed the skirt back into place, the memory lingered with him as he crossed to the driver's side and got in. He hesitated, then had to ask, "Are they always—"

"Always," she said.

He reached for the key, then stopped. "Except for Miss Gracie."

Her straight brows rose for a moment, a look that could have been surprise widening her eyes. "You...met Miss Gracie?"

"Met her?" Mickey didn't hesitate. "I love her. She tried to save me from the pig and she did save me from the dragon."

Her smile widened, upping the charm factor by ten. "My cousin and I got them the same day. They were too big to take with us when we left."

"Too bad," Mickey said, with heartfelt emphasis.

Luci chuckled. "That's what Miss Gracie said when I left it."

Mickey grinned. "She's so...so..." He realized what he'd almost said and stopped.

"So...what?" Luci asked, like she wanted to know.

"Well..." Mickey paused, then decided she'd asked for it. "Normal."

"Really." It didn't sound like a question the way she said. Her face was thoughtful when she added, "How interesting."

He started the engine. "Don't."

"Don't what?"

"Do that. Be like them. Your aunts." He gave a shudder

as he pulled away from the diminishing confusion of the shooting.

"I can't help it. I am like them. You've just been too busy looking at my legs to notice."

Since he couldn't admit that even her legs hadn't kept him from noticing, Mickey said, "Well, they are good."

Luci's laugh was rich and warm. "They have to be. I'm a dancer."

"Dancer?" Mickey didn't mean to make it a question.

"Would you let them go to waste?"

Mickey didn't hesitate. "No."

"Well, there you are then." She relaxed back in the seat as if the discussion were over.

Mickey steered the car onto the freeway. "You're right. You are like them."

"It's a genetic imperative."

"You could fight it."

"I could do a lot of things."

It was a good thing he had three lanes to himself. Her punctuating smile put a swerve in his heart that the car mimicked. He straightened the car and tried to straighten his heart. It wasn't easy with the smell of her, lightly overlaid with smoke, filling the air around him. It was as distinctive as the woman from whom it emanated. Mysterious. Unusual. Somewhat annoying.

She was quiet for several miles before breaking the silence with a soft chuckle.

"What?" Mickey gripped the steering wheel, bracing for another round of the unexpected.

"I was just thinking, I don't have a thing to wear." Her voice was husky with sleepy amusement. He heard a rustle of movement as she shifted and looked at him. "Guess I'll have to go shopping." She didn't sound sorry. "Though my neighbor, Helen, would tell me not to be hasty."

"Why?" Mickey had passed from exhausted into the stupor zone. It gave him a measure of protection from anything weird she might say, so he felt safe asking the question. It was just a dream from which he would soon waken and wonder what he ate that caused it.

"She thinks my stars are out of alignment or something. She's a great believer in stars and convinced there is purpose behind seemingly random events. Like when she hit her husband with her car."

"She hit her husband with her car?" This made a small ripple on the surface of his stupor, but he was able to ride it out.

"He wasn't her husband when she hit him. That's the purpose part. If she hadn't hit him, she wouldn't have met him, wouldn't have married him—so it must have been meant. Otherwise, why hit him?"

"Because he was in the way?" Mickey said.

"Well, just between you and me, that's what I think. I can't see where it's helped her all that much to be married to him, because he's gone to Cleveland every other week. And she has to be Mrs. Maxwell Artesian. Not a name I'd personally like to be saddled with. Especially when she'd almost made it through her life without it." She shifted in her seat to ask, "Don't you think it's kind of a coincidence that we both know people, I mean like Helen and your uncle, who are embarking on late-life marriages?"

This rippled a little deeper, but a yawn cut it off. He hid it behind a hand. "Lots of people get married late in life."

"I guess." She didn't sound convinced, but it wasn't in his job description to convince her. "It's made her obsessed with marriage. Which wouldn't be a problem if she understood about Seymour women. That's why I didn't tell her about the car that almost hit me last week. She'd have had me engaged, even though we don't."

Mickey realized he'd missed a crucial key to understanding what she'd just said. "You don't—what?"

Luci looked surprised. "Get married."

"Ever?"

"Never," Luci reaffirmed.

"Oh." Mickey took the exit on auto-pilot while his tired brain studied this revelation with an interest that wasn't nearly disinterested enough. It seemed, he decided with a discreet look at her legs, that even a really dark cloud had a silver lining.

6
———

Luci's aunts lived in an area of narrow, rutted streets and mixed architectural ancestry just off St. Charles in a house that was a narrow embellished Victorian built just prior to the turn of the century. Set on a corner lot, it had long settled into the midst of an abundant tangle of shrubbery and flowers barely confined by the high wrought-iron fence that circled the property.

Their handyman, Boudreaux, a small Cajun with a speech impediment that made it difficult for the non-Seymour to understand him, kept the house in pristine condition. His tall, spare and mute-by-choice wife, Louise, cared for the aunts. Both had been with the aunts for as long as Luci could remember.

Coming down that first morning, Luci ran into Louise in the hallway outside the breakfast room. She carried a covered tray, so Luci held the door open for her, then followed her in to where the aunts were seated around the long light table in the even longer, lighter dining room.

Despite the long passage of time, they were just as she remembered them. Well, maybe a bit more transparent. They had always looked like they'd just marched off a Russian assembly line, since they were as similar in looks as folk art nesting dolls and not similar in height. Easy to believe that they'd emerged from inside each other rather than the more conventional birthing.

Each had a round white bun on the crown of her head, a round face, round eyes, and round spots of rouge on each cheek. Their skin was white and crepe thin, like tissue paper that had been crushed and then smoothed. Their mouths were crumpled pink bows. Their now faded blue eyes still reflected constant, utter delight with life and living.

Miss Weena, the youngest and shortest, was also the trendiest, favoring caftans in wild colors that were too long and constantly tripped her. She was, Luci recalled as the past made a return engagement, the adventurous sister and the only one who had ever held a brief, but real, job. It was a source of wonder to the family that anyone had actually hired Miss Weena, let alone armed her. Her employer had paid a brief but painful price for his lack of judgment, to his heart and his manhood. But as Miss Weena was wont to point out, he was too old to have children anyway.

It was one of Miss Weena's caftans that Luci had donned for her first foray outside her bedroom. That it landed just below her knees didn't trouble her . Vanity wasn't part of the Seymour profile.

Miss Hermi, the middle sister, favored gray and lavender, which suited her drift-through-life personality. She suffered from the illusion she was a gardener, much to Boudreaux's dismay, and she had a gentle passion for cement gargoyles. It must make the back garden a nightmare to tend but had been a delight to small children with big imaginations.

Miss Theo, the eldest and tallest sister, still wore black, plain and classic. She was considered the sensible sister, though non-Seymours might find this assessment hard to swallow. Her eyes were bright and intelligent, if somewhat remote. She tended to look at life as something quite interesting, but not her concern.

Luci waited until Louise arranged the tray on the table before greeting her. Louise needed both hands free to scribble a greeting on the chalkboard that hung by a chain from her belted waist. Out of deference to Louise's carpal tunnel syndrome, the greeting was brief. Luci kissed each aunt's papery cheek before taking her own chair, feeling most of her twenty-seven years peel away. So little had changed here, she felt like a time traveler.

Until Louise lifted the lid from the tray.

No succulent eggs and sizzling bacon. No pancakes dripping with real butter. Luci looked at what was there, then looked up to ask, "Can I have the Fruit Loops?"

DESIGNED in the early 1950s by the Israeli government to use against the PLO, the Uzi submachine gun is capable of firing 950 rounds per minute. Over time, improved technology has made it the choice of military forces worldwide, including the U.S. Secret Service.

It was also Fern's choice.

She didn't want it because it had a 9mm chamber or a folding metal stock. She wanted it because it was cute and compact. Neat. Manageable. Especially the mini version that they finally chose from Chainsaw Teddy's supply of deadly hardware. On his advice they got the semi-automatic version, which, because of the higher firing cyclic rate, would be easier to control.

Teddy had a smirk on his meaty face when he told them this, but they chose not to respond. Explanations of what had gone wrong were unnecessary. He'd seen the news and been expecting them. Donald didn't even give the AK-47 a regretful glance as they left.

"So, what do we do now?" Fern tucked the Uzi out of sight under the seat of their stolen Ford.

"We head over to where the broad is staying and scope things out." He tossed her a map of the city. "I marked it on the map. But let's get some grub first."

"Drive-through okay? Wouldn't like to leave our Uzi alone in case someone steals our stolen car." Fern rubbed the Uzi with the heel of her shoe and smiled.

"Yeah, just keep it outta sight. Bulls are still jumpy after last night."

"Yeah." Fern looked grimly cheerful. "Read in the paper that they think we're part of a radical senior citizens group. It's too bad we had to be so visible for so long last night." Fern thought back to the moment when it seemed like the Seymour woman was looking right at her. How observant was she? And if she had fingered them? It would make the stakeout more difficult. "We should never have tried it at the airport like that. Planes are never on time."

"Damn Artie."

"ARE you quite sure you don't want to be Unabelle's flower girl?" Miss Theo asked, her spoonful of Lucky Charms quivering just shy of her mouth.

"Completely quite sure," Luci said. She'd polished off the Fruit Loops in crunchy short order. The roof of her mouth was a tad sore, but her sugar craving was at least assuaged, while leaving room for the beignets she had her sights set on.

"But you'd get to strew rose petals in Unabelle's path, Luci dear," Miss Weena said, disbelief predominant in her fluting voice. Fruity Pebbles was her all-too-appropriate breakfast of choice.

"Not everyone wants to strew rose petals." Miss Hermi put her faint but pursuing opinion into the mix. She liked

Captain Crunch. She'd always, Luci recalled, had a soft spot for a man with a mustache.

"I've always wanted to strew," Miss Weena said dreamily. "Or to be strewn." Her hopeful glance slid in Miss Theo's direction.

Miss Theo ignored her, her attention centered on snagging the last soggy Lucky Charm floating listlessly in milk. Miss Weena looked so crestfallen Luci decided to help her out.

"Could she fit in the dress, Miss Theo?"

Miss Theo looked up, her gaze assessing Miss Weena's all too diminutive figure. Miss Hermi threw her lot in for Miss Weena—and the cause of peace—with, "Who else will we find now, Theo?"

"All right," Miss Theo said. "You can strew. Maybe Unabelle won't notice."

Three pairs of eyes widened and looked at her.

"Maybe?" Miss Weena asked.

"She could," Miss Theo said, a hint of defensive taking the burnish off her usual regal style. "She noticed when we tried to switch her puce dress for a white one."

"You'd think," Luci said, "that someone who'd waited as long as Unabelle would be panting to wear white." Luci realized what she'd just said and knew what her aunts were thinking. It was hard to imagine Unabelle panting, let alone—

Luci gave a slight shudder, one echoed around the

table in varying levels of revulsion. Past time to change the subject to one nearer and dearer to her thoughts.

"Speaking of panting," she began. "I was talking to Lila—"

"How is your mother?" Miss Hermi asked, her anxious expression belying the friendly inquiry.

Luci grinned. "The same. She—"

Miss Theo patted her hand. "We all have our cross to bear."

Miss Hermi and Miss Weena nodded. Four gazes drifted toward the fireplace mantel and the row of pictures marching across the surface. Luci was the only one of them to have a Seymour mother, but she shuddered with her aunts at the grim, sensible mother faces casting long shadows over the ineffectual Seymour men they'd married.

Luci pushed back her chair and went to study the pictorial genealogy, a gallery that didn't include her paternity. Was her father the key to her not-quite-perfect family fit? To her split personality? Every other Seymour had a Seymour father to look at, to blame for their mother. Lila wouldn't talk, so somehow the aunts must be persuaded to spill the right beans. A Seymour woman could always be counted on to spill some beans, just not always the right beans.

"Is my father—" she turned back to her aunts. Their reaction was interesting. All three pairs of eyes widened, then narrowed and were directed toward their empty cereal bowls.

After a long, awkward pause, Miss Weena said, "He was a lovely man."

Was? "Lila said he lives here in New Orleans."

Miss Theo looked far too innocent. "Did she? Well, I suppose he might. He was a soldier back then, so we just assumed..."

"Cut a lovely figure in his uniform," Miss Hermi said, hastening to fill the hanging pause left by Miss Theo. "I expect the pictures are still in the attic—"

Two irate stares cut her off in mid-sentence.

"Or...not," she finished feebly.

That subterfuge was alien to them was obvious by how bad they were at it. Had Lila gotten to them first? Why would they back Lila up though? She was the female family black sheep, first for getting pregnant and then for taking Luci away from them. She should have, Luci realized, come back sooner. There was at least one deep spot in the shallow Seymour waters.

She pretended not to notice the worried glances that passed between them, but it was hard not to notice when they stood up and formed a row in front of her.

"What?" She looked from one face to the other, seeking enlightenment that might not ever come. It was obvious they were up to something.

"It just won't do." Miss Theo picked up the edge of the caftan that Luci had borrowed from Miss Weena. Miss

Hermi and Miss Weena both nodded agreement as they circled Luci like vague, charming vultures, their buns bobbing eager approval. "Something in black?"

"Black?" Luci wasn't sure she wanted to know what was coming, but with Seymour fatality, she knew there was no way to avoid it.

Miss Hermi smiled. "To get the police, Luci dear."

"Police?" Luci blinked, but their sweet faces didn't alter one whit. "Police." They nodded encouragingly. Luci pondered for a beat, then agreed. "Definitely black."

Mickey would certainly start mourning when he saw her. Might as well beat him to it. But first she needed to outmaneuver her aunts.

THE DOOR to the attic creaked when Luci pushed it open. Behind her she could hear Miss Weena calling her. She leaned out to call, "Be right down!" then slipped through the door and closed it. And opened it again before she passed out from lack of oxygen. The heat was past oppressive, bordering on abusive. It was a stale and cloying wet blanket that set itself against her need to hurry. But despite the discomfort, there was a kind of magic in the murky semi-dark. Attics were magic and mysterious places in all the best books, where unexpected things could be counted on to happen. Luci had never been immune to magic. That this particular attic might hold the key to her past only heightened the sensation that she'd crossed more than just a wooden threshold to arrive here.

On the other side of that threshold she heard the insistent trill of her aunts and, with a sigh, turned on the lights and drove the magic into the far corners, leaving an ordinary attic with an assortment of boxes and trunks and a lot of shoeboxes. More than a lot, she noted with a grin. The aunts must have decided to challenge Imelda Marcos's position as the Queen of Shoes.

Among the trunks, she found her mother's. It had sat at the foot of her mother's bed until they left town so many years ago. She did a cobweb check and was surprised to find her path relatively free of sticky obstructions. The floor was dusty, so she crouched in front of the trunk and teetered for a moment until she found her balance again. Her elbow bumped one shoebox tower and sent it toppling, but she didn't let the shower of paper that erupted from the boxes distract her.

Now that she was here, she felt a strange reluctance to disturb the past. The musty smell of damp and old assailed her nostrils as her feelings swirled in uncertain patterns. Did she want to do this? She'd been so angry with Lila for deceiving her about her father that she hadn't stopped to think about how it might affect her. What if she found him and didn't like him? What if he was as annoying as her mother? What if—

She stopped, trying to avoid the thought, but it came anyway.

What if he didn't like her?

"This could be such a bad idea," she told the boxes.

She could walk away now. She hadn't crossed any "points of no return" yet. Once she saw a face, had a name, it would be harder to walk away. Unless she'd already passed that point? She looked at the lid and knew she couldn't leave it alone. If she did, her aunts would take her choice away. For whatever reasons their busy and confusing brains had conjured up, they didn't want her to know who her father was. It was her right to know—even if she didn't act on that knowledge.

The trunk wasn't locked, but it resisted opening after so many years. She had to hold it with one hand while she shone the light in.

On top was a framed picture of her mother and a man. Luci reached for the picture with hands that trembled, then let the lid close again. She took a deep breath, then looked at the photograph. It was old and a bit fuzzy. Whoever had been holding the camera wasn't good with it. Their clothes—Lila's the worst the sixties had to offer, and her companion's the uniform Miss Hermi had sighed over —were in the light, leaving their faces in shadow. His was even harder to see than Lila's because of his hat. Only his jaw line, strong and well-defined, gave any sense of his face.

Luci traced that jaw. "Are you my father?"

In the distance, she heard Miss Weena call again. Luci

sighed, then turned her attention to the papers she'd knocked over.

"Dollar bills?" A shoebox full of dollar bills? A quick check of a few more boxes indicated they all contained bills, not shoes. "What? Now they're afraid of banks and large bills? Oh my."

She finished and turned to leave, the photograph tucked under her arm. Later. She'd deal with it and all those unsettling feelings it stirred up...later.

IT WAS easy for Mickey to persuade his partner, Kevin Delaney, to take their break at Cafe du Monde. Delaney was always happy to go where the fat content was high.

Open twenty-four hours to locals and tourists, it served its famous cafe au lait, a strong chicory and milk-laced coffee, and beignets, square doughnuts fried in oil and liberally doused with powdered sugar. Sitting under the canopy, there was always the chatter of people to provide counter-point to the plaintive ballads of the jazz musicians plying their trades for tips, while overhead, slowly spinning fans moved the humid air enough to provide an illusion of cool.

"You want the last beignet?" Delaney asked, his hand hovering over it.

Mickey shook his head, his hand cupping the cooling

coffee as Delaney snagged a lone golden square. Idly Mickey wondered how coffee could cool when it was so damn hot. It was easier, more comfortable to think about coffee than to dwell on last night.

"I guess that means you don't want another order?" Delaney made it a hopeful question. He was a big man with a large, shaggy head of hair, a barrel chest and gentle brown eyes.

Mickey looked at him in resignation. "What do you care? You know you'll eat them all anyway." Delaney gave him an injured look and Mickey sighed. "Fine. I'll take another coffee." He'd need to keep the caffeine level in his blood high if he were going to get through the day. The headache had survived the night.

Delaney placed their order, then turned to look at Mickey. "You really need to lighten up, Ross. You're gonna have a heart attack."

A gleam of humor lit Mickey's glum expression. "You're telling me to lighten up? After you just scarfed six beignets?"

Delaney patted his bulk. "I have a large frame to maintain. Unlike you, my anal retentive friend. You worry the details too much. Get some perspective, step back and look at the big picture once in awhile."

"I tried. But you were blocking my view."

Delaney grinned, his good humor unfazed. He might have retorted, but the food arrived. He leaned forward, trying to ease his wallet out of his back pocket. It was wedged.

Mickey sighed, extracting his wallet from the inside pocket of his last good suit. He tossed a few bills onto the waiting tray and watched as the waiter left without returning any change. Maybe he'd sensed Mickey's building financial crisis and had decided to make sure he got his tip.

"I'll get the next one, Ross."

"You'll have to. By the time I buy a new car and new suits and pay the rise in my insurance rates—that's if they don't drop me—" He shook his head.

"Too bad about your wheels."

"Yeah, that's what my agent said. Right before he reminded me that I chose not to get rental car coverage. I asked him how I'm supposed to get to work? He tells me to take the bus."

"That's cold." Delaney paused in the act of lifting his cup to his mouth. "Did Caroline get hold of you?"

"Yeah. She heard about the shooting. Was worried. Wondered if she could help. Why do women do that?" He rubbed the back of his neck, trying to ease the tension already knotting there.

"What? Want to help?"

"Yeah. What, does she think I can't figure out how to get myself to and from work without a car?"

"So, how did you get to work?"

"Caroline picked me up."

Delaney hid his grin behind his coffee cup. "That's very independent of you."

"Ha, ha. I should've known this would happen when I broke my own rule: never, ever get involved with someone you work with. Especially a woman."

"Well, the only other choice is the men, Ross. Though if you're thinking of a change in lifestyle, maybe you can still find that perp we caught last week. Course, you'll have to wait until after you testify against him before you ask him out." Delaney gave Mickey a shit-eating grin.

"I don't think his boyfriend would like it." Mickey refused to rise to that bait again. Delaney'd been trotting it out all week. It was getting old. "Do I want to know if you heard anything new on the shooting last night?"

Delaney shifted gears. "Not much. You know they found the car—" He stopped, then continued when Mickey nodded. "But don't think I told you it's knee deep in shell casings which forensics is painstakingly dusting for prints. They might be done by the turn of the century. But they might not. At least two murders last night. You weren't the only one getting shot at last night."

"Great. Been a bad year for the NOPD."

"No kidding. Did I mention the memo?" Delaney looked at his cup instead of Mickey.

"What memo?"

"The one about improving our crime stats so the news hounds will quit kicking our butts in print."

"Damn. They might try cutting us some slack." Mickey

knew it would never happen. It wasn't "in" to cut cops slack.

"Ah, well." Delaney sighed before adding, "It does make us look bad when our fellow officers keep getting arrested. 'Course, if the three officers on the scene last night had got off even one shot—"

"Her dress was wrapped around my piece."

"Way I heard it, you were too busy copping a feel to pull your piece. And that lipstick all over your shirt—" Delaney shook his head in mock sorrow.

"Very funny. All you comedians seem to forget..." Mickey's voice trailed off as a pair of real lookers swayed past, their hips eye-grabbing in indecently short skirts. Not bad, he decided, thought the legs weren't as good as—he snapped that thought off before he could complete it. He didn't want to think about Luci. It wasn't a fruitful line of thought. He turned back to find Delaney looking at him with amused resignation.

"Don't you ever get tired, Ross?"

"Of looking? Never. It's the talking and the touching that's getting real hazardous to my bachelor status."

There was a short companionable silence, then Delaney asked, "You never said what happened when you finally got the girl deposited with her family. Were they getting worried?"

"Worried? The Seymours? They don't know how to worry." Mickey tipped back in his chair until he was balancing on the back legs and clasped his hands behind his head.

Delaney grinned. "So what did they do?"

"Do? Nothing. If she had been a kid, her parents would've been crazy to send her to them. Seems they forgot she was even coming."

"Forgot?"

"Yeah, maybe the party they were at distracted them. Was at the frat house across the street. Loudest damn party I've seen since college."

"Uh huh." Delaney fingered his chin. "Didn't you say these were older ladies?"

"Two-feet-in-the-grave old."

Delaney shrugged. "I guess it's true what they say about only being as old as you feel."

"Yeah, well, these birds feel pretty damn young, then. Were having a great time teaching the boys the bunny hop."

Delaney choked, then stretched his legs under the table next to them. "You think anyone past sixty's over the hill, Ross."

"You are over the hill, Delaney. Should've been put out to pasture years ago."

Delaney wadded up a napkin and threw it at him. "So, were they upset about the shooting?"

"I told you, they don't get upset. They wanted to know what it was like to get shot at."

Delaney gave a silent whistle. "I'll have to admit they sound a few bricks short." He had to pull his legs in when a server almost tripped over them.

"More than a few, Delaney. Took me a devil of a time to convince them I'd brought them dear little Luci."

"How could they—?"

"Apparently they don't have a real good grasp of time passing. When I left they were trying to decide if they could alter her flower girl dress to fit or if they should make a new one."

Delaney grinned. "I'd like to meet them."

"You would. You can get along with anyone."

"Yes, well, isn't it lucky I'm so well equipped to be your partner?"

Mickey had to laugh. "All right, all right. It's just that people can be so—so—"

"Human?"

Mickey laughed again. "Yeah. Damn human."

"I heard she had great legs. Worth dying for."

"The legs were good," Mickey admitted. "If they could just be detached from the mouth."

"Too bad I'm married to my job, I'd look her up. Sarge is always telling me I'm late for my mid-life crisis. Just can't seem to get up the steam for it." There was a short silence as he munched contentedly on his doughnut. Then he brushed the powdered sugar off his belly and leaned forward, his gaze serious. "Any chance that shooting was meant for you?"

"Why would it be meant for me?"

"Well, we are on Dante's ass and he's known for not liking that. You find out something you haven't gotten round to sharing with me?"

"Only if it's something I don't know I know. He's been running book for longer than I've been a cop, Delaney. Being a known associate with a dead man isn't grounds to pull him in, much as I'd like to. So unless he's lost his head, I can't see Dante getting hot under the collar over the little we've been able to scrape up on him."

"So what do you think it was then?"

"You saw the report. It was an elderly couple wearing joke glasses." Mickey brushed at the white powder dusted across his trousers, smearing it across the dark surface.

"Jeff Parish guys think they broke out of an old folk's home."

"They would. Only no reports on any breakouts and they haven't made any demands."

"I recognize that look, Ross. Something's bothering you."

"A lot's bothering me—like losing my car." He shoved his hands through his hair, staring into the crowd with a frown. "But, it just seems that if someone went there wanting to make a stink by shooting up a crowd, they'd have done it when there was a crowd. Why wait until almost everyone was gone?"

"Screwing up their nerve?"

"Maybe, but if that's the case, then it took them from

the time the flight was due in, until it actually arrived. That's a lot of exposure for no return." Mickey frowned, his mind replaying the events—while trying not to get stuck on Luci and her legs.

"So, you think they were waiting for someone on that flight?"

"It was the only one left to come in."

"But..." Delaney was thinking hard. "If they wanted to kill just one person, why choose such a hit-and-miss, damn public way to do it? Unless—" He looked sharply at Mickey. "They thought they could avoid focusing attention on their real target?"

"Might have worked if a lot of people died." Mickey considered the idea from various angles. "I could make a case for it."

"I don't know, Ross. It's pretty messy. Risky, too. Why not just arrange a quiet little accident?"

"How do we know they haven't already tried that?" Something twitched at the edge of his mind, then faded.

Delaney nodded. "Makes a little bit of sense, Ross. Your noodle isn't as hashed as you claim. So, if you're right about them, they missed their mark last night and might try again?"

Mickey nodded. "I think it's at least worth looking into. There weren't that many people involved. Maybe five or six coming off the plane. Everyone else had cleared out. If one of them had a near accident lately—"

Again with the twitch. What was he forgetting? What

was he too damn tired to call up from the slippery depths of his brain?

"Something wrong?"

Mickey rubbed his head where the remains of last night's headache lingered. "I'm forgetting something. Hope it'll come back. Feels important."

"Don't sweat it. Thoughts are like women. They only come when you don't want them." Delaney pushed his chair back. "I'll see if I can scare up a list of those names. All it'd take is a phone call to each person. Though I think I should talk to your Luci in person—if only to see the legs."

"You can waste your time if you want to. I asked her the standard questions last night." And got some highly non-standard answers, he could have added but didn't. It would only encourage Delaney. He liked to collect eccentrics. "If you insist on questioning her, count me out. I could die a happy man if I never have to talk to her again—"

The end of his sentence was drowned in the sudden honking of horns and squealing of tires. An old, rattletrap car pulled recklessly across traffic and stopped at the curb. Right next to a "NO PARKING ANYTIME" sign. It was a Volkswagen full of bodies, most of whom appeared to be the male-with-biceps variety. With one exception.

The door creaked open. Luci Seymour delicately began to extricate herself from the young man on whose lap she'd been perched. Her momentary suspension across a hefty knee left a lot of her infamous leg exposed for an enjoyable moment, effectively halting male traffic on the sidewalk for the duration of her suspension. Then there was a collective in-drawn breath of awe, changing quickly to one of regret when, with a wiggle and a twist, Luci freed herself and her skirt from car and man.

7

"Luci." Mickey's brain groaned. A much lower organ signaled delight. He felt Delaney grip his arm.

"You seriously mislead me, Ross."

Mickey studied Delaney's awestruck expression with resignation. Only time and exposure to Luci would wipe it off now. With deep suspicion, Mickey watched her approach. He didn't know why she was wearing what looked like mourning clothes on a hot weekday morning, but the drifting lace and floppy-brimmed hat made her look deceptively harmless and far too charming. Let Delaney take the ride this time. He'd be the one to keep his wits about him in the bright hot light of day.

"Mickey." Her voice was rich with a mournful Southern accent she hadn't had last night as she held out her hand to him. "How fortunate. I was just on my way to see you. The boys..." She made a vague gesture with a black-gloved hand in the direction the Volkswagen had gone. "...were going to buy me breakfast before taking me to you."

Fighting a rearguard action against another lust surge, Mickey took the hand and resisted a need to kiss it by shaking it. "Aren't those the same guys who wanted you to strip on the hood of their car?"

"Well." A fan appeared from somewhere and was used to good effect. "Sort of, though it wasn't exactly a strip, just a more progressive version of the bunny hop."

"Strip, bunny hop, uh..." Delaney's confusion turned Mickey's and Luci's attention his direction.

Luci looked him up, then down, and extended her black gloved hand and sultry smile in his direction. "Hello?"

Delaney slanted a laughing glance at Mickey before pressing a gallant kiss on her wrist above the glove. "I'm Kevin Delaney, and you have to be Miss Luci. Mickey's just been telling me about last night. I hope it hasn't put you off New Orleans?"

"Well, I haven't been asked to strip before—"

"He means at the airport," Mickey said.

"Oh." Luci blinked, trying to remember what about last night was supposed to have upset her. Mickey's pained expression prompted her to say, "Men have tried to kiss me—"

"The shooting," Mickey snapped, avoiding looking at Delaney.

The urge to grin had the edges of her mouth twitching. "Oh. That. Right. The shooting. Did you catch them?" The two men shuffled their feet, making it even harder to keep the grin at bay. A sweet smell crossed her nose's path, pulling her attention abruptly from them. "Yum. Those beignets look lovely. It's been years since I had one."

She gave them a hopeful look and saw Mickey open his mouth to cut off this blatant solicitation, but Delaney forestalled him.

"Mick and I were just going to have some. Would you like to join us?"

"I would adore it." She pretended not to see the obvious signs—streaks of powdered sugar on their suit pants—that they'd already had some, and slipped a hand through Delaney's crooked elbow. "So kind."

Mickey stood his ground, but neither of them appeared to notice, so he stomped after them, reaching the table too late to stop the order going in.

"We'll have to make it quick, Delaney," he said, going for firm and authoritative. "We have to get back—" The words died in his throat when she turned towards him, her eyes large and sad in her face. "Is something wrong?"

"Wrong?" She turned back to Delaney. "Do I look like something's wrong?"

Delaney looked uncomfortable. "Well, yes."

She leaned forward and patted his arm. "I am sorry. Sometimes I emanate."

Mickey looked at Delaney and found the same bewilderment in his eyes, so he looked at Luci just in time to see her give a tiny shake, casting off sorrow like a cat shakes off water.

"It's these clothes my aunts picked out. They were somebody's funeral outfit. Death and mourning are very strong auras." She leaned closer to Delaney, giving him a confidential smile. "Auras are very useful in my profession. Did Mickey tell you I'm an actress?"

Mickey choked.

"No, he didn't." Delaney leaned in to meet her halfway. "I'll bet you're a great leading lady."

"That's so sweet of you!" Mickey couldn't believe it when she rapped him lightly with the fan. "But I'm not really the leading lady type. I do character parts." She gave Mickey a quick look, her eyes wide and mischievous, before turning them back on Delaney. "I just finished a run in Arsenic and Old Lace."

"One of my favorites." Delaney covered her hand with his. "And you were—?"

"Abby, one of the crazy aunts who kill old and lonely men. It's an amazing coincidence, when you think about it, because when they showed it to me, I had an over-whelming urge to say my lines, only there was no Mortimer to freak out." She turned to Mickey. "Then I thought of you. Isn't it interesting the way fiction and reality sometimes collide?"

Mickey's eyes narrowed. Was that humor lurking in the

depths of her eyes? He leaned towards her and asked with calm emphasis, "What are you talking about?"

She looked surprised, then demure. She looked away, then back. "How can I say this?"

"Try words," Mickey suggested.

"It's...a...stiff."

"A...stiff?" Mickey had been expecting a curveball from her, but he still wasn't ready for it. Perhaps it wasn't possible to be ready for her curveballs.

She looked down, then back up at him, her eyes deep, green and utterly mysterious. "Stiff in...every...way."

LUCI DIDN'T GET her beignets. She looked longingly over her shoulder as Mickey and Delaney hustled her to their car and inserted her in the back seat.

"Shouldn't we call in the Crime Lab and the Coroner's office?" Delaney asked Mickey across the top of the car.

"You heard what she said about fiction and reality, Delaney. What if she's mixed too much fiction with her reality?"

Delaney's face was a study in the journey to enlightenment and then to horror as he processed this.

"Right. We wait." He pulled open his door and squeezed in, no car being wholly capable of accommodating his bulk.

Mickey grinned and slid behind the wheel. The grin faded as he watched Luci. In the back seat, she straightened her body and dress, removed the floppy hat and fluffed her hair back up. She settled in, dead center, her hands folded in her lap like a Vanderbilt in a limousine. Her pose settled, she looked around her with something less than enthusiasm.

Mickey felt his hackles rise again, but couldn't seem to help it. He didn't want to ask, didn't want to turn and look at her when he did, but couldn't help that either.

"What?"

"Is this a real police car?"

He opened his mouth but closed it when he realized he didn't have an answer. He turned around and started the car, leaving the field of battle to Delaney. He'd wanted to meet Luci. Here was his chance. Mickey put the official light on the dash and used it just long enough to force their way into traffic.

Delaney propped an elbow on the seat and said to Luci, "It's unmarked for undercover work."

"I see." Luci nodded wisely. "No siren?"

"Sorry." Delaney looked almost guilty. "Dead bodies aren't exactly emergencies."

Luci smiled, her face partially framed by the rear view mirror. "Certainly not a frozen one."

"Frozen?" Mickey's question was a quick echo of Delaney's. Like Delaney, he looked at her, though his look was, of necessity, very brief, because of the swerve the front wheels made, followed quickly by the honk from the car behind him.

"I said he was a stiff," Luci reminded them, as she quickly hunted up the seat belt and secured it. "What did you think I meant?"

"That he was—" Delaney stopped and gave Mickey a help me out here look.

In the rear view mirror, Luci saw Mickey's bug-eyed "I wish I could help you" look and barely managed to hold back a grin. She cleared the chuckle from her throat and said, "He's that, too." They were both showing their whites when they looked at her this time. Thank goodness for red lights. Luci tread lightly, using her look of gentle inquiry in hopes of bringing the tension down a few notches.

Mickey choked. Delaney managed a strangled, "And you'd know this because he's—"

"Naked," Luci finished for him.

It was Delaney's turn to choke. Mickey seemed to have recovered, though his voice sounded like it was being squeezed past a painful obstruction. "So your aunts have—"

"A naked dead man in their freezer." She used the rear view mirror to make sure her expression was approving enough to reward them for their comprehension without further antagonizing them.

The skin above Mickey's right eye developed a twitch. He realized the light had changed and put the car in gear —after earning another honk from the car behind them.

"It could be an accident," Delaney said without conviction.

"Only if bullets are a natural cause of death in this city," Luci said.

"Bullets?" Mickey sounded more despairing than questioning, but Luci decided to ignore that part.

"Well, bullet. Could be bullets, though there's just the one hole. I'm not a trained professional, but Miss Weena said he's been plugged right through the heart with something small caliber."

Mickey swallowed, a dry raspy sound, before producing with extreme dread, "Miss Weena?"

"She's had...limited experience with small caliber firearms."

Mickey got the feeling she was avoiding eye contact with him, and he made a mental note to investigate Miss Weena's firearms record before exchanging an uneasy look with Delaney. "It's field-day time for the press, with our asses in the kick position here, Delaney."

"They've been there since we signed on to be cops, Ross. Kind of getting used to it." He turned back to Luci, his face showing strain. "You say you discovered the body this morning?"

"Oh, I didn't discover it. My aunts found it, or it might have been Boudreaux. You'd have to ask them about that." A slight frown appeared between her brows, as if this was a question she hadn't expected or thought about. "He's their man. Does the gardening and odd jobs around the place."

"Uh huh." The grunt could have meant anything as Delaney busied himself writing in his notebook, asking without looking up, "Anyone recognize the victim?"

"Oh, we all did, but we don't know him, you understand."

Mickey didn't. "You all did what?"

"Recognized him." Luci sounded like she was explaining, but she wasn't. Mickey knew an explanation when he heard one, and this wasn't one. Especially when she added, "But we don't know him."

"How the hell can you recognize someone but not know them?" He could hardly see for the twitch above his eye.

Luci shrugged. It was an elegant, vaguely European shrug and caused him to twitch again, but lower down this time. He tried to think that twitch away, but Luci's mysterious heady scent was winding its way through the air currents and into his nostrils. Both twitches got worse instead of better.

"I didn't think it was possible," she said. "But it really is."

A red mist formed around the edges of his vision, mixing with the lust. St. Charles narrowed to one lane. If he could just hang on a little longer...

He slowed down, trying to keep the car at the center of the red tunnel.

Luci looked at the heirloom timepiece Miss Hermi had pinned to the front of the dress, did a little math and said,

"Could we pick up the pace a bit? They've been alone with him for quite awhile now."

Mickey felt his eyes widen as the red tunnel narrowed even more. It took him a long beat to realize there was a red light at the center. He hit the brakes and turned to look at Luci. Delaney was already staring at her, showing whites all around the brown.

"They know about evidence, don't they?" Delaney asked.

"I did explain to them about evidence and preserving the crime scene, but it's hard to know what they understand because they're aging Seymours, which makes it worse. Like wine, aging seems to bring out the bouquet more." Then she added in a confidential aside to Delaney, "You notice I was careful not to say fine wine, out of deference to Mickey's headache?"

"Mickey's head appreciates it," Mickey said, making no effort to sound appreciative. "Mind explaining why you didn't just use the phone?"

"I told you, they don't have one. The technology thing?" She looked at Mickey, then Delaney, but found only increasing confusion.

"How can they not have a telephone?" Delaney rubbed his face, but the confusion stayed where it was. He sounded dazed when he added, "It's not safe!"

Luci sighed. "I know. Uncle Willy got them one of those 'I'm falling and I can't get up' gizmos, but they buried it under the phlox." She frowned. "I wouldn't have chosen phlox. Hydrangea maybe but not phlox."

They both looked at her, then each other, then her again.

"It's genetic," she said. They didn't blink. "The light's green." Another long pause. "That means we can go now."

Mickey faced forward and went. Delaney was either comatose...or praying.

Luci relaxed. That had gone better than she expected.

8

I t wasn't that he didn't trust Fern and Donald, Artie told himself as he slid out of the cable TV truck he'd "borrowed." The overalls he'd found inside were a nice bonus. He'd had enough time to get new shoes before heading over to the Seymour's to wait for a chance to get inside. Too bad he'd forgotten about the old ladies' thing for electronics. Miss Hermi took one look at him, shrieked and slammed the door. The first time on his foot. He limped back down the walk and almost limped out in front of Fern and Donald. A quick turn took him away from them just as an unmarked police car came around the corner with lights flashing.

He turned again but didn't see the dog that had come out to sniff him. One minute he was upright. The next he was lying on his back in the grass behind a small white fence staring at a big scratch on his new shoes.

The dog, panting helpfully, jumped the fence and stuck his nose in Artie's crotch.

WHEN THEY'D STOPPED in front of the house, Delaney hopped out and opened the door for Luci. Mickey looked past him, then pointed towards the yard with a half-grin that still had dazed around the edges.

"Look. A gnome."

Bent precariously over the porch railing was a short round man with a Humpty Dumpty body and stumpy legs. His inverted bald head was visible through the porch railing.

"Boudreaux," Luci said.

Mickey watched him over-balance, then tumble into the azaleas. There was a shudder of leaves, then he emerged, leaves clinging to pate and clothes. He started to brush himself off, but stopped when he saw them.

"Would you tell the aunts we're going to look at their stiff?" Luci said.

Mickey watched in horrid fascination as Boudreaux approached, his pants slipping further down his hips with each jogging step. His cracked lips opened and out came a Cajun-tinged garble of words, none of which Mickey could decipher. He looked at Delaney and found him suffering from the same lack of comprehension.

"Uh oh." Luci shook her head. "How long have they been there?"

Boudreaux responded with another burst of gibberish.

"Oh, dear." She looked at the two men. Boudreaux trotted back to his azaleas. "We'd better hurry."

Mickey didn't move. He couldn't. Not yet. Not until he had one moment of understanding. It didn't have to be a big moment, but he damn well wanted to understand something.

"What the hell was that?"

Luci didn't answer right away. She appeared to give it serious consideration. "Two people...communicating?"

"That," Mickey said, positively, "was not communicating. That was...not even in the same star system as communicating!"

Luci looked at him the way someone looks at a lunatic. "Okay. We weren't communicating. No problem. But the aunts are still alone in the garage with your stiff."

"The garage?" Mickey heard his voice rising and cut it off at the pass. "It's in the garage?"

"Yes." She hesitated, then added, "Louise is getting tea."

"Tea?" Delaney looked uneasy. "Why?"

"I'm not sure," she admitted. "It's not like there's a lot of room in there between the Nash and the freezer. Unless we set it on top of the freezer. Oh, well." She gave them a cheery smile. "We'll just have to see what they have in mind, won't we?"

This time they didn't look at each other. Perhaps, she decided, they didn't want the other to see the stark fear in each other's eyes?

Mickey followed Luci and Delaney along the sidewalk that bordered the long side of the property. Due to the dense growth that mingled in and around the fence, he could only catch the occasional glimpse of the area behind the house. The fence barely contained the plant life and couldn't begin to contain the rich scent of leaf and bud, strangely mixed with a hint of disinfectant.

Trying not to look at Luci's swaying hips just ahead of him, Mickey's gaze bounced off a small Ford that was parked under the shade of an oak tree. Inside was an elderly couple studying a map. He wasn't in the mood to be helpful, and before they could notice him and ask for help, he re-directed his attention toward the small gate that closed off the garage area from the street.

"I'm trying to get the Nash up and running," Luci explained, or at least giving the Seymour equivalent of an explanation. "So I can get around. I wanted to rent a car but the aunts freaked, and now I can't get one because of this proctologists' convention."

"Your aunts have something against rental cars?" Delaney asked.

"Only against children driving rental cars. They have no problem now that I'm a grownup. Or they wouldn't if I could get one. Won't matter if I can get the Nash running."

"You're going to fix a Nash?" Mickey didn't try to hide his skepticism. "I suppose now you're a mechanic, too?" It was getting hard to keep up with what she did.

"Oh, I wouldn't claim to be a mechanic. That implies professional knowledge of car repair, and I repair by intuition. I expect it's something I inherited from my father's side, because the Seymours are dangerous around engines." She stopped at the gate, pushed it open, and then stepped into the tiny courtyard.

Mickey, with a sense of foreboding, followed Delaney inside.

Like many in New Orleans, the courtyard still retained its other-century feel. Small, with a meager cobbled driveway and a high wooden fence around the perimeter, it had been adequate in the days of horse and carriage. Now there was barely room to navigate an automobile, if the paint on the posts was any indication. There were also ominous signs that cleaning had taken place recently. The cobblestones still showed signs of damp in the high hot sun, and the latches of the gate and garage's double doors had been polished and oiled. The scent of disinfectant was much stronger here, too, mingling with the smell of green growing things and horse. From the partly open door could be heard the murmur of several high-pitched voices.

Against a rising instinct to run, Mickey went to the garage and pulled open the door. At the rear of the stable/garage, on the other side of a Nash that matched the paint on the posts, three old ladies stood in a semi-circle around the open freezer—which had flowers arranged on either side and a big, black bow hooked over the latch.

"What are we supposed to envy about that?" Miss Hermi asked, in her fluting, fluttery voice.

"I was a little surprised, too," Miss Theo admitted.

"Well, I'm disappointed." Miss Weena said flatly.

"I always suspected that men blew it all out of proportion," Miss Theo said. "But then, men have never made any sense to me."

Her sisters nodded their agreement like small faded vultures.

There were a lot of things Mickey would have preferred doing besides stepping into that garage. This included facing serial killers and drug dealers with assault weapons. But Luci pushed the other door open, letting sunlight flood in and alerting the old ladies that the law had arrived.

Seemingly oblivious to their discomfort, she sidestepped past the Nash and joined her aunts. For a long, unnerving beat, they stared into the freezer, the four heads angled the same direction for half of it, then the other direction.

"I see you found a place for the cake," Luci said

"Well," Miss Theo said. "He wasn't using that spot under his knees and I only had to move him a very little to get it there."

"It was my idea to put the point of the heart between his cheeks," Miss Weena said with obvious pride.

Luci smiled and put her arm around her little aunt. "Sheer genius, Miss Weena."

Mickey choked, drawing their attention to him. Miss Theo directed a sweet smiling look at Mickey. "Oh, good. You've come to get him out. He's in the way."

"WELL, THAT TEARS IT," Fern said. "They've found whatever it was Artie wanted to move and brought in the cops. Any guess how long it will be before they find the money?"

"They didn't go into the house," Donald muttered. He scratched his crotch as he considered the situation. "Might still be able to pull it off."

"Why don't we walk past, see what they're doing?" Fern was tired of sitting in the car. Even under the shade of the old oak and the windows down, the temperature was way past uncomfortable. She could feel Donald thinking, and the effort sent the temperature in the car up a few more degrees.

"Just wait a minute, Fern, they ain't been gone that long."

Fine. She'd tried to be nice. Now it was time to get nasty.

"I want to get out of this car, Donald," Fern said with

pointed calm. "I'm not as young as I used to be. And I won't be getting any older if I don't get some air."

"All right, all right. You can take a stroll...but take it slow! Careful-like. Don't want to draw no attention to us."

Right. Like the biddies peeking out from behind their lace curtains hadn't seen them sitting here for the last couple of hours. Donald might be cunning about killing, but he was clueless about the suburbs.

Fern opened the door and had one foot out when the water erupted in the yard next to them. Only a narrow sidewalk and low white fence separated them, so she got a face full of water. She slammed the door closed, just as Donald grabbed her arm.

"What?"

"Listen" he hissed, pulling the map into position again.

She didn't want to listen. She wanted to get out. The water had cooled her off until it evaporated, leaving her hotter than before. And now she was shut in the hot map tent again, where even the sultry air couldn't get at them. Then she heard it, too, and forgot about being hot. The distant sound of sirens. Lots of them. And the passing of each sweaty second brought them steadily closer.

"New Orleans has lots of crime, Donald," Fern pointed out. "I'd be surprised if we didn't hear sirens."

"Getting an itch, Fern."

Fern's eyes widened.

"Maybe we ought to get out of here..."

"Good idea."

Donald shoved at the map, the folds resisting as Fern fumbled for the ignition where the keys dangled.

"Take it slow!" Donald's hand clamped over hers, his expression anxious, sweaty. "Easy. Casual-like."

Before he finished speaking, two police cars, their lights flashing but without the warning sirens, turned the corner, coming at them from two different directions.

"Donald!"

"We'll go down fighting, Fern!" he cried, groping for the Uzi he'd stashed under the seat, even as the map tangled around his head.

As her heart accelerated to dangerous levels for her age, weight, and physical condition, the cars bounced across the rough road surface, coming closer...closer...closer...while in the distance the wail of more sirens got steadily nearer.

"I think I'm having a heart attack, Fern," Donald moaned, clutching his chest.

Fern's sweat-soaked hand slipped on the keys as she tried to fire the engine. The first police car drew level...then slid past them and screeched to a halt at the foot of the driveway the Seymour woman and her escorts had disappeared into. The other car never even came close. It slid into position near the first car as its officers slid out and hurried up the drive and out of sight.

For one long, agonized moment, Donald and Fern stared at each other in bewilderment and shock.

Then Donald quavered, "Get the hell out of here, Fern! Before the rest of them get here!"

She got, the car wobbling as she headed for the corner. In the rear view mirror, she thought she saw a man sitting in the midst of the sprinklers before she turned the corner. She forgot about him or anything else until she'd put several blocks between them and the cops and that terrifying official noise...and until the air conditioning had cooled the car to a breathable level.

Donald scowled, his recovery assured with the passing of immediate danger. "What the hell is going on?"

"I don't know." But she didn't think they'd be going to Disneyland anytime soon.

THOUGH THAWING AROUND THE EDGES, the corpse was still solid. Huddled in the bottom of the freezer with a wrapped cake under his sprawled knees, his arms were at his sides and his head was back against the edge of the freezer. His skin was tinted blue and frosty from the warm air that mingled with the cold. And, Mickey was forced to concede, frozen solid, the corpse was not a credit to his sex.

The only comment Delaney made before he went to call in the crime boys was that he must have frozen before rigor set in. This thinly veiled reference to the fact that rigor can sometimes add some emphasis made Mickey choke. While waiting for the reinforcements to arrive,

Mickey had ample opportunity to study the corpse and to realize what Luci meant when she said she recognized the corpse but didn't know him.

Their John Doe had one of those faces that you feel like you just have to know, if you could just remember where.

"ID's going to be a sonofabitch," Mickey had muttered to himself, but Luci's aunts heard.

"Really?" Miss Theo said, moving in for another look.

"I didn't realize men were so—similar." Miss Weena stared at the corpse, then looked at Mickey.

For the honor of his sex, he'd tried not to look self-conscious. Now he looked at the Crime Lab technician. "You find anything?"

"Didn't leave much to find." The tech gave him a glum glance. It was hot in the garage and the smell of disinfectant was almost overpowering.

"So, are the old broads nutty or just naive?" The forensics investigator from the Coroner's office grinned at Mickey and Delaney. He could afford to grin. He only had to deal with the stiff.

Mickey shrugged. "Probably both." He stretched, then rubbed at his temples where the ache was now a sledgehammer pounding away at his concentration.

"If you didn't find much, what was in those bags you hauled out of here?" Delaney mopped at the sweat beading along the worry lines that creased his forehead.

"Have to give the taxpayers their money's worth.

Besides, you never know. Might be something there we can use."

Mickey looked at the CI. "How long before we can get the results from the autopsy?"

He shrugged. "You won't even get a prelim for three or four days."

"Why so long?"

"Gotta thaw him first. This ain't no Thanksgiving turkey, Ross. We can't shove him under running water."

"We need an ID."

"We'll be able to get his prints by tomorrow or next day. Extremities thaw first. Looks like his family jewels are already starting." He grinned.

Mickey didn't want to talk about family jewels. He looked at the tech. "Anything unusual?" Everyone stopped and looked at him in disbelief. "Anything else?"

The tech rubbed his chin. "I did notice one thing, but I'm not sure what it means."

"What?"

"I think he might've been hosed before he was froze."

There was a moment of silence as each of the men assimilated this. It was a long moment, because this was not easy to assimilate.

"Hosed?" Mickey asked, looking at Delaney instead of the tech.

"Think so."

"How can you tell?" Delaney asked.

"He's shining like a new penny. Practically polished.

Smells like PineSol, too." This produced shudders all around as the tech turned to spit. He caught the eye of the CI and turned the action into a cough instead. Coroner hated anyone contaminating the crime scene with outside bodily fluids, even crime scenes that had been scrubbed.

"I noticed some of the usual gunshot indicators were missing," the CI said with a frown. "No external bleeding. No powder or burns. For a violent death, he's uncommon clean."

"Just some gunshot tattooing that couldn't be scrubbed away," agreed the tech, sending another round of shudders through the group. "Surprised the perp didn't take a Brillo to that. Not that it would help. Can't scrub away tattoos. Just surprised he didn't try."

"Maybe the perp knew it wouldn't help. Thanks to television, every school kid in America knows the basics of forensics," said the CI.

"Yeah, but—hosing a body?" Mickey asked.

The tech shrugged. "Maybe the perp had a thing about cleaning?"

Delaney and Mickey exchanged glances at this remark. Was there a connection between their scrubbed John Doe and the not-exactly-normal Seymours?

"Maybe the old ladies did it," said the CI, echoing Mickey's thoughts. "They sure cleaned this place up good."

"I don't want to jump to conclusions," Mickey said, not entirely honestly. He really did want to jump to conclusions. It would wrap things up, if not neatly, at least quickly, if the old ladies did it. With a caseload up the whazoo on his desk, quick was nice. The old broads would never see jail, wouldn't last that long. And if they did? Well, just pity the poor schmucks who had to do time with them.

Trouble was, his gut was telling him the easy solution didn't quite track. Damn his instincts, he thought. They'd gotten him in more trouble than he cared to remember. In a city of complex, not entirely straight-forward political relationships, good instincts weren't always wonderful to have.

"It's possible," Delaney said, "that someone familiar with this setup and crime scene techniques is our perp. Other than the stupidity of leaving the body frozen, there is a calculation to this that isn't completely insane."

Mickey nodded agreement, looking at the tech. "You notice anything else?"

"Well, I'm not the doc, you understand, but the lividity seems...well, odd."

"How?" Delaney crossed his arms over his chest and watched without expression as the body, resisting efforts to reduce it to a discreet, flat bundle, was wheeled away.

"I don't know how freezing effects lividity, but it looks to me like he was moved. The blood pooled along his buttocks and legs and along his front. Like he lay on his face for a while."

Mickey thought for a moment. "What does that mean?"

The tech shook his head. "Don't have any idea. Just thought it was unusual."

"So basically, we don't have much to go on?" Delaney said.

"Not much that I can see," agreed the tech.

"Sorry," added the CI. "Maybe after the autopsy?"

"And our ID?"

"Gonna be a bastard if he's not local. You know how slow the FBI is. But we'll do the usual. Circulate photo, prints, dental. Might scare up someone who knows him." The CI frowned. "Who does know him, I mean."

"You know you haven't a hope in hell of getting a time of death, don't you?" The CI turned to go, then looked back to add, "Guy could've been in there for years."

"Not years," Mickey protested. "The old ladies must have used it recently." Though, how, he had to ask himself, likely was it that they'd be using a freezer stored in a garage?

"Ought to ask them," the tech suggested with a smirk. "And tell them thanks for the tea."

He gave an evil chuckle.

Mickey gave him a stiff smile with a glare attached.

"Good luck," said the CI. He was smirking, too. "Think you're gonna need it."

～

THE GARDEN WAS VERY MUCH like her aunts, Luci decided. She looked with interest at the long, narrow space nestled behind the house as she made her way towards the slider swing tucked under the blossom-weighted branches of the magnolia tree.

Some of it she vaguely remembered from those long-ago visits, like the cement cherubs, urns, and gargoyles that Miss Hermi was so fond of inserting in the middle of the flower beds. But the brick pathway, winding between those randomly placed flower beds, circling the thick trunks of magnolia, oak, and cypress and passing close to the bougainvillea before finishing at the small patio crowded with metal and wicker patio furniture, seemed new. And of course it all looked smaller than she remembered.

Only one small corner had escaped the ordered disorder that was Miss Hermi's gardening style. Near the shed, and mostly out of sight of the house, was a raw scar of bare ground with lumber stacked near it.

Luci looked at it, frowning as she kicked off her shoes and sank onto the slider swing. Before relaxing against the over-sized cushions that made the wooden surface bearable, she poured herself a glass from the tall pitcher of lemonade on a tray that Louise had left perched on a cement birdbath.

A long drink, a sigh, and she relaxed back, settling her feet on the arm rest opposite. A gate creaked over near the garage, but she didn't look. Being emotionally tuned in to the easily irate Mickey Ross wasn't what she'd have chosen, but Luci was not one to kick against the vagaries of life. And it was amusing to watch him struggle against it like a fish on a line. He couldn't know she wouldn't be reeling him in.

When they came into view, both he and Delaney looked grim and hot. Though Mickey still retained his powers of observation, Luci noted. For a long moment he stared at the bare patch in the corner of the garden, before following Delaney over to join her. What was his busy brain making of that, she wondered?

She snuggled deeper in the cushions and rotated her tired feet. When they were close enough, she gave them a sleepy smile, widening it to a grin when she noted their interest in her generously exposed legs. She gestured toward the birdbath, her voice purring as it left her throat. "Help yourselves—to some lemonade. Or I can ring for some tea or coffee?"

"Lemonade's fine." Delaney's voice sounded a little husky and he still wasn't looking at the birdbath.

Taking her time, her gaze on their wide eyes and slack jaws, Luci pulled her legs down, straightening enough to tuck them discreetly under her skirt. Then watched the red run up both their faces.

Delaney turned to pour, but Mickey, after a tug on his tie and a pause to clear his throat, nodded towards the raw ground. "What's supposed to happen over there?"

"Miss Hermi claims it's to be a gazebo. She wants the

bride and groom to stand in it on the big day. Like cake decorations." She tipped her head back, giving Mickey her best wide-eyed look.

Mickey met her look and had to smile because she looked so cool and fresh after the hot garage, and because the thought of Eddie in a gazebo was the silver lining to today's cloud. "There is a God."

Luci's smile became edged with satisfaction, starting a different kind of heat coursing through Mickey's mid-section. She snuggled down in the cushions with a movement that was feline and fetching. He stopped. Where and when had "fetching" found its way into his vocabulary? That place above his eye seemed inclined to twitch again, but before it could get going, Delaney put a cold glass in his hand. Mickey applied it to the spot for a long moment before taking a long drink.

"Uh, Luci." Delaney rubbed his glass on his neck. "We need to talk to everybody connected with the house. Would your aunts mind if we commandeered a room?"

"You could commandeer the whole house and they wouldn't mind. Minding isn't in our programming." She hesitated, then asked with a casual air, "Any ideas yet who did this?"

Delaney shrugged. "Not a clue. It's too early to even guess."

"What about my aunts? You don't think they are involved, do you?"

"We're not allowed to think until we've talked to more

people." Mickey took a long drink of lemonade, then grimaced.

So he did suspect them, Luci thought, noting how he avoided looking directly at her. She supposed it was a natural reaction for someone like Mickey, who liked things ordered, controlled. Neat and tidy. The clues lined up like obedient soldiers on parade. Of course she couldn't let him pin this on her aunts.

"They didn't do it, you know."

Both men looked skeptical, though they tried not to.

"You're sure about that, are you?" Mickey took another long drink. "Look, whatever your personal opinions about this, a body was found in their freezer on their property. That means we have to talk—"

"Talk? Don't you mean interrogate?"

This time Mickey did look at her. "Talk. Ask a few questions. But if you'd like to call the family lawyer—"

Who was older than her aunts and still in love with Miss Theo. She didn't think so. Luci straightened her body until her feet were on the ground, holding his gaze with her own the whole time. "I'll just sit in on the talk, if you don't mind?"

Suspicion flared in his eyes and narrowed them to slits. The little lines at the edges and on the bridge of his nose were kind of cute.

"Why would you want to do that?" he asked, his voice as suspicious as his face.

Luci widened her gaze, mixed in innocent and said, "Why, to help."

"When hell—"

"Thanks," Delaney interrupted smoothly. "But we'll let you know if we need you."

Luci shrugged like it didn't matter. "If you don't think you need an interpreter—"

"An—" Mickey shook his head. "Why would we need an interpreter?"

"Last time I checked we all speak the same language," Delaney added his two cents, though he looked more amused than affronted.

"Yes, but without the Seymour accent. It can be confusing." She stood up. "I wouldn't want you to be. Confused, I mean."

"No," Mickey said. "I'm sure you wouldn't."

HER EYES GLITTERING WITH AMUSEMENT, Luci showed them into a room at the front of the house. The front parlor, she called it. A subtle hint at the more than just personality differences that separated Mickey from Luci Seymour and her aunts.

Delaney went straight for the table, but Mickey paused just inside the doorway and looked around. The parlor was a clean room, with long narrow windows that overlooked the street and a decor that indicated no single personality had directed its planning. Dim and cool, the furniture was a mixture of old and new, good and tacky, trendy and venerable. Not unlike the Seymour ladies.

Delaney tested each chair for soundness before taking one that still creaked a protest when he sat down. He waited a beat, but when nothing happened, pulled out a notebook and a pencil with a nearly flat tip. He licked it, then looked up.

"Start with the help?"

Luci opened her mouth, but Mickey quelled her with a look. She closed her mouth, then curved it into a slight, unsettling smile.

"I'll send them in."

Was it his imagination or did her tone add, *it's your funeral*?

Mickey picked a chair near Delaney's but didn't sit. "One at a time, please?"

Luci paused at the door. "Of course."

When she left, he was sure it was his imagination that she took the light with her. He widened the gap between the curtains and then sat next to Delaney, removing his notebook and sharpened pencil.

Louise came first. A small dour woman, she was so thin, Mickey wondered if life with the Seymours had sucked all her animation out of her, leaving only this pale husk. Was the small chalkboard and chalk she carried an intimation of trouble ahead?

"Did you know she was mute?" Delaney whispered

when she seated herself across from them without comment.

"No—" Though now that he thought about it, she hadn't said anything to him when he'd come for the pig. With some unease, Mickey noticed that she'd already written her responses on the board: no, yes, I don't know.

Despite these ominous signs, he trotted out his first question, her full name. By the time she'd squeaked her way through it, he and Delaney were twitching. And determined to limit their questions to ones she could answer with her pre-written responses. It didn't help that they didn't really know what to ask, since the only thing they knew for sure about their corpse was that he'd been shot, hosed, and then froze.

They both heaved sighs of relief when Louise left as silently as she'd arrived.

They took a short break, then summoned Boudreaux. He entered, some of the leaves from his fall into the azaleas still clinging to his person. Though vocal, they already knew he wasn't a great communicator. Between his heavy Cajun accent and an apparent speech impediment, he succeeded in communicating only his agitation.

When the door shut behind his round form, Delaney turned to Mickey. "He knows something."

"No shit. How do we find out what that something is?"

"Is it too late to take Luci up on her offer?"

"We don't need her. Besides..." Mickey looked sheepishly at Delaney. "I checked while you were in the can. She's not here. She went out to buy some clothes."

"Great. Are we screwed?"

"Of course not. How hard can it be to question some old ladies?" Mickey asked.

There was a stir in the doorway and they looked up to find Miss Weena standing in the doorway dressed as Sherlock Holmes.

"My good Wats-men," she said as she waved her pipe at them. "Why are you sitting around when the game is afoot?"

9

Over their muffelatta lunch, Donald went broody. Munching his sandwich, he stared ahead, his lids blinking to a rhythm only he could hear.

In between supplying him with food, Fern did some thinking of her own. It was obvious what Artie had wanted to remove from the Seymours before the cops found it. Now that his secret was out, would he still be able to get to the money hidden inside and pay them their money? Donald was confident it wasn't over yet, but Donald was an idiot who didn't want to leave his last job undone. Men and their egos.

Leaving Donald to his thoughts at the paper-littered table, Fern strolled over to the lunch counter for a refill on her coffee. As she waited she looked out the window. St. Charles was a pleasant prospect with its tree-lined vistas sliced by a picturesque streetcar. Only she wasn't in the mood for picturesque. Not when what she wanted to see was a view of Luci Seymour in the sights of the Uzi.

It took her a moment to realize she did see Luci Seymour—though not in the Uzi sights. She was getting on a streetcar.

"Donald!" Fern hissed. "It's her!"

He freed himself from the table and trotted over just in time to see Luci Seymour passing in front of them, her distinctive profile framed in the window of the streetcar.

"Pack your camera, Fernie. We're going to Disneyland." He stuffed in his last bite of sandwich, wiped his face on his arm and looked at her. "Let's follow that broad."

MICKEY HAD PRETTY MUCH RESIGNED himself to a state of permanent headache before they managed to persuade Miss Weena, aka Holmes, to sit down across the table from them. Her cupid's bow mouth pursed in a manner that he suspected was supposed to be thoughtful.

"Before we go hunting we need to get some details cleared up, Miss Weena," Mickey said, smiling in what he hoped was an encouraging manner.

"Of course." She chewed on the end of the pipe, then removed it to point at them. "I've been giving this a lot of thought. With my law enforcement experience, deduction comes naturally to me."

"Law enforcement experience?" Delaney asked like someone who didn't really want an answer.

"As a security guard." She gave him an encouraging smile. "Packing heat satisfied a deep need that I didn't know I had until I packed it."

"A...security guard?" Delaney croaked out.

Mickey just croaked.

"I had to cut the gig because I couldn't keep the gun belt up. Kept falling down around my ankles. And if you loop it around your neck, it's hard to get the gun out." She leaned forward to confide, "That's how he got shot."

Mickey swallowed. "Shot—who?"

"My boss." She looked at Delaney, whose mouth was twitching, but not producing words. "It was just a flesh wound." She looked at Mickey, who knew he was doing the landed fish, gaping thing, but was unable to do anything about it. "He was too old for children anyway."

It was, Mickey decided, a nightmare. An amusement park nightmare where you wander around getting on safe rides, but they all turn out to be the roller coaster to hell.

Delaney, dazed but trying, got up and pulled out Miss Weena's chair.

"We'll call you," he said. He held the door for her. Mickey saw her give him a flirty smile, then pat his butt before sashaying out the door. Delaney shoved the door closed and looked at Mickey.

Mickey grinned. "Hey, you're the one who thought they sounded interesting."

Delaney shuddered. "I must have been out of my mind."

MISS HERMI WAS A WELCOME RELIEF, a brief respite in the Seymour storm. She didn't try to squeeze anything, kept her distance, and tried to answer their questions. Her problem was a simple lack of interest. She wanted to talk about Eddie and Unabelle's honeymoon, something Mickey preferred to never think about.

"It's so important to get a good start to the marriage, don't you think?" Miss Hermi's voice flowed out her papery lips, like a gently babbling brook.

Mickey looked at Delaney, who looked as clueless as Mickey felt. They both shrugged, which she seemed to take as encouragement to continue.

"Men think all that's important is good sex, but what about shopping? Sex is slam, bam, thank you ma'am, but you take mementos home with you."

It was a wild guess, but Mickey had a feeling that Miss Hermi was probably responsible for the collection of National Park shot glasses scattered around the room. It was easier to focus on this thought than the one where Eddie was slamming, bamming or thank-you-ma'aming Unabelle. Or that sweet little Miss Hermi had just said that.

Delaney pulled himself together and managed to dig

out the meager information that Miss Theo had jurisdiction over the freezer and Miss Hermi ruled the garden.

"We came through the garden," Mickey said. "It was very—interesting."

Pink flaked her cheeks. "Well, I do think it's coming along nicely. In days past, I wouldn't have chosen cement as a medium for expression, but it's turned out rather well and far less costly than marble." She frowned. "Not too sure about that gazebo, though. That was Reggie's idea. He said it wouldn't matter if it wasn't in the middle of the garden, because I couldn't cut down a tree, even for art's sake. Normally I wouldn't listen to a Seymour male, but Reggie's a little less asinine than one might expect."

"Reggie?" Mickey pulled the name out of her jumble of words. "I don't think anyone's mentioned Reggie?"

"Well, he's easy to forget when he's not here. He's in Cleveland. He has business interests there. When he gets back he's giving the bride away. In the gazebo. After he finishes it, of course."

"Of course," Mickey echoed, looking at Delaney. Cleveland. Luci had said something about Cleveland last night. Something about her neighbor. He realized what he was doing and gave himself a mental shake. Focus, Ross. Focus on Reggie. He might not have the legs Luci had, but he could be a real, viable suspect.

≈

EVEN AFTER TWENTY MINUTES EXPOSURE, and twenty years living in New York City, Fern couldn't quite believe what she was seeing. Perhaps it was the sluggish economy that had driven the mall manager to attempt the Christmas in August theme, complete with several truckloads of imported snow and, inexplicably, ten Elvis impersonators.

The snow was piled next to the escalator and heaped to resemble a mountain slope, with plastic evergreens randomly impaling the white surface for realism. Then the pile was opened up for snow play to hundreds of children. The only person who seemed surprised when the children ran amok was the organizer of the event.

Next to the snow hill was a gaudy stage where the Elvises were assembled, each attired, like the stamps, to represent a different period in Elvis's life.

Beside her, Donald choked for the third time. Fern looked at him. Judging by the amount of eyeball white showing, he was approaching heart attack level. Not that she blamed him. It had been a long, discouraging day, broken only by that brief moment of hope when they picked up the Seymour woman's trail at the streetcar stop. Why she had to visit four malls besides this one, not to mention ride the bus across the bridge over the river—

Fern's blood pressure wasn't doing so hot either. Oh, how she wanted to do her, Fern thought, staring at the now-hated profile browsing in a store across from them. This hit was taking on the trappings of a Quest. Something to do for the pleasure as much as for the money.

But first she had to get Donald calmed down. Or he would do her right here in the mall in front of everybody, and they'd never get to Disneyland.

"Why don't you sit on that bench there, Donald, and I'll get you a Coke or something?"

He nodded, and she paused only to make sure of her bearings before heading for a food counter she could see in the distance, her orthopedic shoes not protecting her aching feet from the stone floor. As she collected their drinks and made her way back to where Donald waited, she could hear the discordant wailing of the Elvises turn into synchronized sound. Easing through the crowd that had gathered, she could see an Elvis in black leather with slicked-back hair crooning a love song into the mike.

But no sign of Luci.

"Here." Fern shoved the drink at Donald and scanned the crowd. "Where is she? We haven't lost her, have we?"

Donald ignored Fern's impatience, taking a long drink before answering morosely, "Nah, she's still there. In the front, by the stage."

Fern craned her neck, her height enabling her to see over most of the crowd. "Where—?"

Then she saw her. She was, as Donald said, right at the front and center, in the heart of the action, swaying to the music, a look of appreciation lighting her face.

Fern didn't blame her for the appreciation. He was a fine Elvis, especially in the hip area. Fern turned to

Donald. "You know, he kind of reminds me of you. Give him a switchblade and a gat—"

Her voice failed, so she gave Donald a grim, misty smile. His narrow shoulders squared, and without speaking, Donald stood and pulled her against his beer belly, steering her around their corner of the court with an air of sleazy aplomb.

When the music faded into applause, he stopped and looked up into her eyes with a look that peeled away the years, leaving a young thug and a rebellious girl facing each other once more.

"Oh, Donald!" Fern's scant chest swelled with her sigh. She started to lean her head on his scraggy shoulder, but he stiffened and pushed her away. "Donald?"

"Damn! She's gone!" He frantically scanned the crowd. "Damn the woman! We lost her, Fern!"

A snowball hit him square in the face.

MISS THEO DIDN'T ENTER, she made an entrance. There was much of the grande dame about her, from her elegantly styled white hair to her old-fashioned buttoned down shoes. Of the three, she reminded him the most of Luci, particularly around the eyes, which were intelligent and somewhat amused.

He held her chair, then resumed his. Seated, the differences between the sisters seemed to fade away, leaving only the similarities, especially in the way she looked at him, her gaze calm, yet distant.

"You're all very much alike, aren't you?" Delaney said, echoing Mickey's thought.

Her fine brows arched, enhancing the sense of familiarity.

"Yes, though dear little Luci doesn't quite fit. Sometimes she doesn't seem like a Seymour at all, she's got so much of her father in her. Very forceful gene pool, he had. It's interesting to see how she turned out, because we all wondered, her being the first in so many years."

"The first?" Delaney asked with a hint of caution.

"Offspring of a female Seymour. The men have produced a hutch-full, of course, and a pretty dismal bunch it was, too. And then Lila's beaux, not that I didn't like him, but so forceful and determined he could change us. You can imagine how worried we were when we found out she was increasing. Thank goodness our worries were ill founded. She turned out to be quite sweet and almost normal. Of course, we love her so dearly that we don't mind her little eccentricities." Her smile was refined but filled with a child-like wonder from another distant time.

Mickey had no idea how to respond to this, so he looked at Delaney.

Delaney cleared his throat. "We were wondering about the freezer, Miss Theo?"

"Well, isn't that interesting. So was I. It will have to be

cleaned and aired, but do you think that's enough? I wouldn't want to upset our guests."

"Your...guests?" Delaney's face showed his difficulty in following this.

"The party. For dear Eddie and Unabelle. It's this weekend, so it's important to get this resolved as soon as possible." A wisp of handkerchief fluttered when she used her hands to punctuate the urgency of the situation.

"Uh huh." Dumbfounded staring was getting them nowhere. Time for a change of tactics. "I can see this is of grave concern to you, and we'll get back to you on it as soon as we can," Mickey said. "In the meantime, we need to figure out how the body got there in the first place."

Delaney gave Mickey a look of respect as Miss Theo stared at them, her brows once more arching toward her white bun. He could see her processing this, see it all playing out in her faded blue eyes.

"Well," she finally said. "Isn't that interesting? I never even thought about how he got there. So, do you think someone put him there?"

"Well." Delaney still sounded like someone was strangling him. "I don't think he got there on his own."

"Is it possible," she asked as she leaned toward them, her voice dropping to a more confidential level, "that the person who shot him put him there?"

"We think so, yes," Mickey said, a shade too heartily. "Can you think of anyone who could—or would—do something like that?" Her wide gaze stared at him without blinking for a long beat. Mickey found he couldn't fight the imperative to fill the silence. "It would have to be someone who knew about the freezer, was familiar with the garage area and the comings and goings around the house."

"But it would also have to be someone who would do that, who would shoot someone and put them in a freezer, wouldn't it?" Miss Theo's face showed only gentle inquiry. There was no awareness that this criteria could include her or her sisters.

"That's a good point," Delaney said, with obvious flattery. "Anyone who springs to mind?"

"Well, I hate to be ugly, but—Reggie springs to my mind."

Mickey and Delaney straightened and exchanged hopeful glances.

"He is a Seymour male," she added, as if this were a crime, too. "And he's been in prison."

This turned a weird lead into a hot prospect. Mickey asked, "Really? Prison?"

"I'm afraid so." She looked pensive. "Perhaps he missed it when his mother died. She was the matron in a women's prison. His father married an IRS agent a few years later."

Delaney blinked, probably because he'd run out of the more extreme repertoire of responses. "That would...affect a kid."

"Particularly one who is already marked by the Seymour curse."

Mickey looked up from his notes. "Seymour curse?"

Even as the words left his mouth, he knew he'd made a mistake. This was one of those roads that shouldn't be traveled. He knew it in his gut.

"Ineptitude." Miss Theo looked wise. "There's not a Seymour male, dead or alive, who isn't a waste of space." She gave them a bright smile that seemed to say, "Aren't we glad we've got that behind us?"

Mickey decided the better part of valor would be to leave it behind them and try another tack. "Do you know if the garage is kept locked? Or the gate to the street?"

"Oh, you'd have to ask Boudreaux that, but I would imagine so. I mean, we haven't been out in the Nash since his eyes went. He's nearly blind, poor man, but still very eager."

"We noticed," Mickey said, dryly. "I understand Reggie is in Cleveland?"

Miss Theo nodded. "On business."

"And when is he due back?" Delaney asked.

"Well, for the wedding, naturally. He's giving the bride away. But also for the party." This appeared to worry her, too, if the crease in her brow was indicative of worry. It was hard to know with a Seymour, Mickey was learning. "He promised to help Boudreaux pour the cement for the gazebo. Case of the inept leading the blind, I'm afraid. Hermi's much too easy to get round, I'm afraid."

"Cement?" Mickey spared a quick, thoughtful look at Delaney. He made a note while Delaney tried again with the freezer.

"Back to the freezer, Miss Theo. When was the last time you looked in it?"

"Last week. I wanted to get it started. I mean, you don't just turn it on and get cold air, you know. It has to warm up, or would that be cool up?" A slight dark look lowered her gentle brow, then she brightened. "Luckily it was already on."

For the first time since the mention of Reggie, Mickey felt a surge of hope. "So that means the body was stashed there sometime between when you looked in it and today—"

Miss Theo shook her head. "Oh no, it had to be before that."

Mickey didn't want to ask, because he was afraid he already knew the answer, but he had to. It was his job. "Why?"

"The body was already there. I'm guessing that's why the freezer was on. Quite the heat wave we had this month, don't you think?"

Her pale, helpful gaze beamed on Mickey, then shifted to Delaney. Mickey tried to ask, but the words couldn't get out his constricted throat. Delaney tottered in to fill the gap. "And the time before that—that you looked in the freezer?"

"Oh, my," she leaned back, her mind obviously going back in time. "It would have to be at least twenty."

"Days?" Delaney asked with faint hope.

"Years, dear."

"But—" Finally Mickey managed to speak. "But—why didn't you call us when you first found it?"

"How could I call you, dear boy, when I didn't know you?"

FERN LEANED against the railing that overlooked the mall's center court, lifting first one foot, then the other in an attempt to relieve the pain from her corns. Below her, the shrieks of the snow-crusted children rose in painful spirals of sound as the snow hill melted beneath the combined assault of bodies and heat.

Mercifully the Elvises were on break, reducing the crowd enough for Fern to pick out Donald's forlorn figure propped against the central pillar. Soon she would descend the escalator and admit defeat in her attempts to find Luci Seymour, but there was no hurry . . .

Almost as if he read her thoughts, Donald looked up and saw her. She straightened, giving a disheartened shrug to the question she knew he was asking. Time to join him. She turned, almost missing his sudden outbreak of frenzy.

"What?" she mouthed, shaking her head.

He calmed down, managing a gesture to her right. Bewildered, Fern looked left, doing a full one-eighty turn before her gaze collided with the profile of their quarry: Luci Seymour leaning against the rail barely twelve inches from Fern. Fern gripped the rail as her heart rate surged.

Through the mist that formed over her eyes, she saw Donald jumping up and down. She turned. Luci was heading for the escalator. In a daze, Fern turned to follow her. A crowd formed behind Fern, frustrating her desire to maintain a distance, and Fern was forced onto the escalator right behind Luci. What Fern could see of her, she looked happy, serene, cheerful. It was so unfair. Anger started deep but moved upwards, focusing on her, Luci, the cause of all Fern's problems.

Just as the escalator began its drop, Luci leaned over the side to stare at the children playing in the snow below.

"Poor little mutts," she said. "Someone ought to show them how to play in the snow."

Luci arched up on her toes, craning for a better view. The action made it all blindingly clear for Fern. Someone should show the little mutts how to play in the snow.

She was jostled from behind. Instinctively Fern softened her knees, allowing herself to be thrust forward against the off-balance Luci. A judicious upward thrust and Fern had the satisfaction of seeing Luci sail over the side of the escalator and disappear from view.

Too bad she couldn't enjoy the sensation. Or keep herself from tumbling down the moving stairs.

THEY TRIED to ask Miss Theo more questions, but the momentum was gone. She told them more about Reggie than they really wanted to know, something about the family crest that they didn't understand, about his stepmother getting strangled by an irate tax evader and his father getting struck by lightning while using the toilet—thereby ending all hope of Reggie having brothers and sisters. Miss Theo seemed to think this was a good thing, Reggie's side of the family being even more useless than was "normal." Though she did concede that Reggie was less useless than she'd expected, given his maternity, paternity and jail time. When she left, Mickey and Delaney were both exhausted.

Delaney stared at the ceiling, his hands behind his head. "She did warn us, you know. She said we didn't speak Seymour."

Mickey stared at the floor. "The Captain will have to take me off the case when he finds out Eddie's a suspect."

"Eddie's not a suspect."

"He will be. I'm going to make him a damn suspect."

"If Eddie's a suspect, so's the Pope. Give it up." He sat up and rubbed his face for a moment, then a look of determination replaced woe. "Instead of making up evidence, let's figure out what we've got."

"You know what we've got. We got nothing."

"I'm not saying we got a lot, but there's got to be something here."

Mickey looked at him, his expression incredulous. "Like what?"

Delaney looked at his notes, then at the flat pencil,

discarded them and picked up Mickey's notebook. "Let's look." He looked down. Under Louise's name Mickey had written: uncommunicative. His lips twitched. "So Louise didn't say much. We're supposed to look for non-verbal clues, too. What was your impression of her?"

"That she's good at not giving non-verbal clues. Or any other kind of clues."

Delaney grinned. "True. You think she might be protecting the old ladies?"

"I don't know," Mickey said, then added, "I did wonder if Boudreaux was. He seemed, I don't know, more incoherent than he was with Luci. He wouldn't meet our eyes."

"Okay! Now we're cooking!" He made a mark beside Boudreaux's name, then looked up. Question marks don't take long to make. "Anything else?"

"I say we pin it on Reggie and be done with it. He sounds like someone it'd be easy to pin something on."

"Hey, works for me. How we go about it?"

Mickey paced across the room, then jerked the curtains back and stared out at the street.

Police activity was starting to wind down, thereby reducing press activity also, leaving only the terminally curious to hassle the uniform left to guard their crime scene. The harsh midday sun was beginning to soften to afternoon gold. A few streets away he could hear rush hour beginning to gear up. Somewhere, people thinking of supper, evening TV, or hot dates. Somewhere there were people who could go to bed right now if they wanted.

None of those people were in this room.

"Any bright ideas?" Delaney asked.

"The last bright idea I had was—" He stopped, swiveling to face Delaney, an arrested expression on his face. "Of course. Why didn't I think of her before?"

"Her? Who?"

"Gracie. The normal Seymour!"

THOUGH BOTH MEN had been awaiting her arrival, they didn't hear Miss Grace Seymour come in, bringing a wave of fresh, cool air with her.

"Did you wish to speak to me?"

Like thirsty men in a desert, they turned towards the oasis of serenity she brought with her. About the same height as Luci, Grace exuded normality like a subdued perfume. Her light brown hair was pulled back from the plain lines of her face and bundled at the nape of her neck. She dressed simply, neatly, in a dress that was somewhere between blue and gray. Her eyes were calm and inquiring.

Delaney pulled out a chair for her, almost tripping over it in his hurry.

He must, Mickey realized, be more tired than he thought, because for a moment her profile wavered into near transparency before getting solid again. Or maybe it was this place getting to him. And them. He rubbed his eyes, trying to force them to wakefulness.

"Thank you," she said, with merciful brevity. While the two men seated themselves, she watched them in comfortable refreshing silence.

"Miss Seymour—" Mickey began, because Delaney seemed content to just stare at her.

"Oh, please, call me Gracie."

"Sure." Anything she wanted. "This is my partner, Kevin Delaney. We were wondering if we could ask you a few questions about the murder?"

She nodded, looked at Delaney and got caught in his rapt stare. Mickey grinned, cleared his throat and launched into their spiel, but it was pretty much a no-go. She didn't know much more than the others. At least she let them know it with three words or less answers. Mickey could have cried with relief. The only time he felt cut adrift was when they got to Reggie.

"Yes, he lives in Cleveland. Business interests, I understand."

"So we heard," Mickey said. "Can you tell us a little more than that?"

"It's hard to find more to tell about Seymour men, I'm afraid."

"Could you try?" This from Delaney, whose expression bordered on fatuous. She cast him a shy glance, followed by an even shyer smile.

"All right." She thought for a moment before speaking.

"Well, they're kind of stupid and inept, really. All of them. Their only real skill is this strange ability to persuade terrifyingly competent women to marry and take care of them."

"Oh." Mickey didn't know what else to say.

"You know, you ought to talk to Velma. She lives next door and is hoping to be Mrs. Reggie. Of course, she thinks she's psychic, but you mustn't hold that against her. Otherwise she's pretty sensible—or Reggie couldn't, wouldn't, look at her. It's sort of a biological imperative." She directed a grave, flickering smile at them.

"Oh." Mickey looked at Delaney, but he was looking at Gracie, so he made a note. "Anything else you can tell us?"

"Well, you might want to talk to Unabelle."

"I'd planned on it," Mickey said. Shit. Was his uncle's fiancée mixed up in a murder? "Anything in particular I should ask her?"

"I'm not really sure. I just think she—absorbs more information than she lets on. You'll have to ask the right questions, of course, because I doubt she knows she knows anything. Be creative."

"Creative? Great." There was already too much creativity around here for Mickey's taste.

Gracie smiled. "The girls are difficult, I know. Navigating the Seymour Zone is difficult for outsiders. We're like curious children."

The girls? Mickey had to smile at that. While he was

smiling, she rose and glided to the door in a single, liquid movement.

"You're not like that, Gracie," Delaney said. "Why is that?"

She stopped, then looked back. "Because I'm no longer curious?"

She left, her passage so smooth and silent they didn't see or hear the door's movement, and took all the cool from the room with her.

The silence was long, like that after a stellar performance by a diva, then Delaney said, "I like her."

Mickey grinned. "I noticed."

"She's so—so—"

"Normal."

"I was going to say nice." There was a moment of silence, then Delaney said, half to himself, "If I were a marrying man—"

Mickey looked up from his notes. "They don't marry."

Silence. "Why don't they marry?"

"I have no idea."

Another longer silence.

"Damn shame."

"Maybe," Mickey said, his mind's eye reluctantly fixed on a different, younger Seymour's face. "Could be a blessing by a merciful God."

10

Dante, aka Harvey Mertz, didn't look dangerous. Dressed in quantities of baggy silk and an oversized wool coat, he had a young smooth face, round surprised eyes, and standup blond hair. With practice, he kept his soft mouth sardonic, but he didn't have to practice the cold glow in his pale eyes. That came naturally. As did his affinity for criminal activity.

He'd started out with an illegal gambling operation and then expanded into anything that offered a profit—except drugs.

"Drugs lack artistic appeal," he told Max, his assistant-in-crime. "Besides, you either have to go national or wind up dead." Neither of these options appealed to Dante. It was nice staying alive. And staying local it was easier to watch his back. He knew where his friends were if he needed to kill them.

When he wasn't figuring ways to amass tax-free funds, he designed and constructed Mardi Gras floats. It served as a useful cover, being located in the warehouse district where comings and goings were hard to monitor, and gave him an outlet for his creativity.

Dante also liked being atypical.

Because of the revolving nature of his friendships, Dante kept close to what family he had, particularly to his Aunt Cloris, who had assumed his upbringing when his mother got tired of her husband being in jail and caught a bus out of New Orleans when Dante was eight.

Their relationship was almost Oedipal, until Cloris married a year ago and moved to Miami with her new husband, Arvin Maxwell. Arvin had taken a powder with all her money just six months later.

"Still no word on Arvin, Mr. Dante."

Dante turned from his perusal of a recent float design and frowned at his assistant, Max.

"That's not acceptable, Max. It's been six months."

"I know, Mr. Dante, but the guy's dropped off the earth."

"Even rats have to go to ground somewhere. He's out there, Max. I want him."

"I've got everybody looking, Mr. Dante. We'll find his hole."

Dante nodded, his face brooding. "You arrange for Cloris to get picked up at the airport?"

"Yes, sir. Cain and Abel are going. You want them to take the limo?"

"Yeah. Have them get her some candy and flowers. Daisies. She likes daisies. And tell them to have lots of tissues on hand. She's still upset."

"Right."

Max didn't leave, just waited until Dante asked, "Was there something else, Max?"

"Benny the Book's here. Wanted to know if he could talk to you."

"Benny? Am I angry with Benny, Max?"

"No, Mr. Dante."

"Is Benny angry with me?"

"No, Mr. Dante. He says he has something to show you."

"If it were anyone else, I'd have you just kill him, but Benny is innocuous. Send him in. Let's see what he wants to show me."

When Max ushered Benny into his office, a sardonic humor lit Dante's pale gray eyes. Benny was "old school" criminal, back in the days when underlings cringed into the "Boss's" presence. He even had a satchel clutched to his chest. He removed his cap and fiddled nervously with it.

"Park it, Benny, and tell me what's agitating your bone box."

"Huh?"

Dante sighed. Why couldn't henchmen have intelligence,

a little humor? It would have been nice to have a little give and take, a tiny clash of minds. But that just led to nasty power struggles and dead bodies to hide. He sighed for lost opportunities as he indicated a chair with a movement of his head.

Benny perched obediently but uneasily.

"So what's on your mind?"

Benny's eyes bulged. Perhaps he wasn't aware he had a mind to have anything on? He licked his lips several times, his fingers playing with the handle of the satchel as he began to sweat and talk.

"Ya know I pick up a bet or two around the old-timers bins, boss? Oldsters, they like to play the odds now and again, but they can't get out, so I go in when I can. Pick up a pretty good sum there. Honest."

"A bookie that makes house calls. How quaint."

"Huh?"

"Nothing." Another sigh. "Please, go on with your fascinating story, Benny." He leaned back in his chair with a discreetly concealed yawn.

"Uh, right." Agitation always made Benny breathe heavily through his nose, so his words came out nasal and accompanied by little puffs and grunts. "'Bout a year ago I meets this broad, calls herself Jane, but I figure she made it up. Some do, when they know somebody won't like 'em to bet. Me, I don't worry none, cause most pays cash anyways and they's easy enough to track down if they don't. You know, Boss."

"That's right, Benny. I know. You're obviously a prince

among pedestrian bookies. So what's the problem, if it's not a bad debt?" It was amusing to toy with Benny, but not for very long. No challenge to it.

"This Jane, she brung me somethin' strange today. To place a bet." Benny popped to his feet, opened the bag, and extracted a shoebox. Then another and another until there were six of them on the desk. When blank looks met his efforts, Benny opened one box and dumped the contents onto the desk, creating a mini-money-snowdrift.

Max looked at Dante, then popped the lids off the other boxes. "Holy shit!"

"Indeed." Dante leaned forward, caught a handful of the bills and fanned them in his hand. "That's a pretty big Christmas package, Benny." He looked closer, then up again. "Ones, Benny? Are they all ones?"

"All of 'em, boss. Jane, she never placed this big before. Small bills, small bets, but not this small." He looked bewildered by his own logic and added, "But not this big, if you know what I mean."

Dante gave him a quick resigned look, his long fingers playing with the pile. "These good? They aren't queer?"

"I never been suckered with no queer bills, Boss. Not now, not ever." Benny spoke with a seedy dignity.

Dante let the bills flutter back to the pile, then leaned back again. "What's the bet?"

"Saints. Sunday."

"Excuse me?" Dante straightened again. "She bet on the Saints?"

Benny nodded mournfully. "To win."

"Sucker bet," Max said.

Dante nodded, leaned back in his chair and stared at the money. "Why all single digits? Kind of bulky."

"Dunno, Boss. But... " Benny looked even more mournful. "They's more where this come from."

"Really?" Dante's eyes narrowed. "How do you know that?"

"Cause she tole me so."

"She told you?"

"That's right, boss. Said it were too many to carry all at once."

"Well, well." Dante picked up a handful of the bills and let them shower back down while Max and Benny watched. "That's very interesting, Benny. Very interesting."

"You got something, Ross?" Delaney topped off his coffee cup then relaxed back in his chair.

"I don't know. Maybe." Mickey sat back, arching his back to relieve the stiff area, his fingers beating a tattoo on the table. They'd been going over their notes and the statements collected by the uniforms canvassing the neighborhood while they waited for Unabelle and Velma to return. "Since we don't know who, I've been trying to concentrate on why. Why hose him? Why put him in the freezer? Why keep him at all? Why a gazebo?"

"A gazebo?" Delaney gave Mickey a skeptical look. "Would you like some more coffee?"

Mickey grinned, albeit tiredly. "Stay with me on this. I think I can tie it all together. We agree he was probably stripped and hosed to remove forensic evidence. But then why freeze him? The smart thing would be to get him decomposing as fast as possible, right?"

"Right," Delaney agreed, "unless you're a wacko—"

"Or you don't have a good place to stash a body. This is the middle of the city. It's not that easy to find bare ground and bury someone. Unless you have a garden and just happen to be putting up a gazebo."

"Ah, I see where you're going. You think Reggie planned on inserting our John Doe into the foundation?"

Mickey shrugged. "Him or someone in the neighborhood. There are mostly old ladies on this street, but we've got three possibles also away right now. Jacob Arthur supposedly is visiting his daughter. Arthur Will is away on a singles cruise. And Arturo Degas is visiting family in Mexico."

Delaney looked amused. "Three Arthurs? Pretty unlikely sounding suspects."

"Yeah, but my scenario could stretch to include them. We've got a perp who kills, probably unpremeditated or the body would already be stowed. If it was Reggie, he talks Miss Hermi into installing a gazebo for him to stash the body under, but gets sidetracked when he has to go to Cleveland. If it was a neighbor, same thing, unplanned killing. Sees

Seymour ladies starting a gazebo, but then the work is interrupted so he stows the body in the unused freezer."

"And then leaves town, too? Pretty thin, Ross."

"Hey, I didn't say it was a good scenario. Just that it was one. Personally, old Reggie's got my vote. Everybody we've talked to expects Reggie back for the party this weekend. A local perp would know that and could plan for it. What they couldn't plan for was Miss Theo deciding to restart the freezer for her cakes."

"True. Hey, if nothing else, it gives us something to plump up this report to the Captain. Hopefully Miss Velma will be able to tell us more about Reggie. I'll admit he's got my vote, too, and if she doesn't, well, if she doesn't, maybe her muse—or whatever it is psychics use—will be able to—" Delaney grinned.

There was a knock on the door and a uniform poked his head in. "Captain's been trying to get a hold of you two.
"

Mickey and Delaney looked at each other, then checked their cell phones.

"Mine's dead," Mickey said.

"Mine, too," Delaney said.

"He wants a progress report before PR issues a statement to the news boys."

"My suggestion would be a brief, succinct, no comment," Mickey said.

"To the news or the Captain?" Delaney asked.

Mickey thought for a moment. "Both. No one's gonna like what they hear anyway."

CAPTAIN HENRY PRYCE WAS AN ERECT, stern-featured man with dark, graying hair, hazel eyes and a straight, humorless mouth. Fortunately for the men under him, it was only the mouth that lacked humor. A healthy sense of humor was a necessary ingredient for surviving the roller coaster that was the New Orleans Police Department.

While Delaney delivered their Laurel and Hardy report, Mickey prayed for that sense of humor to surface. Delaney finished and the silence stretched beneath the Captain's cool assessing stare.

Mickey tugged at his tie. Delaney swallowed, the sound echoing around the silent room.

"You call this a report?" Pryce looked at Mickey.

"A—preliminary report, sir." Mickey punctuated this with a large swallow of his own.

Pryce turned to Delaney.

"An extremely preliminary report," Delaney added.

"Really?" He wheeled to stare out the window, his hands clasped behind his rigid back. "And which part do you think we should share with the press?"

"As little as possible, sir," Mickey said with heartfelt conviction.

Pryce wheeled around. Mickey flinched back—until he saw the humor melting the ice in the Captain's eyes.

"Had an interesting time with the Seymours, did you, gentlemen?"

Mickey and Delaney exhaled at the same time.

"Yes, sir," Mickey agreed. Interesting was the non-profane term for their time with the Seymours.

"We do have a viable suspect, sir," Delaney pointed out.

"I hope so. The Seymours have connections all over this state. They helped arrange or were present at a lot of prominent weddings. Some for people presently sitting on the bench."

The significance of this allusion was not lost on the two detectives who were well acquainted with the dangerously complex nature of political connections in Louisiana. Mickey shifted uneasily as Pryce frowned, one hand fiddling with the papers scattered across the top of his desk.

"How are the ladies?"

"They seem to be fine, sir," Delaney said, giving Mickey a puzzled look. Mickey shrugged.

"Upset over this business?"

"If you think they are upset, you must not know them, sir," Mickey said.

The edges of Pryce's stern, straight mouth twitched, his version of a grin.

"Any   connection   between   this   murder   and   the shooting last night? I understand their niece was with you at the time?"

"We don't think so, sir," Delaney said. "Why?"

"Quite a coincidence. Sure it's one?'

"We can look into it," Mickey offered, wondering how they'd do that. They knew so little about both incidents. Which was a connection—of sorts.

Pryce shook his head. "Just keep it in mind, in case a connection does emerge. What about Eddie? His fiancée clear?"

"Well, we can't rule out anyone," Delaney pointed out. "We've found no connection, though we've received information she might know something without realizing it. She wasn't home when we left, but we're planning on questioning her as soon as she gets back."

"If you're worried about conflict of interest, sir—" Mickey began hopefully.

"If I worried about that, Ross, I'd have to disqualify most of the force from every case we have. Just mind how you go. The Seymour's' political connections go way back. It's a—tricky situation. The department will support you, of course, even if you step on some toes. As long as you don't step unnecessarily."

"Yes, sir," the two men chorused. Mickey stirred restlessly. The mandate to investigate was double-edged. But, this was New Orleans. Double-edged mandates were invented here.

"What's your case load look like right now?"

Heavy to impossible, Mickey wanted to say, but he didn't. "We're putting in a lot of time on the Dante thing."

"You got something on him you haven't told me about?"

"No, sir."

"Anything else?"

"Just twenty or so on-goings that aren't going anywhere right now," Delaney admitted.

"Then give the Seymour investigation top priority. It could easily go high profile and we want to be ready. But don't neglect your other cases, of course."

"Of course."

Mickey and Delaney exchanged glum looks as they shuffled out. It seemed ironic, Mickey decided as they drove past the prison, to know that the people they arrested would get more rest tonight than they would.

ARTIE GOT out of his car, adjusted the Pizza Party shirt he'd lifted from the back of the store and then picked up the pizza he'd bought from the front of the store. The old ladies didn't like technology, but they loved pizza. The whole situation was costing him way more than he counted on, but inside the house was all the fruit of his scamming labors. Now, when it was too late, he could admit it had been stupid to put all his dollars in one attic, but it had seemed so safe, so secure. And he hadn't been lying when he told Fern no one wanted to launder dollar bills.

He hadn't counted on that or that he'd get so many. They'd just flooded in and continued to flood in, one at a time, no matter how fast he spent them. Already he had a trunk full. When he'd seen the nearly empty attic, the urge to fill it had been irresistible.

He hadn't counted on Luci, of all people, coming here, of all places. The one person on the face of the earth who could bring scrutiny upon him—a scrutiny that would bar him forever from Helen.

It was unfortunate they'd found Hermann, but they didn't seem to have found the money. Somehow, someway, he had to start moving it out. But to do that, he had to get inside. The pizza would be his calling card. Louise always left people standing in the hall. Once he was alone...

He started up the steps, but was only halfway up when he heard a car stop behind him. With deep foreboding he turned and saw the cops getting out of the car. His turn became a dive into the shrubs by the steps. No, not shrubs. Ivy.

"Ouch," he said before he could stop himself.

When the sun beats down on New Orleans, it's easy for outsiders to think it's just another frenetic city with the requisite old buildings and a swamp for contrast. But with the creeping dusk comes, not a cooling down, but a heating up of the other New Orleans as the night-lifers heed the siren call to pleasure. For the street cops, it's the siren call to pissed off as they struggle to keep the peace against increasing odds. Night, and the strange allure of the yellow moon, makes their job harder, enhancing what is worst in the violent, the dishonest, and the insane.

Mickey was thinking about the insane as they once more pulled to a stop in front of the Seymour house, which was dark and quiet, except for bits of light that crept past the heavily curtained windows.

The frat house was quiet, too, though light streamed abundantly from each of its uncurtained windows. Mickey shut his door and looked at Delaney over the roof of the car. "Did you hear something?"

Delaney listened for a moment, then shrugged. Together they used the light from the frat house to pick their way toward the Queen Anne house where Velma Verlain, presumed psychic and girlfriend to "business interests in Cleveland" Reggie Seymour dwelled.

The name and the legend were exotic. The lady wasn't.

Short, pear-shaped, a bit nearsighted, and attired in a polyester pantsuit, she had intense gray eyes that peered at them from under the gray fringe of her plainly cut hair.

Totally concerned citizen, she ushered them into a room that was homey-scented and even more ordinary than she was. She maintained the sensible facade through the opening gambit. Stayed with it throughout a careful perusal of the photo of their John Doe from the freezer, who she felt she should know, but didn't. Even offered to show the photo around. Her calm facade showed its first crack when Mickey broached the subject of Reggie.

"You surely don't suspect Reggie? That would be ridiculous! He's a businessman with interests in-"

"Cleveland," Mickey interposed. "We've heard. No one's been able to pinpoint the exact time he left, or when he'll be returning. We were hoping you'd help."

"If you're going to involve Reggie in this, I'll have to ask Hugo," she informed them, her sensible face turning mulish.

"Hugo?"

"My channel. He's my conduit to the space/time continuum. He's a little upset by all the police cars and sirens because he was a criminal in a past life, but I'm sure he'd cough up something to help me. Though I won't mention it's for Reggie. He doesn't like Reggie. Claims Reggie is a con artist. It's absurd, of course. Reggie is a businessman with interests in—"

"Cleveland." This time Delaney finished it. "That seems to be about the only thing we do know about Reggie. We'd really like to know more."

"Why? So you can bully and brutalize him? He's sensitive. Kind, caring. But why should you care about that? You just want someone to pin this murder on."

Mickey and Delaney shifted uneasily. It was hard to

summon a credible protest when they had been hoping to bring it home to Reggie. Pinning it on him would be unethical. And difficult. Though not impossible.

Mickey opened his mouth to say something soothing, but lost his train of thought when the lamp next to Velma began to spin in a slow circle. Next to him, Delaney stiffened as he, too, caught sight of the lamp.

With some difficulty, Mickey collected his thoughts, which wanted to spin faster than the lamp, and managed a question. "It's helpful to get your...views of Seymour, Ms. Verlain. The others—"

"Oh, I know. They think he's next to useless! They have no conception of the damage they do with their lowered expectations! Reggie has been marred, marred I tell you, by this ridiculous dysfunctional family thing! So, he finally manages to rise above it, and then the police come sniffing around. It's an unjust world. An unjust world, indeed." She tipped her head back, looking at them through lowered lids while the lamp began to spin faster.

"Yes, well." Delaney cleared his throat, his eyes fixed with horrid fascination on the lamp. "We really need to ask him a few questions. When he calls—"

"He doesn't call. Reggie and I are connected by something better. Something deeper than mere wires and signals. Our souls joined the moment our eyes met—"

With a vicious jerk, the lamp spun across the room and crashed into the opposite wall.

Velma shook her head, leaning forward to say, confidentially, "I'm afraid Hugo has descended to unbecoming jealousy."

As soon as she came in, Luci could tell her aunts had searched her room. They had tried too hard to leave things as they were, so of course, they had failed. Luci had anticipated this move and hidden the photograph between the two mattresses. Even if the aunts had suspected this move, they wouldn't have been able to lift it up. Luci had barely managed it.

With some difficulty, mostly caused by the sling and the elastic bandage on her left arm, Luci removed the photograph and held it up to the superior light by her bedside. The face still eluded her efforts, but she could see the medals in strict rows across his chest and the way his hand gripped Lila's.

Not too surprising he'd gotten what he wanted, even from an elusive Seymour, Luci decided with a slight smile. Though he hadn't gotten all he wanted. Lila had eluded him in the end, taking her secrets with her.

The frame was a heavy one, not really suitable for the photograph it housed.

"I wonder..." Luci turned it over, removed the back and freed the photograph from confinement. With rising excitement she realized there was faded writing on the bottom right hand corner. She held it up to the light—

"To love cheeks from your pooh bear?" She lowered the picture and stared at herself in the fading mirror. "I think I'm going to be sick."

THERE WAS no middle ground in this investigation, Mickey decided morosely. The participants either had too much personality—or too little. His uncle's fiancée came in on the too little side, possessing less animation than Velma's lamp. This seemed symbolic somehow, but Mickey was too weary to figure out why.

Medium height, medium build, straight brown hair, blank brown eyes, late fifties to early sixties, with no distinguishing marks whatsoever. Sitting opposite them, she stared at the wall. The one with nothing on it.

Mickey had long ago decided his uncle was marrying Unabelle because he knew only the personality-less could put up with Eddie's powerful personality. It still didn't make much sense. Zero times zero was still zero. But if Eddie wanted to marry the equivalent of a slightly warm, inflatable person, that was his business. And if she kept Eddie from messing about in Mickey's life, so much the better.

In an attempt to ease her non-existent unease, Mickey

gave Unabelle a false smile. "I don't know if you remember me, Miss Fraser? I'm Eddie's nephew, Mickey Ross."

Her blank gaze got, if anything, blanker. After what seemed like a long time, she asked, "Eddie?"

He looked at Delaney and saw the same desperation in his eyes that he felt in his own.

11

The humid air was slow to bring the soft sound of a blues-laden love song from the frat house across the street as Luci came out and perched on the porch railing, pondering her few options. If her aunts wouldn't help her, it wasn't going to be easy unraveling the mystery of her paternity. That Lila had called him her pooh bear was not something she wanted to admit to anyone.

She pushed her paternal thoughts to the back burner and let her mind home in on the distant hum of traffic as the city geared up for the night. The air was heavy with the scent of too many green growing things to sort out the alien foods that enticed and teased one to venture forth from comfort zones. This place, with its lazy decadence, was the polar opposite of her sturdy, duty-minded Wyoming, and had her feeling very unlike her Seymour self.

She'd come here in search of her father and found murder, mayhem and a strange stirring she hadn't known she was capable of. Was it the city that was making her wish for things a Seymour didn't? Or was it someone?

With some reluctance, she let herself think about "someone." Men had passed as tiny blips across her horizon. Better looking, far less uptight men. Why did this one disturb her thoughts? Stir yearnings to which she was supposed to be immune? All the nerve endings in her body seemed to have awakened to the fact that they were nerve endings and could feel. Could feel so much so that she now felt the soft stroke of air across her skin. Was aware of each thud of her heart and the in-and-out of her own breath. Inhaled a thousand heady scents and heard the most insignificant bug's mating cry.

That she even knew it was a mating cry was pretty amazing.

Was this how her mother had felt before breaking who knows how many years of family tradition? Had her flaky, infuriating mother felt this languid and this filled with want?

It was a terrifying thought. She'd come to find her father, to discover the roots of her strange duality, but he wouldn't just be her father. He was her mother's lover. She was the by-product of something that had been meant just for them. Did she really want to open that Pandora's box? Her fright and flight instinct clamored for equal time with the "jump his fine bones" instinct. It might even be ahead of the game, but how could she leave with her aunts mired in the mess of murder?

She was caught between the rock of murder and the Seymour hard place.

Murder was a messy, untidy business, even without her aunts factored into the equation. The family would expect her to factor them out, but the object of her lust wasn't going to let that happen until he was sure they weren't in it.

As if her thoughts had conjured him, the door behind her opened and Mickey and Delaney emerged.

"Don't feel bad," Delaney said. "You do the best bad cop on the force. There just wasn't anything to get a hold of there."

With night-accustomed eyes, she noted the discouraged slump to their shoulders and their glum faces.

"I just don't get it," Mickey said. "What does Eddie see in her?"

"He's got enough personality to animate ten people," Delaney pointed out.

"I have to meet Eddie," Luci said.

They both started with surprise. Mickey peered into the shadows until he found her, framed against the round moon riding just above the tree line in the night sky.

For a moment he contemplated a meeting between Luci and Eddie. What would Eddie think of Luci? She was in a picture perfect pose on the porch railing. The moon had maliciously chosen to bathe its light across her mouth, to stroke light and shadow in just the right amount to highlight the curve of breasts and thighs, and left her heart-stopping legs lost in shadow. About halfway through his examination of her, he quit thinking about what Eddie would think of her and started thinking about what he'd like to do with her.

Delaney gave him a forceful nudge that cleared his head, but not the heat that had built in his mid-section.

"Huh?"

Luci's smile was slow and sultry. "Gracie tells me you had a little chat with Velma."

"Gracie?" Delaney said.

Mickey bit back a sigh as Delaney went into "moon" mode again, turning his bulky body to send a hopeful look at the house.

"Is she—"

"Turned in for the night? I'm afraid so," Luci said. "How was Hugo?"

"He was jealous," Mickey admitted reluctantly.

"Oh? He just tried to cop a feel off me."

Mickey realized his hands had fisted and deliberately straightened his fingers. "Velma didn't mention you'd been there."

She stretched languidly. "Miss Weena assigned her to me when you declined to be her Watson. If you feed me, I'll tell you what I know." Her hopeful look had a generous helping of humor and sympathy.

Mickey started to sigh again, then realized he'd been doing it almost continually since he'd met her and stopped himself. Hadn't he vowed to take the tough line with her? "You'll tell us what you know or we'll charge you with obstruction."

Luci looked at Delaney, her sunny good humor belying her words. "You're right. His bad cop is good."

"Don't—" Mickey fought his way to control. "Just tell me about Reggie's police record."

Luci folded her hands demurely in her lap. "He tries to cheat people."

Mickey looked at Delaney. "A bunco artist?"

"You give him far too much credit," Luci said.

Mickey grinned. "Velma says it's the family's fault, that you all marred him."

Luci smiled. "He marred himself without any help from anybody. Unless you count the body piercing.

Mickey looked at Delaney. "Body piercing?"

"Intimate body piercing. Lila calls it his small vanity, but I think that puncturing your—private areas—with cheap jewelry, no matter how specially designed, is not a small vanity."

Mickey looked uneasy. "Specially designed jewelry?"

"Yeah, according to the family grapevine, it's a variation on the family crest. Poison oak and a weasel head. It was designed by a great aunt of mine. She had a rather wicked sense of humor. I don't think Reggie got the joke, else why would he be flaunting it? If you can call it flaunting to wear it—there."

Both men flinched and Luci bit back a smile.

Mickey shuddered. "Does Velma know?"

"If she's a psychic, she should." Luci looked toward Velma's house just in time to catch her closing the drapes. Luci frowned as the feeling that she knew her from somewhere else swept over her again. But how could that be? Velma had moved in after Luci and her mother left the area.

"Something wrong?" Delaney asked her.

Luci stood up and shook off all the feelings and impressions like a dog shedding water. "Do you hear it?"

Mickey and Delaney looked at each other, then at her. Their mutual blankness made her smile.

"A pizza," she explained, "calling my name. I swear I can smell the sauce."

On Mickey's face, blank gave way for annoyed, with just a hint of resignation. Delaney tilted his head and listened. "Yeah, I think I do."

"Not a chain pizza. Something more upscale, I think?"

"There's a place on Magazine that does gourmet pizzas," Delaney said, giving Mickey a hopeful look and rubbing his stomach. It obliged him by growling.

Mickey shoved his hair back. "Fine. Whatever." Luci's delighted smile made his head spin so fast, he didn't notice the sling on her arm until they got to the car.

"Did I do that when I tackled you last night?"

Luci patted his arm reassuringly. "I took a header off an escalator."

Delaney looked worried. "You okay?"

Luci nodded. "Just a slight sprain and a touch of snow burn."

Mickey shook his head. "Snow burn?"

"From showing the kiddies how to make a snow angel." She slid into the car and smiled up at him. "Bad idea in a dress."

In a daze, Mickey closed the door and looked at Delaney. "When did I stop knowing what was going on?"

But he already knew the answer to that. The moment Luci Seymour walked into his life. He started the car and pulled away, his stomach rumbling happily at the thought of upcoming pizza.

ARTIE WAITED until they were out of sight before he emerged from the ivy. Pizza sauce liberally splattered his pants and the stolen pizza shirt, but his shoes had suffered more vilely. Even his Instant-Polish kit couldn't fix them. It had been a bad week for shoes. Something else to add to Luci Seymour's account.

IT WAS dark in Fern's hospital room when Donald pushed the door open and peered in. Fern was huddled in the regulation bed in the regulation gown, a cast adorning her arm. He started to back out, but she stopped him with, "I'm awake."

He slipped through and closed the door behind him.

"You forget who's the bopper in this family, Fernie?"

Fern looked up, her face so downcast, Donald felt sorry about ribbing her. Ponderously he trod over to her and patted her broken arm.

"Never mind." His voice was gruff. "Weren't such a bad idea, you know. If it had worked, our troubles'd be over. Weren't your fault it didn't, neither."

"She sent me flowers, Donald." She nodded toward the tasteful arrangement brightening the darkest corner of the room.

"Damn! Anybody else take a dive off an escalator, they'd be pushing up daisies 'stead of sending them."

"What are we going to do now?"

Donald pulled the chair close to the bed. Seated, he was on a level with her. "I been thinking on that very thing. Took a run past the house. It's all nice and quiet. Even the bulls are gone."

He kept his voice low, but Fern heard his underlying excitement.

"What?" She sat up, leaned toward him as a lust for revenge coursed through her veins. "Uzi time?"

"I wish. Give me a lot of pleasure to blast that bitch to hell and back. But," he said with a regretful look. "We'll have to settle for blowing her into little bits instead."

"Blow—Donald, are you thinking of a bomb?"

"I am."

"But—how?"

"I told you, I've been by. Somebody had backed a car out of the garage. I saw her look under the hood." He didn't mention that Luci's long, bare legs had made him want to look under her hood. You didn't cross a woman like Fern. Not if you wanted to keep all your parts. "Like she was trying to get it running." He waited a beat, then added, "A Nash."

Fern sat straight up in bed, oblivious to the pain the movement caused. "A Nash?"

He grinned. "Nash has always been lucky for us."

Fern looked almost girlish and almost blushed. "Back seat of one, anyway."

"This time the whole car's gonna bring us luck. Gonna take us all the way to the Bahamas. Who's gonna be surprised when a little gal blows herself and a car up? Ain't natural for her to be working on a car. Though I hate to do it to a Nash."

"Yeah," Fern agreed, hesitated, then said with decision, "I've got to get out of here."

"Just what I was thinking myself." He held up a sack of clothes he'd packed for her. "I'll help you."

12

"I do love a woman in uniform," Delaney said appreciatively the next morning as he watched Caroline walk away. Mickey nodded morosely. Caroline had been real possessive this morning when she picked him up, even straightened his tie. Mickey shuddered, as the feeling of being hunted had him hunching in his chair. Caroline sure as shooting had the software and the hardware to take him down and wrap him up.

"Yeah," another detective drooled his agreement. "The only thing better'n watching her leave is watching her come." He leered and pumped his arms suggestively.

"Don't you gentlemen have anything better to do than stand around being sexist?" The cold voice of Captain Pryce sent them all scrambling for their desks—except for Mickey and Delaney, who were already at theirs. "You have time to give me an update on the Seymour investigation—unless you're not finished lusting after Officer Cory?"

"Yes, sir, of course, sir!" Delaney tried to bring his bulky body to attention while Mickey grabbed for the folder that represented their cumulative knowledge of the Seymour investigation. It was a very thin folder.

"Things are finally starting to move," he stated, avoiding saying thaw, "at the Coroner's office. They took prints this morning and forwarded them to the FBI with an ASAP request. I believe they're hoping for dental x-rays this morning, and the autopsy is scheduled for tomorrow morning."

"Word is, you've got a possible perp on tap. A bunco artist?"

Mickey looked at Delaney. "Not exactly an artist, sir." The report on Reggie Seymour was in their basket this morning, confirming what Luci told them last night. Was it the idea of her being right that made him so uneasy—or something else?

He handed the report to Pryce, who flipped it open. "Any prior record of violence?"

"No, sir, but Miss Weena's gun is missing. Same caliber."

"And," Delaney spoke up, "most cons aren't violent unless someone threatens them. It's possible our John Doe is a former cellmate, trying to cut in on his action."

"What makes you think he was running a con this time?"

"If you look at his record, sir, you'll see he's either been running a con or doing time for one since he hit puberty."

"We're compiling a list of his known associates, sir," Mickey added.

Pryce acknowledged this with a slight nod, his finger hovering over text in the file. His brows rose. "Body piercing?"

Mickey picked at an imaginary piece of lint on the sleeve of his suit. "Yes, sir."

"This doesn't track with what I know of the Seymours."

"Apparently the male Seymours are—different from the women."

"Really?" Pryce frowned, staring off into space for a long moment while the two men watched uneasily. He finally gave himself a slight shake and directed his cold gaze back towards his detectives. "You got a plan?"

"We'd like to pick Seymour up," Delaney said.

"Why do I hear a 'but' in there?"

"We don't know exactly where he is," Mickey admitted. "We have information that he's in Cleveland—conducting business, but no one seems able to be more specific than that."

"Not even the girlfriend?"

Mickey flinched at this description of Velma.

"She seems content to maintain a psychic connection with the suspect, sir," Delaney said dryly.

Pryce's lips twitched. "You have been having an interesting time, haven't you?"

Mickey and Delaney exchanged quick looks. They'd left the really good stuff from their meeting with Velma out of the report.

Pryce snapped the file shut and tapped it against his hand. "Well, one thing you can probably be sure of."

"What's that, sir?" Mickey asked, suspicious of the sardonic look in Pryce's eyes.

"With his record of ineptitude, he's bound to surface soon. Just be ready when he does." He tossed the file onto Mickey's desk. "You know the drill. Start with the Cleveland PD. Then head back out to the Seymour's, see if one of them will cough up an address—any personal details. The press is already turning this into a circus. Let's wrap it up quickly, okay?"

"What are our chances of getting a warrant to go through his room?" Mickey asked.

"It would be better if we could search the whole house," Delaney added.

"Did I mention these people have friends in high places? You'd be better off to just request their permission, get them to waive their rights."

"I hate to tip our hand if they refuse," Mickey said.

"The Seymours? I doubt they're that devious, Ross."

"Not the old ladies, sir, but there's a niece that's smarter than she likes to let on. She's making protective noises. I don't think she'll let us search without a warrant."

Pryce considered this. "I'll see what I can do. Still have a few favors I can call in. When do you want to do it?"

"As soon as possible."

"Okay." Pryce didn't shrug, he never did, but the "it's your funeral" was implied by his tone of voice.

Mickey watched Pryce stalk to his office before he asked, "Why do I get the feeling Captain's laughing at us?"

"Probably because he is." Delaney looked up from some sheets he was scanning. "Did you get someone to check out our three Arthurs? Before we get too hot after Reggie, we ought to clear them."

"It's in the works."

"Your Uncle Eddie doesn't make any mention of Reggie Seymour. Didn't he meet him?"

"When he was questioned, no one knew to ask about him." Mickey felt a surge of hope. "If anyone can give us the straight scoop on Seymour, it'll be Eddie."

"Let's do it. Be nice to have some nice, real facts to plump up this file." Delaney grabbed his suit jacket off the back of the chair. "We can get some coffee on the way. Fortify ourselves before we tackle the Seymours again."

DANTE'S current Mardi Gras float was loosely modeled on Persephone emerging from the sea after her long sojourn out of the sun. He was particularly pleased with the visual impact of her large, mostly bare breasts just cresting the wave that mingled with the flow of her long hair down the length of the float.

He made a minor adjustment to a measurement, then looked up as Max came in and cleared his throat.

"What is it, Max?"

"I have some information on Arvin—not much—but it's a start."

"Ah." Dante leaned back. "Took you long enough. Tell me where the bastard is."

"Thing that's made it so hard is Arvin Marvin didn't appear to exist before he met your aunt. Had to be an alias. I put out some feelers. One of Giancarlo's men remembers seeing a man answering Arvin's description in Salt Lake City." Max hesitated. "Seems he was married to twins there. He relieved them of their savings and disappeared about three months ago."

"He's a bigamist?" Max shrugged. Dante leaned back in his chair. "Cloris isn't going to like this."

Max looked as sympathetic as he was capable.

Dante frowned into the distance. "Keep looking. I don't want him anymore—at least, not breathing."

"Yes, Mr. Dante. I'll arrange the contract. Anyone special you want to do it?"

Dante looked at Max. "Let's find somebody that knows the bastard. Guy like that must have done time. I could tell he was a screw-up first time I met him. If he hadn't already married her—" He scowled, his clenched hands breaking in half the pencil he held. One piece flew across the room and hit the wall. It made him feel better. He straightened. "The boys here yet? Got a little job for them to do, too."

Max signaled them in and retreated to a corner.

The boys, Cain and Abel—though if those were their real names was anybody's guess—were tall thin twins, with a useful facility for looking like federal agents. Presentable, but with the ability to be vicious, loyal and mildly ambitious, they were intelligent enough to actually get Dante's jokes. A couple of thugs a wise guy could depend upon.

"You wanted to see us, Mr. Dante?" Abel, the spokesman of the two, asked.

Dante nodded. "Got a little job for you to do. A simple locate and pick up. With kid gloves, boys—for now."

"Sure thing, Mr. Dante. Who you want us to grab?"

"Ah, that is the problem. She's a client of Benny's. You remember the oh-so-dull Benny?" They nodded. "Ask him where she lives, then pick her up, and bring her here so we can have a little chat, do a little business."

"No problem, Mr. Dante." As the two men slid out, Cain checked his gun and then stowed it back under his jacket.

Max turned to leave, then hesitated, a slight frown on his face.

"You got a problem, Max?"

"Just seems like small potatoes, Mr. Dante. A scam that nets dollar bills?"

"Normally bills that small wouldn't interest me, but so many? Where did she get them? And why small bills? Why not an assortment? All these questions I don't have answers for." He looked blandly at his henchman. "You know how I hate unanswered questions. They disturb my sleep. Make me cranky. Next thing I know, I want to kill someone. That son-of-a-bitch Ross and his large partner are riding my ass pretty close, Max. Don't want him to find something to smell."

"Yes, Mr. Dante." Max was silent for a moment. "You think she's running a scam?"

"The idea does rather spring to mind."

"Pretty penny ante scam when it only nets dollar bills."

"Our bird is clever enough to start small and works up. Not much in one box, but according to Benny, there's more where that came from. How much more? Now we can wait patiently for our bird to bring it to us package by package and lose it gambling. Or, we can find out what scam she's running on my turf. If it's big enough, I might let her live long enough to cut me in. Any way you slice it, she's taking money from me."

"WHAT DO YOU WANT?" Eddie asked brusquely. He stood impatiently by his car, looking pointedly at his watch. Edward "Eddie" Ross was as tall as Mickey, but thinner, with just a hint of a stoop starting to curve his shoulders. But age couldn't blunt his forceful manner or lengthen his patience span.

Mickey shifted uneasily. He was over thirty, not a kid,

but he still found it hard to remain cool when Eddie looked at him like that. "We need to ask you some questions. Won't take long."

"Gave my statement yesterday to that flunky you sent over here to snoop through my life."

So that's what was bothering him. Mickey relaxed. "Come on, Eddie, we could really use your help. We're trying to find out about a guy named Reggie Seymour. The old ladies say he sometimes stays with them."

"Reggie?" Eddie relaxed, too, leaning against his car with his arms crossed over his chest. "You think that worthless piece of dirt did the killing?"

"It's possible," Mickey admitted. "We don't have anything solid on him, except a bunco record."

Eddie nodded as if this made sense. "Only met him once. Sorry piece of work. Probably a punk when he was young. Now a gigolo wannabe. Made my skin crawl, but the ladies—" He shook his head over the gullibility of ladies. "That nutsy neighbor of theirs was fawning all over him."

Delaney and Mickey exchanged glances. "Sounds like he ran true to type," Delaney said.

"True to type?" Eddie asked.

"According to the ladies, their family men aren't—great," Mickey explained.

"Yeah, real screw-ups," Delaney added.

"Well, I told you he was an asshole, didn't I?" He was impatient again, looking at his watch. "Are you through with me? Cause I gotta meet Unabelle. We're applying for the license today."

"Just one more question, Eddie, okay? Did he seem capable of violence?"

Eddie hesitated. "Violence? Didn't they teach you anything at the academy?"

"What?" It was stupid to get defensive.

"Anyone's capable of violence. If they're cornered." He slid in his car and slammed the door. Through the frame of the window he glared at his nephew.

"I knew that." Mickey looked at Delaney. "We just have to figure out how our John Doe cornered him."

Eddie nodded agreement, then pulled away with a discreet squeal of tires.

"Eddie seemed a bit on edge," Delaney commented as they clambered into his car.

"Oh, he was just pissed because I didn't talk to him myself yesterday." Mickey didn't want to talk about Eddie. It made his head ache.

When they got to the house, Luci was helping Boudreaux weed the ground around a bougainvillea. To his relief, neither of them appeared to notice the two detectives. He wasn't in the mood to spar with Luci right now. Or to get within lust range. Still mute, Louise showed them into the dining room where they found the old ladies knee deep in preparations for the party they were giving for the bride and groom this weekend. It wasn't easy, he found, to get them to focus on the murder. Or even, he realized, to remember there'd been one.

"Murder?" Miss Theo didn't look up from her sheaf of lists. "Weena, is dear little Luci done fixing the Nash? This list of errands is getting longer."

"She's helping Boudreaux in the garden," Miss Hermi said, flecks of pink coloring her cheeks. "She said she'd go do the errands right after lunch."

"The garden?" Theo looked up from her lists.

"I noticed the bougainvillea looks a little tense."

"Boudreaux—" began Miss Weena.

"—is the one making it tense! You know he never liked it."

Delaney gave Mickey a panicked look.

"You're senior," Mickey said.

OUT IN THE YARD, Luci tossed the last weed into a wilting pile and paused to brush stray hairs back from her face, then winced when her wrist reminded her it had been twisted recently. There was something very soothing about having her hands in moist brown soil. All the things that worried at her Seymour imperturbability couldn't seem to get a foothold on her thinking here, where the present was hard to separate from the past.

She looked at Boudreaux. "I've done this before, haven't I? Worked in the garden with you, I mean?"

Boudreaux nodded, the wrinkles carved into his sun-scorched skin deepened by his delighted grin.

"I can't believe how much I'd forgotten about this place." Luci picked up a hand rake and started smoothing the disturbed dirt. And how much I never knew, she added to herself. She gave Boudreaux a speculative glance. Might he know the secret of her paternity? He'd been around at the critical time. It was worth a try—if she still wanted to know?

She raked a little harder. "I've been thinking a lot about the past." Her rake caught on a large clump of dirt. "I know it's not very Seymour of me." She whacked the clump with the rake and the clump partially fell apart. "But there's part of me that's not Seymour, isn't there?"

She looked at Boudreaux, but he wasn't looking at her. He was looking at the ground. Luci looked down, too. Amid the broken pieces of the clump of dirt there was a gleam of gold. Luci exchanged a puzzled look with Boudreaux before picking it up. She had to use water from her bottle to wash away the dirt that clung to it before she could see what it was.

"It's the Seymour family crest," she said. She frowned. "But the only person who wears it is—"

She looked up at Boudreaux. They both looked at the dirt, then at each other. "Mickey isn't going to like this."

Boudreaux muttered an emphatic, mostly incoherent agreement.

MICKEY HADN'T EXPECTED the interview to go well, but he'd thought it would go. Somehow the tables had been turned. He shuffled his feet and avoided Miss Theo's gaze. "Your cake, ma'am?"

Delaney rubbed his temple like it pained him. Maybe he won't be so quick to espouse the cause of eccentrics, Mickey thought with perverse satisfaction. He lowered his head when Miss Theo gave him a severe look.

"My cake. Which has mysteriously disappeared."

"Oh. That cake." He gave Delaney a help me look.

He squared his shoulders and stepped into the line of fire. "I'll dust my men for crumbs, ma'am, but I'm afraid we may have to wait for weight change to find the perpetrator."

Her smile took them both by surprise and was potent enough to remind Mickey of Luci.

"I can see why Gracie likes you." Miss Weena and Miss Hermi both giggled their agreement.

"She does?" Delaney said with revealing hope. Not that Mickey hadn't suspected Delaney was badly smitten. He got a goofy look every time Gracie's name was mentioned. He gave him a pointed nudge. Delaney started and cleared his throat. Due to his large chest, it was an impressive sound.

All three old ladies looked at him like inquiring birds.

"Yes, dear boy?" Miss Theo asked. Miss Weena patted

her bun and then sidled closer to him with a simpering smile.

"About Reggie. We need to find him—"

"Um, I think I know where he is," Luci said from the doorway.

Mickey hadn't seen her arrive, so he didn't get time to prepare himself for the sight of her in her grubby shorts, her skin still dewed from her recent earthy efforts. His throat dried up and closed like a noose drawing tight, leaving Delaney to ask the obvious.

"And that would be?"

"We already told them," Miss Weena said, "that he's in Cleveland, Luci dear."

"Actually..." Luci's gaze was all sympathy when it met Mickey's, giving him some warning of impending doom. "I think he's under the bougainvillea."

Miss Theo blinked her surprise. "How odd."

"Not really," Miss Hermi said, going immediately defensive. "He's very fond of the bougainvillea."

Mickey looked at Delaney. "I'll flip you for who gets to call it in and who has to go look under the bush."

MICKEY LOST THE TOSS. He knew he would. It had been that kind of week, he decided as he followed Luci outside to see Reggie's remains while Delaney went to call it in.

"How do you know it's Reggie?" Mickey asked, for something to say rather than a strong desire to know.

"I don't know. Not for sure."

Mickey stopped and looked at her. Big mistake. Her grubby, slightly damp tee shirt hugged her breasts. Her shorts hugged her hips and generously left ninety percent of her legs bare. The muggy confines of the garden immediately got several degrees hotter. He tugged at his tie, but that wasn't what was tightening his throat—and parts much lower.

As if she knew he couldn't talk and why, she put a bit more distance between them. "I found this." She extended a grubby hand to him, opening it to show him what looked to be a small piece of jewelry.

Mickey picked it up, his fingers brushing against her palm for a heated moment before he could break the contact. He looked at it for a long moment before his vision cleared enough to start showing him detail.

"Looks like some kind of animal head surrounded by leaves—" he managed to say almost calmly.

"It's a weasel head. And poison oak." A brief pause, then she added, "The Seymour family crest."

Mickey looked at her warily, as his brain pulled up her comments about Reggie from last night. "The family crest? You mean—"

"I'm afraid so."

He wanted to toss it down and rub his hands down the sides of his pants. He wanted to toss her down, too, and make love to her until his blood quit running hot for her. He did neither. "According to his file he—"

"I know." She looked down instead of at him. He appreciated her tact.

Mickey swallowed. It had to be asked. "Was it still—"

"No." She seemed to be looking everywhere but at him as they approached the bougainvillea. "At least, not after I raked—"

He tried not to flinch, but he wasn't made of stone.

"Sorry." She hesitated, then said, "He didn't feel it, you know. It's not even attached—"

Mickey shook his head. "I'll get your—statement later."

She nodded soberly, her hands clasped behind her back, as she looked straight ahead. "I suppose it's a— touchy subject for a guy."

If she smiles, he decided, I will shoot her with my gun. And no jury on earth will convict me. Not if I call the old ladies to the stand.

Perhaps she read his thoughts. Or his intentions. She didn't smile, didn't even look at him as sirens once again wailed in the distance.

Artie didn't like the rock and hard place he found himself in. Fern and Donald were positioned at one end of the street doing something pretty odd again with the map they'd been pretending to study. Sirens could be heard coming toward them from the other direction. And he'd scuffed his new shoes and couldn't do anything about it because the blind guy he was pretending to be wouldn't know he had scuffed shoes. He hadn't thought this particular disguise through, but he had to get into the house, and who could say no to giving a blind guy a drink of water? Not even Louise the Heartless. Now the cops were coming and he was boxed in.

Not that anyone was likely to bother a blind guy, but he was sticking out like a sore thumb on the soon to be less quiet street. He'd just have to continue tapping his way toward Fern and Donald, but would they penetrate his disguise? And why weren't they getting out of here with the cops coming? He'd had a bad feeling when he'd seen Luci and Boudreaux digging near the bougainvillea. Just went to show you couldn't even count on a bush to keep your secrets for you.

As the sirens got louder and closer, he backed up and up. One minute he was watching Fern and Donald's car, the next he was wrapped in leaves and branches. Sharp little buggers, but at least he was out of sight when the cop cars came squealing around the corner.

13

"What the—?" Donald's voice faded into choking incoherence as he stared at the police cars that once more engulfed the house.

"There's the forensics van." Fern looked at Donald. "These people have done more killing than we have, in less time!"

"What're we doing wrong?"

"Everything, apparently." Fern shifted in the seat. It wasn't easy being a wheelman with her arm in a sling, but the Town Car with the automatic was a big help. "Let's go. We can't plant the bomb with the police crawling all over the place." Just being this close to police made her skin crawl.

"Wait. Look." He pointed past the confusion down the street. On the edge of the action, but not in it, sat the Nash, alone, unattended under a shade tree just past the driveway. "Busy bodies'll be watching the bulls. Bulls'll be work-ing. I'll just be an old man tinkering with a car. Bet no one will even remember me."

"I don't know, Donald." Fern was uneasy. Everything that could go wrong with this hit had gone wrong. Why should today be any different? And when it did go wrong, what chance did they have of getting clear with half the police department crawling everywhere?

"Sit tight, stay cool," Donald directed, sliding out the door with the bag containing the bomb, also purchased from Teddy.

It wasn't east to sit quietly, her arm throbbing in sync with her pounding heart while Donald strolled over to the Nash.

After a quick look around, he popped the hood, opened the bag and installed the bomb with a deftness that peeled away the years. Dang, if the old boy can't still surprise the hell out of me, she thought with a half grin.

The grin froze when the gate opened and Luci came out.

ARTIE SAW his opportunity and untangled himself from the tree, adding only a few more scratches to his face and hands. He righted his glasses and started tapping his way down the street away from Fern and Donald. He had to pass Luci, but that seemed like the lesser of two evils right now. He considered warning Donald, but discarded it. With Donald on the verge of discovery, this was not a good moment to link himself to him.

Luci turned to close the gate as Donald closed the lid of the Nash and dusted his hands down the sides of his pants. Donald started back to the Town Car while Luci started toward the Nash. They passed within a few feet of each other, but with their backs to each other, neither was aware of it. Donald slid into the passenger side of his car as Luci tossed her handbag onto the seat of the Nash, then slid behind the wheel.

When Fern started the car, it only took Artie a couple of beats to realize what Donald had just done to the Nash and what was about to happen. Yes, it would solve his little problem, but it could also end his problems permanently. Tapping faster, he turned and almost stepped out in front of a painfully familiar black Buick. It honked, giving him a good reason to jump back. He did a quick about-face. At the moment, bombs and the hit couple seemed the lesser of the evils confronting him.

He didn't know how Dante's boys had managed to find him, but maybe, just maybe, they wouldn't recognize Cloris's erstwhile groom in the blind man with scuffed shoes.

～

"WELL." Donald's voice was a couple of octaves higher from the close call, and he dabbed at the sweat breaking out on his forehead. "Least we get to see the show."

Fern let the car roll forward, her whole attention directed to the rear view mirror and the girl taking a long time to settle herself in the seat, find the keys and get ready to insert them in the ignition.

"I put it on a delay. Ten seconds after the engine starts, its Disney World here we come," Donald said hoarsely.

ARTIE HAD TO LOOK. He pretended to stop and feel his watch. Only shock kept him from showing how shook up he was. And then Dante's goons grabbed Luci out of the Nash, slamming the door, but leaving the keys dangling in the ignition. He turned away as the dark car snaked past him and turned the corner. Was this the solution to his problem? Or an escalation of his problems? Why would Dante want Luci—

He didn't have time to finish that thought. It was replaced by the realization that Fern and Donald's car had drifted off course with the street and on course with him. It was moving slow, but not so slow it didn't clip him as he tried to leap out of the way. He landed behind a familiar looking small hedge. In a distant sort of way, he heard the car continue on until it crunched into a large oak, releasing a shower of acorns to pelt it and him.

DANTE WAS WORKING on a new sketch when Cain and Abel thrust Benny's "Jane" into his office. For purposes of intimidation, he kept writing. First there would be the inevitable burst of indignation. Then the demand to know what was going on, why she'd been brought here. When he didn't answer, she would subside into an uneasy silence. A full minute after that, he would look up and ask his questions. And she would rush to answer them.

So he smiled and continued to fill the silence with the scratch, scratch of his pen...until she strolled past him to stare out the glass window of his office into the warehouse where his Persephone waited the Mardi Gras call.

He looked at his guys first. They lifted their shoulders in identical shrugs. And, he noted with a deepening frown, they looked odd. Cain and Abel didn't do odd. He tapped the pen against the desk, faster and faster as hope faded that she would crack first. Okay. He spun his chair around. Her back was to him, but even so, she wasn't at all what he imagined Benny's "odd bird" would be. Tall and reed slim, she was wearing a yellow sundress with clean, graceful lines that flattered the greyhound lines of her body. On her feet was something that might have been sandals, so brief were they, and on her head she had a bright red cap with the brim pointed back.

He got up and joined her, finding no sign in her pure

profile that the elongated silence or getting snatched by his boys troubled her in any way.

A feral smile edged up the corners of his mouth. He did love a challenge, and "Jane" looked to be a bit of one. "Benny didn't say half enough about you, Miss Jane."

"Who?" Luci gave him a brief, questioning glance before returning to her examination of the float, a critical and assessing look on her face that seemed to assume he'd invited her here solely to get her opinion on it.

Not sure whether to get mad or laugh, he shoved his hands into his pockets.

"Not that I buy your name is Jane."

She looked at him for a long unnerving beat. Her eyes were green x-rays that seemed to look right into his soul.

"I would hope not." She returned to her study of the float, her head tipped, as if a new angle would solve the conundrum. After a pause, she added, "Luci Seymour. And you are?"

"Dante." Seymour. He'd heard that name before, but in what context?

He looked at her, but before he could ask, she said, as if she heard him thinking, "The stiff in the freezer. On the news."

"Oh yeah. Guy looked exactly like my tailor. They find out who it was?"

Luci shook her head, her thoughts still missing from her expression.

For a moment he could feel his temper—or was it

something else?—trying to slip the leash. Cain and Abel, who knew what happened when he lost his temper, reached inside their jackets for their guns.

"The boobs," she said, turning to face him. "They aren't—"

"Aren't what?" His temper jacked up another notch.

"Very real. I mean, look at them. They're the same size. Real boobs aren't the same size." She didn't say it, but the question was implied: didn't you know that?

"Of course I know that," he snapped, adjusting his jacket in a defensive movement. "They're art."

She looked at him, one brow arching. "They're fantasy."

Cain and Abel started to pull their guns clear of their jackets as Dante teetered on the brink of letting his temper turn deadly.

"If you had them you wouldn't be so fascinated with them." She turned from the float and her gaze passed over the goons as she surveyed his office. "Have you been doing boobs long?"

It had been a long time since anyone had tried to startle Dante, let alone succeeded. He examined the novel feeling from all sides and decided it was rather intriguing. He laughed. Not loud, not long. More of a snort, really. But a snort with amusement in it.

Cain and Abel looked at each other, as surprised as they were capable of being. Then they put away their guns.

"Benny was right." He trailed a finger down her cheek. "You are...unusual."

Luci stepped away from him, toward the desk and the plans spread out there, so as not to appear to be avoiding him.

"Benny?"

"He works for me."

No surprise there. Not that she had a clue what he was talking about, but it didn't seem prudent to tell him that. "Oh."

"The shoebox he brought me was most interesting."

Not only did the light bulb go off, so did alarm bells. He wasn't one of her aunts' intimates, so how did he know about the shoeboxes? It was all weird enough to keep Mickey's headache going into the next new millennium if she were stupid enough to tell him about it. It was obvious she needed more information. Could she get it without giving any away?

She arched her other brow, thanking the powers that be for the Seymour-ness that kept her expression bland and cool despite the intensity of his very dangerous regard. "Really?"

Cool, very cool. Obviously a woman after his own heart. Dante smiled his satisfaction. "Absolutely."

He joined her by the desk, letting his body brush against hers.

"I found them so interesting I'd like more of them."

Luci traced the line of the float with her finger, the

action moving her around the desk and away from him. "Would you?"

Dante leaned across the desk and trapped her hand against the paper. Trapped her gaze with his. "Yes, I would."

She didn't even blink. "They aren't mine to give."

He studied her face with interest. There was charm in the angular lines that wasn't apparent to the undiscerning eye. He prided himself on having a discerning eye—particularly where women were concerned. Initially, he'd planned to ferret out the scam, eliminate the principals and take it over for himself. But she was an unexpected bonus. Perhaps, if she wasn't too clever, he'd keep her. For a while anyway. It might be fun.

"You gave one to Benny."

Luci slid her hand away from his and took his chair, sliding back and crossing her legs. Both movements worked the skirt of her dress up enough to draw attention. The three men practically created a vortex with their collective and simultaneously indrawn breaths. When they turned a touch blue around the lips, Luci smoothed the dress back in place.

There was a combined exhaling that ruffled her hair. Luci waited until Dante's dazed gaze found her face again before she said, "I'm afraid that wasn't me. I couldn't have given Benny anything yesterday, since I only arrived last night."

"What?" He wheeled to look at his suddenly worried

men. They both gulped, swallowed and backed into the wall. "Idiots."

"I wouldn't be too hard on them." Luci stood and walked around the desk. "This Benny doesn't sound like a person who pays a lot of attention to detail."

"That's right, Boss," Abel said hoarsely. "Benny said it were the younger one. That the rest are old. Wouldn't know about her, now would he?"

All three of them looked at him. He wasn't a fair man, but he liked to appear to be one, so he nodded. "Then who was it?"

"I suspect, though the idea fairly boggles my mind— and you should know a Seymour doesn't boggle easily— that it was Unabelle." For the first time she looked more than mildly curious. There was a tiny frown between her oddly straight brows. He studied it and decided to like it. "Though I wouldn't have her picked up if I were you. Her fiancé is a retired cop. Eddie Ross?"

Dante scowled. "Ross?"

"You know him?"

"Let's say I've had some...interaction with his nephew."

Luci smiled. Dante wasn't ready for it and he thought he was ready for anything. He kind of heard the boys inhaling again, but all he could do for the space of it was stare and bask in it.

"We have something in common then." She turned off the smile. Rational thought took a bit longer to be restored. "I've had a few encounters with him myself."

Dante took a shaky breath, then said with assumed calm, "Then you know how unreasonable he can be?"

Luci laughed. The sound invoked an extraordinary feeling of delight that once again blurred rational thought and made him want to grin like a fool. He looked at his men and saw they were grinning like fools. He realized his mouth was starting to turn up and stopped it.

Get a grip, man. She's just a woman. One who made him want to sit up and beg, but just a woman. He rubbed his brow, hoping to clear his head. What—oh yeah.

"The boxes. What I'd really like to know is how the boxes got that way." He chose his words with care, not anxious to use the actionable ones like scam and defraud. It didn't seem possible that she was wired, since no one knew she was going to get grabbed, but he stayed in business by not trusting anyone, especially anyone as attractively packaged as Luci Seymour.

"Another thing we have in common." This time the wattage on her smile was turned down, as if she knew its danger to the male brain.

"Is that a problem?" he shot back.

"No." Her shrug was a study in the elegant. "The contents just don't seem to be your style."

He stepped in front of her. She was as tall as he, so he had to use the force of his personality to intimidate her. He gave her a deliberate once over, mentally stripping her. "What's in those boxes will always be my style."

She looked amused instead of intimidated. "Okay, but my aunts—"

"They're your partners?"

"I'm not in it at all. I'm just here for the wedding."

"But you can talk to them? They'll listen to you?"

She looked at him, her gaze closed and cool, with no sign of the charm that had taken his breath away. "Maybe. The situation is...complicated."

She'd piqued his interest now. He was accustomed to people experiencing a full range of emotions in his presence, but he'd never met anyone so politely indifferent. Maybe a change of tactics was in order? He captured her hand and gave her his most charming smile.

"Luci, I hope it's all right for me to call you Luci? And you can call me Dante. I'm counting on you to uncomplicate it for me."

Luci studied him. He wasn't just going to go away. And it would really be annoying if his men kept grabbing her off the street. Not to mention what it would do to Mickey's blood pressure if he got involved, which she had a feeling he would.

"It would help if you met them. They're giving a party on Sunday. You should come, bring a friend."

His eyes gleamed. "I like parties. And I'm quite good with old ladies, aren't I, boys?"

"Sure, boss."

It was hard not to grin at their less-than-enthusiastic

endorsement, but Luci knew it wouldn't be wise. This guy's ego was probably more fragile than Dresden.

Dante squeezed her hand, his eyes broadcasting his confidence that he was good with ladies her age, too.

"I probably ought to warn you," she said. "There's more than just the freezer stiff that you saw on the news."

"Oh?" Was she warning him, perhaps even threatening him? Only if she didn't know who she was dealing with. She couldn't be that stupid. Not with those eyes. When dealing in word games and innuendo, it required good instincts to tell what was bluff and what wasn't, but he wasn't getting a clear read from her. She was too unexpected, too far outside the norm. He toyed with the idea of being blunt—but it was such fun to match wits with someone who actually had some. He'd give her a little more slack before he pulled her in. Add a little spice to the game.

"I found another body. Under the bougainvillea."

He blinked and let loose her hand. "Another one?"

"I'm afraid so." She gave a rueful shrug. "The police suspect my aunts. Because of Arsenic and Old Lace. You know the story?"

He nodded. "Did they do it?"

Luci looked thoughtful. "It's hard to tell with my aunts."

Dante's eyes narrowed. Definitely a thinly veiled threat. Behind him Cain slid his hand back into his jacket.

"If that's a problem for you," Luci went on, "we can just forget everything."

He smiled wickedly. "I don't think so." Cain and Abel smiled, too. "I'm really looking forward to meeting your aunts. Now more than ever." He held out his arm. "Why don't I buy you lunch and you can tell me all about them— and all about you?"

Her eyes were friendly but cool as she smiled and said, "I would love to, but I'm supposed to give a statement to the police. I don't dare keep them waiting. Just make for more questions."

Dante smiled. "So it would. At least let me run you home."

Luci smiled back. "How kind."

The sarcasm went right over his head, just like she'd expected. He was a clever thug, but not a bright one.

THERE WERE advantages this crime scene had over their last one.

This one hadn't been cleaned and disinfected before their arrival—just raked a bit. They had a possible ID. And they'd been able to keep the old ladies away.

And then there were the disadvantages.

The smell. The ribald commentary from the forensics boys. The fact that Reggie had surfaced as a corpse instead of a suspect. All the important and influential people who were going to be unhappy about this.

"Captain did say he'd turn up." Delaney looked as morose as he sounded. "You're hot and pissed. These clowns can handle things here for half an hour. Let's go get some lunch."

Mickey had no argument with this plan, so he nodded and followed Delaney through the garage courtyard to the side street where they'd parked Delaney's car. They arrived at the street the same time as a long black limo. A rear door opened and Luci slid out. Behind her Dante, aka Harvey Mertz, was framed in the opening.

"Until next time, sweet thing," he purred, saluting her extended hand with a lascivious kiss. Then, with a mocking two-fingered salute to the slack-jawed detectives, he pulled the door closed so the limo could snake around the corner and out of sight.

"Hi, guys. Did you finish digging up the rest of Reggie?" Luci asked cheerfully. Instead of joining them she headed for the Nash parked at the side of the road with the door hanging open, as if it were waiting just for her.

"I'm going to kill her this time, Delaney. Don't try to stop me."

"Now, Mick. Think of the paperwork."

"I don't care. I want to know—"

"Why don't we just ask her? It might work." Delaney kept a firm grip on Mickey's arm. They got there as Luci was reaching for the key in the ignition.

"Uh, Luci?" Delaney tapped her shoulder.

"Hi, guys," she sounded abstracted. "I've been trying to see if my thingamajig works, but I got abducted. I hate it when that happens."

"Abductions or failed thingamajigs?" Mickey asked, heavily sarcastic.

Her smile was fast and lethal. "Both."

"Which thingamajig is giving you trouble?" Delaney asked hastily.

"The one that makes the engine do stuff."

"Oh, the thingamajig. You know, Delaney—"

"Yeah, I know. Why don't you try it, then we'd like to ask you a few questions. Okay?" Delaney's smile was hopeful, his eyes considerably less so.

Luci's lips twitched, despite her best control efforts.

"Yeah." Mickey crossed his arms over his chest. "We don't mind halting our murder investigation while you try out your thingamajig."

Luci gave him a sunny smile. "Thanks. I've never worked on a Nash before. Not sure how good my intuition is with a strange car. Cross your fingers."

Both men held up crossed fingers.

She turned the key, but instead of a smooth purr there was only a repeated clicking sound. She tried again.

"I was afraid of that. It didn't really feel right. Oh, well. You know a good auto parts store?"

Delaney uncrossed his fingers and pulled the door open. "We'll take you there after lunch."

"Wow, my second invite—"

"Dante? You had lunch with that wise guy?" Mickey burst out. Arms akimbo, thumbs hooked in his belt, he glared at her.

"No, but it was a good guess." She studied him thoughtfully before adding, "He doesn't seem to like you either."

"Ha!" Mickey almost choked on the word. "No surprise—"

"Let's all calm down, okay?" Delaney asked , looking at Mickey.

"I'm always calm," Luci pointed out.

"Look." Mickey shoved aside Delaney's restraining arm to loom over her. "I've had a really bad couple of days and I'm not in the mood for any of your crap. If you're as smart as I think you are, you'd better not say anything until I get some food. Or I won't be responsible for the consequences. Got that?"

Luci nodded, then immediately contradicted herself. "I need to powder my nose."

Mickey inhaled, his hands clenching and unclenching at his sides, but there was no good answer to this unanswerable euphemism. He gave a curt nod and stepped back.

With movements both slow and cautious, she angled off the seat, sliding one leg from under the wheel and lowering it to the pavement. The slow drag gradually unveiled more and more leg as her skirt stayed put—

until ground zero was reached, when it dropped like a curtain.

Both men exhaled. Mickey tugged at his tie and said, "Hurry up. I'm hungry."

She saluted without speaking and headed through the driveway gate. Mickey watched until she was out of sight.

He angrily rubbed his hot face. "She does it on purpose, Delaney!"

"Yes, and she does it very well." His voice was thick with laughter and lust. "What are you going to do about it?"

"I have no idea." Mickey paced away from him, then back again.

"Well, you'd better decide before you do kill her. It's a real bitch getting strip-searched."

FERN WAS afraid to look at Donald. He'd been ominously quiet since they hit the tree. They'd managed to leave the area without attracting attention, but it had been a close call. She'd patched up the cut on his forehead but could do nothing for the bulging veins at his temples except exchange the damaged car for a sporty little Ford. He hadn't even said anything when the goons brought the girl back and she'd climbed behind the wheel of the Nash. He'd choked when the cops came out and whimpered when the Nash wouldn't start, then subsided back into a silent simmer when they all left again instead of getting blown up.

A bead of sweat formed on her forehead, then ran down between her eyes, hovering on the end of her nose for a long moment before dropping into her lap. Even under the shade of an oak it was hot with the motor off. It was time to do something. She cleared her throat and looked at Donald, but whatever she was going to say died in her throat at the look in his eyes.

Maybe it wasn't quite time yet.

Mickey was waiting for Luci when she started back downstairs, her nose presumably powdered. Delaney had spotted Gracie and abandoned Mickey to Luci's caprice. Halfway down, Luci stopped, her brows rising in a question.

"Delaney made other arrangements for lunch. So he won't be here to protect you if you annoy me again," he informed her. He'd used the time she was gone to lecture himself into a more rational frame of mind. It was ridiculous to let her keep pulling his chain. He was a trained officer of the law. A highly trained officer of the law. So she was annoying—and unexpected. He could handle both of those things. All he had to do was keep his cool. Think before he spoke—and after she spoke. Count to ten if he must. Or a million. Whatever it took.

Luci nodded, but a wary light crept into her green eyes as she let him steer her outside to the car.

Good, Mickey thought as he held her door, then slid behind the wheel.

"Delaney got a better offer for lunch, did he? Should I be insulted?"

"Only if you prefer older men," Mickey said, expertly swinging the car onto St. Charles, "and if you're inclined to be jealous of your Aunt Gracie."

"She's not my aunt," Luci said, her voice oddly neutral. "She's sort of a cousin. Delaney's not interested in Gracie in a romantic way is he? He's just questioning her again about the murders?"

"Why shouldn't he be interested in her? She's a very charming lady. A very normal lady."

After a brief pause, she said, "Only in comparison with the rest of us."

Mickey's eyes narrowed. Here it comes. Another one of her outrageous conversational roller coaster rides. He mentally braced himself. "What? You might as well tell me. What's wrong with Gracie?"

"There's nothing wrong with Gracie—except for being dead. And she's kind of cold to be around when the temperature drops, but that doesn't happen often here, thank goodness."

It was fortunate he had to stop at a traffic light. Because she'd done it again. He gripped the steering wheel. Hard.

Counted to ten. And kept going. At one hundred and ten he managed to choke out, "Dead?"

"Yes." She hesitated, then added, "I really thought you'd notice—what with all your experience with dead people."

"You—" He choked a couple of times, then snapped out, "The dead people I deal with don't walk and talk!"

"You noticed right away she wasn't like any living Seymour."

"I said she was normal!"

"I suspect that dead is as normal as we can get."

He choked some more, then settled for glaring at her until honking interrupted him. The car jerked forward as he mentally fought back. "No way. Not this time—"

"You can check if you don't believe me. She's buried at St. Mary's not far from the house. The aunts put flowers on her grave the last Sunday of every month."

Mickey had the strangest urge to laugh. It was funny, in an insane sort of way.

"She's dead?"

"Yes."

"She doesn't look—dead."

"She likes to keep herself up."

This prompted another round of counting before he could say almost calmly, "Really?"

"Yes, really. She's dead. Not married."

A tense silence filled the car for a couple of blocks.

When he turned the car into the parking lot of a Shoney's restaurant, he finally looked at her.

"All right. She's dead. How did she die?"

"She was killed by an irate suitor."

It was the first thing she'd ever said he could understand.

Fern pulled in across the street from Shoney's and watched Luci Seymour and the cop go inside. Only then did she look at Donald for direction. He was looking better now that they had something to do. His color was almost normal again, though she wasn't sure his eyes would ever stop bulging out of the sockets.

"What should we do now?" she asked.

"Wait," Donald said, like he was praying. Under cover, his hand stroked the Uzi like it was his best friend. "They can't stay in there forever."

Inside Shoney's, Mickey told Luci what to order for him, then retreated to regain his cool. Nothing like a urinal to put things in perspective. He leaned his aching head against cool tile and spent a few glorious moments mentally strangling Luci—until he started hurting himself. Then he pulled his clothing and his brain together and made a few decisions. First, he would check out her outrageous claim about Gracie. He stopped and used his cell phone to call in a request for any background info on Grace Seymour. He felt somewhat better, but wouldn't be one hundred percent until he had food in his stomach. Only then would he question Luci about Dante. After that, well, he'd just have to see.

His food was there when he joined Luci, and he could see that she had made a run at the salad bar. To his relief, she just smiled at him. Did she sense how close he was to losing it? He hoped so.

Luci ate quietly, aware of how close Mickey was to losing it. She deflected his brooding looks with bland ones. When he wiped his mouth and hands and tossed his napkin aside, she knew the truce was over. The question was, how much of what she suspected about Dante should she share with him? Until she knew how far her aunts were involved in whatever was going on, did she dare let him start stomping around in things?

The men in her family had not prepared her to trust in male finesse. The men she'd met outside her family had only re-enforced her conviction there was no such thing as male finesse.

She met his determined gaze with a disingenuous one. He wasn't going to be easy to sidetrack. Or to fool. But she'd never backed down from a challenge before. She wasn't about to start now.

"What were you doing with Dante, Luci?"

"Looking at his enormous boobs?"

"Don't mess with me, Luci. I'm not in the mood. Just tell me what I want to know. Or I'll arrest you for obstruction of justice. You ever been strip-searched?"

"Not by a cop."

"You surprise me."

Luci gave a mock sigh. "And I thought I couldn't anymore."

He glared at her, but instead of wilting Luci found herself thinking that even mad he was darn cute. Those little wrinkles fanning out from his eyes made the pads of her fingers tingle with a desire to trace them. And his mouth, well it was tantamount to carrying an unconcealed weapon.

She realized he was picking up on her thoughts because his glare started filling with a different kind of heat. Heat, she was beginning to discover, could be caught. In the space of a heartbeat, a tidy blaze started in her mid section. It started to do an arc between them but got stopped by the waitress coming up to clear their table. Mickey waited until she was gone, then pulled his handcuffs out and dangled them in front of her. Somehow she didn't think he had bedroom games in mind.

"All you have to do is ask," she said, not sure she was talking about Dante or the games.

She saw him swallow. It seemed to take a long time. He had to do it again and shove his hands into his hair before he managed a hoarse, "Why were you with Dante?"

Luci eyed the spiky ends he'd created in his hair, wanting to smooth them back in place, knowing it could lead to more than a better hairdo. Focus, she reminded herself. She felt a need for something to occupy her hands and picked up her discarded napkin, folding it once, then again as she said in the tones of one making a confession, "I don't know, but I promise it wasn't fun. The guy's an octopus."

She gave a delicate shudder. "Yuck."

She couldn't resist a peek to see how he took this news. His reaction was better than she expected. His hands clenched into fists and his eyes turned from a blue glare to something that was almost...green? Was it—jealousy? She couldn't stop her smile anymore than Canute, whoever he was, could stop that flood.

"An—" He stopped, cleared his throat. "Did he say why?"

The glare turned blue again and irate. She refocused on the question. "Something about Benny and shoeboxes?"

"That would be Benny the Book, but—" Mickey gave her that look again. "Shoeboxes?"

Benny the Book. Gambling? And Unabelle? Her mind was getting boggled again. Must be some kind of record. Luci nodded, then studied the folded napkin. She began to tear it. "He told me he liked what was in them."

He blinked several times and sort of looked like he was...counting. "I don't think so."

"He had his gun-toting henchmen looming over me. What was I supposed to do? Tell him he's full of crap?" She made the last tear in the napkin and realized she'd made a question mark. Symbolic and possibly Freudian. Mickey was having a most unsettling effect on her. She fashioned a circle to add to it.

"So what did you do?"

She shrugged and smoothed her question mark. "I invited him to my aunt's party on Sunday. It's their shoe-boxes he wants. I figure they can deal with him better than I can."

The thought of Luci's aunts and Dante in the same room gave him a twitch next to his right eye. He stopped it with his hand and tried to think his way to sanity, but he was too close to her. She created, he decided morosely, a sanity-free zone for at least a yard or so around her.

"I did some thinking while you were freshening up."

Mickey braced himself. "Oh?"

For a long beat, Luci stared at him. With some effort, Mickey managed to meet her look without flinching or lusting.

"You are," he said, finally, "on the inside there."

"That's true." Luci picked up the pen the waitress had left for Mickey to use to sign the credit card receipt. "One thing I was thinking. I know we found Frosty the dead man first, but I think Reggie is really victim number one."

"There's no forensic evidence to support it," Mickey said, "but I happen to agree with you."

"Really?" Luci looked delighted, then bent to write "Reggie" and "Frosty" at the top of her question mark.

"Is that all of your thinking?" Mickey asked in his most dampening tone.

"By no means. There's the weddings." She frowned.

"Weddings?" Mickey wasn't ready and his stomach did a drop.

"They seem to be a sort of theme that runs through this whole thing. That and naked bodies. Which sort of goes with weddings, too. At least the honeymoon part of weddings."

"Other than Eddie and Unabelle—" Mickey began.

"And my neighbor, Helen. And while he was driving me back, that Dante person mentioned his aunt, the one he wants to bring to the party? Well, she got married not long ago, too. It ended badly, which is why he wants to bring her, but, still, it's a wedding. And Velma. She wanted to marry Reggie." Her look was loaded with see?

Mickey patted his pockets, looking for his aspirin bottle as the headache made an abrupt return. "I don't see—"

She frowned, her expression turning thoughtful as she added Velma's name to the others on her question mark.

"What?"

"Velma." Luci traced her name with the pen. "There's something just not right with her."

There was, in Mickey's opinion, more than a mere "something" not right with Velma. There was a host of "somethings" not right with this whole case. He'd be lucky to get through it without something going wrong with him.

"Gracie noticed it, too," Luci said, as if this were the clincher.

Mickey flinched. He had to. He didn't want to believe her when she said Gracie was dead, but it was something easy to prove or disprove, unlike, say, her theories on the relationship between marriage and murder. If Gracie was dead, Delaney was in serious trouble. Mickey hadn't seen him this smitten since...well, fact was he'd never seen him this smitten.

Pain did a tap dance on his temples, apparently immune to the aspirin he'd ingested. He had to get back, warn him—something. He dug out his wallet, found some cash for the tip and tossed it onto the table. It wasn't until he stood up that he realized Luci was studying him, her gaze unreadable.

"He'll get over it," she said, then stood up, bringing her face almost even with his. The compassion in her eyes was mixed with something that could have been regret.

"What?"

"Gracie. Seymour women. Men fall for us, but they get over it. Or they kill us." Without being asked, she started for the exit.

"Do you read minds?"

"Just faces. Yours isn't exactly poker."

"Oh." He followed her, frustration giving him some protection against the sight of her graceful, sexy body and glorious legs. Some, but not nearly enough. Not when her scent trailed after her, filling his nose and fogging his brain. Regret for Delaney and for himself cut through the fog, leaving too many questions to rise to the surface of his mind. He tried to call it back, but one escaped from his mouth. "Why don't the Seymour women marry?"

His question took her by surprise. Where had that come from? She opened her mouth, stopped, then said with utter truth, "You know, I have no idea."

14

"Max," Dante said as he rocked back in his desk chair, hands clasped behind his head. "It's a pity you weren't here to meet Benny's Jane. I'd have been interested in your opinion of the lady." He waited for Max to look appropriately regretful, then asked, "You get everything taken care of?"

"Yes, Mr. Dante. Henry won't trouble you again."

"Good." Dante frowned. "Miss Luci said I could bring Cloris to some party on Sunday. Think you'd better go with me, too. Keep your eyes open, let me know what you think. Oh, and Max?"

"Yes, Mr. Dante?"

"Find out all you can about the Seymours. She says the scam is her aunts'. They're the ones with the body in the freezer."

"Right." Max made a note.

"Miss Luci tells me they've had another one turn up under some bushes. If they did do these guys—" Dante looked thoughtful. "Why don't you put someone on to watch the place? Like to have a feel for the setup before we go in."

FERN AND DONALD picked up lunch at a walk-in joint across from where their quarry lunched. The food calmed Donald but left his determination to blow Luci Seymour away undiminished. As he stuffed food into his mouth, his brooding gaze never left the entrance to the restaurant. The busy street with its complicated restrictions on turning wasn't suitable to their purpose, but after lunch, they followed them to a narrow quiet street and watched as they parked in front of an auto parts store.

"All right. This is good, real good. Drive by slow so I can check it out, then turn round. When I give the word, hit it. Then get out of here."

Fern nodded, concentrating on getting the car into optimum position for the kill—and an easy escape. She was aware of the pain from her broken arm, but hovering just past the dingy rutted street was the vision of the Disney castle in all its glittering glory—

The cop took the girl's arm as they crossed the street.

"Now?"

"No, let'em get inside. Last time the cop saw us coming.

This time he won't see us 'til too late. I'll frame them in that nice big window and cut 'em in half."

There was a brief glare as the light hit the open door, then it swished closed, shutting the pair inside.

Donald nodded, his voice casual as he said, "Let's do it. Real slow and real casual-like."

The Uzi was cradled in his lap. Light, easily handled, ready to become deadly with the flick of a switch.

Fern idled the car into position, just for a second using her broken arm to hold the car steady while she brushed the sweat from her eyes.

"Damn." Donald rested the Uzi on the window frame as he peered at the shop.

"What's wrong?"

"Lights glaring on the glass—but I think—yes, got her!" He lifted the Uzi and released the safety, his finger tightening on the trigger.

Luci placed her order for a starter, then turned and leaned against the counter. "This shouldn't take too long—he seems to have a good grasp of his doohickeys and thingamajigs."

"So do you," Mickey said, his voice wry. "Sure you're not a mechanic in your other life?"

"What I am in my other life would surprise you."

"What you are in this life surprises me."

Luci couldn't stop the surprise, the delight or the smile that spread across her mouth. Dang, he was good. It would be wise to limit her contact with Detective Mickey Ross. She broke eye contact with an effort, her gaze bouncing to the car moving past the shop. Absently, she noted the window was down, the ominous barrel slightly protruding.

Barrel? It was an effective distraction.

No time to think or speak. Only time to act—

She hit Mickey hard. It felt good, but there was no time to enjoy it as bullets smashed through the plate glass window, shattering it into hundreds of deadly missiles. The line of fire traced across the counter toward Mickey at chest height as Mickey staggered once, then went down with Luci attached to his chest.

The sound, the fury, the smell of cordite mingling with the smell of auto shop in the enclosed space was overwhelming. She felt Mickey grope for his gun. The cold metal brushed chillingly against her bare thigh, then he rolled, reversing their positions. His gun flared and she couldn't control a flinch. Funny, she thought as she stared at the column of his throat inches from her eyes, smelled his aftershave mingling with the smell of dust. She thought she'd been broke to the sound of a gun.

"Damn!" Mickey looked down at her, his face grim. "Are you all right?"

Luci fought against the adrenaline surging in her body, even as she felt the adrenal beat of Mickey's body working against her good intentions.

"We've really got to stop meeting like this." Was that her voice, so throaty, so breathless? She saw the change of focus in his eyes first, then felt it in his body. But there wasn't anything she could do about it. He was on top.

"No, we've got to stop meeting like this," he said and bent his head. In the distance, a siren began to wail, the sound getting louder and closer.

His mouth tasted as good as it had looked, maybe better. So this was what all the shouting was about. No wonder people didn't want to stop. No wonder her mother didn't stop. Dimly, on the other side of pleasure, Luci heard the shop owner beating a frantic tattoo on the counter above them.

"You see that, man? They just blew hell outta my store! That's what I get for not paying protect! That's what I get! I tole him I weren't gonna pay no protect and now he try to kill me! Damn it to hell! This no time to be suckin' face, man!"

Mickey quit sucking face. Luci tried not to smile as he looked up and snapped, "Call 911!"

"I don't want no police! They try to kill me again! I didn't see nothing! I don't know nothing! Beside, cain't you hear? They coming! Oh, man, I'm dead!"

"You are the police." Luci felt impelled to point this out, since it appeared to have slipped his mind. "Shouldn't you do something?"

So he did something. He kissed her again. Not what

she meant. But not bad. The second kiss was better than the first one—though that didn't seem possible.

"What the hell—Mickey?" A shrill voice, rising in disbelief, cut between them. Mickey looked up.

"Caroline?"

Through the dust—and the lust—Luci looked up, too. It was immediately obvious that Caroline was having a non-business response to the intimate arrangement of Luci and Mickey's bodies. Her nostrils were flaring and her eyes were shooting glare bullets.

"Is she your girlfriend?" Interestedly, she made note of the stocky well-endowed figure. She let her gaze linger deliberately on how well Caroline filled out her uniform and felt Mickey tense. Her gaze found the drawn weapon. In a semi-undertone, Luci asked, "Is it a good idea to cheat on someone who has her own gun and carte blanche to use it?"

ON ONE SIDE, Caroline glared at Mickey while snapping questions at Luci. She ignored him while an EMT attempted to determine who was bleeding and who was merely bled upon.

After a period of probing and poking while the ache in Mickey's head got worse and the pain in his side built, the EMT patted Luci's knee and said, "Well, doll, you lucked out. Minimal damage."

The EMT taped a final bandage over a gash in her arm, grinning in a way that made Mickey want to smash in the guy's teeth. Not because he was jealous. He just wanted to hit someone. To vent a little.

Luci's smile was too sunny, too friendly. She was getting back at him, and for what? A couple of kisses that were little enough recompense for all the pain and suffering she'd caused him? She wasn't that good. Well, yeah, she was. Who'd have thought a mouth that straight could taste that good?

"It's amazing," her mouth said now. "After the week I've had, I should be dead. This is my second drive-by shooting this week, not to mention the nosedive off that escalator. And almost getting hit by that car back in Butt Had."

Caroline's whole face twitched and Mickey bit back a grin. Luci was right about one thing. Caroline wasn't a good person to piss off.

The EMT turned with obvious reluctance to Mickey.

Caroline turned to Luci with even more obvious reluctance. "You saw the car first?"

Luci nodded. The EMT poked around in Mickey's gash with cheerful callousness.

"What did you do?" Caroline asked through gritted teeth.

"I jumped on Mickey—"

"What?" Caroline's voice rose to an ear-painful pitch.

The EMT poked harder, eager to finish his work.

"Only to save his life," Luci said reassuringly.

"Nasty, painful, but not serious. You're gonna need a few stitches plus your head x-rayed." The EMT stepped back.

Mickey felt Caroline's unspoken but emphatic agreement hit him in waves.

"You might have a concussion—" the EMT added.

"I doubt it. He's got a hard head."

Mickey looked up and found Delaney standing in the doorway, surveying the scene with a resigned expression.

"I can't let you go anywhere alone, Ross."

Mickey grinned weakly. Finally someone to protect him from the women.

"And the kiss?" Caroline snapped. "What was that?"

Luci was quiet for a moment, then brightened. "Mouth-to-mouth?"

Caroline gave a low growl. Delaney leaned close to Mickey. "I wouldn't count on her for a ride to work anymore, bubba."

"Do you have any aspirin?" Mickey asked the EMT.

LUCI INSISTED on collecting and paying for her thingamajig —even though the store no longer had a cash register— before she would allow Delaney to convey them to the hospital. The irony of Delaney's car escaping the recent carnage didn't escape Mickey's notice as he slid inside.

"How'd you get here so fast?"

"Hopped a patrol car. Wanted to make sure you hadn't got my car shot to pieces. Glad to see you kept it out of the line of fire."

When the hospital finished with them, Delaney took Luci home first. It took less energy to follow Delaney and Luci to the Nash than to argue. They both had orders from the doctor to rest. Mickey leaned against the Nash's fender and watched Delaney and Luci install the new starter through a haze of exhaustion that went deeper than his soul.

Not that tired stopped him from appreciating the sight of Luci bent over the front fender, one exquisite leg bent as she subdued the Nash's innards. It was obvious God had made her too cute to kill to protect her from herself. A thing of beauty was a joy forever—from a safe distance, he decided, then moved a step closer when Luci exchanged the fender for a seat behind the wheel.

He didn't want to lose sight of her legs. Who knew how long they'd be where he could see them? She'd go back to Butt Had after the wedding. And he'd be glad. Really. Okay, not glad, but relieved. Definitely relieved.

Luci clicked the key once, then again, but the engine still didn't respond. Delaney poked his head around the edge of the hood. "Try it now."

Luci did. "Nope."

"There's a wire hanging down from under the dash," Mickey said, figuring he ought to do something to move this forward or he'd never get gone. He crouched down and grabbed the wire. "It looks like it should be plugged into something."

"Really?" Luci slid her legs to one side. "I was sure I plugged everything in before I left. Can you get it?"

"Sure." Mickey forced his attention away from her legs and groped for, but failed to find, the other side of the connection. With some difficulty, he got his head under the wheel and a partial view of the under-the-dash area. "Ah, there it is."

He made the connection. "Try it now."

Luci's leg brushed against his cheek as she applied gentle pressure to the gas pedal. Above his head she turned the key and the engine caught. Out of the darkness of the under dash, two numbers glowed red. Six. Zero. Then five, nine. It took him five more seconds to realize what he was seeing.

"Shit!" He hit his head on the wheel, trying to get clear. "Get out of the car!"

"What—" Luci looked at him, confusion visible in her wonderful eyes.

Delaney strolled around the side, wiping his hands on a rag. "What's wrong?"

Mickey managed upright and pulled Luci off the seat. "Bomb!"

Delaney grabbed her other arm.

Luci looked at Mickey, then Delaney. Saw the same thing in their eyes. Urgency. Fear. It was contagious. She started to run, stretching her legs to match their frantic race toward the dubious cover of Delaney's parked car.

They dove, a tumble of arms and legs and bodies as the Nash went up like a rocket. The explosion, which lifted the front end of the Nash off the ground, vibrated through the gelatinous swamp and shattered the windows of Delaney's car. Glass pelted them, and fire, reaching out from the blast, scorched across their backs for a searing moment. Then there was only the sound of fire and metal hitting the ground.

"What—" Luci, who'd landed on top, started to look up.

"Wait." Mickey held her down as a second explosion rocked the street, this time from the Nash's gas tank.

Luci, her ears ringing, shook her head, then extricated herself from her rescuers and stood up. The heat from the blazing car sent her back a pace.

"I never had a starter do that before."

With a rough jerk, Mickey turned her to face him, his face as angry as she'd ever seen it.

"So? Tell me, Miss Seymour, just who the hell is pissed at you?"

ARTIE HEARD and felt the explosion. He smiled his delight as he bent to unlock the door to his car. He'd stopped to buy Band-Aids for his numerous cuts and scrapes and they now liberally adorned his face. Good thing his new shoes were without flaw, he decided with a sigh of contentment. Things were really starting to look up. He raised his gaze to give thanks and saw something falling out of the sky toward him. What—

There was just time to identify it as a large, old-style steering wheel before it wrapped itself around his neck. His skull still ringing from the impact, he saw stars and blood dripping on his new shoes.

15

"We did it, Fernie! I'm sure of it this time! Break out the beer. Let's celebrate!" Donald tossed the Uzi on one bed and did a half-leap onto the bed next to it. With hands clasped behind his head, he grinned so wide she saw the gums above his plates.

Fern nodded abstractedly as she bent over the cooler. She was wondering if she would be able to get her picture taken with Mickey Mouse. She'd have to keep Donald away from Winnie the Pooh. They were built too much alike to be photographed together, but she couldn't tell that to Donald. He loved that bear.

In honor of the occasion, Donald shook the first two beers and sprayed her with one. She sprayed him, then they fell on the bed, laughing like a couple of kids until Donald got jabbed in the privates with the Uzi.

"Disney World here we come!" He staggered over to

the sorry TV and fumbled with the dials until a fuzzy picture formed on the screen. "I want to see them haul her outta there in one of them black body bags."

"News won't be on for awhile."

"Someone's liable to have one of them news break things soon." He turned through the three channels until a plastic newsman highlighting the top stories filled the screen.

"Violence again broke out in the streets of New Orleans this afternoon. An auto parts store in downtown New Orleans was the target of a drive-by shooting. Police have no motive for the incident which left two people, one an NOPD detective, with minor injuries—"

Whatever else the newscaster had to say was drowned in Donald's howl of rage as he kicked in the TV screen, pulling his hernia in the process.

DANTE WAS STUDYING his Persephone when Max slid into the room.

"Yes, what is it?"

"I think we got something solid on Miss Cloris' husband, Mr. Dante."

Dante wheeled to look at his assistant. "Tell me, Max."

"Found a snitch that thinks he recognizes him from prison. Seems he's a con artist, name of Arthur "Artie"

Maxwell. Has a string of aka's—and a penchant for preying on older ladies with cash."

There was a long pause as Dante assimilated this information. "Your snitch know where he is?"

"I got everyone looking, but word is, he's gone to ground. I don't think you're the only one looking for him."

"I want to be the one who finds him."

"Yes, Mr. Dante."

Dante resumed contemplation of his masterpiece.

"I like the boobs the same."

"So do I, Mr. Dante."

THE FIRE DEPARTMENT CAME. And more police cars. The bomb squad, paramedics and the news media, both print and electronic.

And Captain Henry Pryce—looking especially grim.

"Can we be cashiered or are we gonna be shot at dawn?" Mickey watched the determined approach of the Captain, the clusters of official humanity falling back for their stern-faced leader.

"If we're lucky we'll only be shot," Delaney said. He examined the series of neat plaster strips the EMT had applied to his arm, voiced his thanks, and stood up. Rolling down his sleeves, he waited for Pryce while the same EMT as before turned his attention to Mickey.

"You got a death wish, man?"

There was no time to answer as Pryce stopped in front of them.

"Gentlemen." Pryce's hooded gaze was as cold and green as his stare, long and unnerving. "Care to explain what happened here?"

They didn't, but had to anyway. When they finished, there was another nerve-wracking silence until Pryce said, "This has gotten completely out of hand. What's the motive?"

"No clue," Delaney admitted. "Does seem like they have to be related to the murders, though."

"Thank you for stating the obvious, detective," Pryce said.

A distraction seemed in order, so Mickey jumped into the fray. "Speaking of the murders," he asked, "has our autopsy come in yet on the John Doe from the freezer?"

Pryce's gaze swiveled to Mickey like big guns homing in on a small target. "Funny you should ask about the Coroner. He's been asking about you."

"Really?" Mickey tugged at his tie.

"If I were you, I wouldn't expect any—favors—from them for quite a while. At least until they've had time to forget the riot. Always assuming that's possible."

"Riot?" Mickey and Delaney looked at each other.

"It seems a pair of our detectives gave a picture of the frozen corpse to some crazy psychic. Who made copies and handed them out for all her friends to show around. Which helped the TV people get hold of one and run it on the noon news. Seems like everyone in town thought it was a picture of someone they knew and came down to make sure it wasn't. Now which detectives do you think would do something so stupid?"

"I'll check around, sir." Mickey avoided looking at his Captain, but it didn't help. He wished looks could kill so he'd be out of his misery, but knowing Pryce, he'd just set his eyes to maim.

"You do that. In the meantime, your autopsy is at the bottom of the priority list."

"So—are we suspended?" Maybe it wasn't a total loss.

"Not—yet."

"The Seymours—" Delaney started to protest.

Pryce cut him off at the knees. "...are the only reason I haven't suspended you. I know, none better, how—difficult they can be. But if you keep your head, your perspective, you can handle a few eccentric old ladies.

"Yes, sir."

Mickey noticed a uniform approaching and turned to him with relief at the distraction he hoped he would provide.

"Ross, Delaney, Miss Seymour said she was going to change, but she'd meet you in the garden—oh, sorry, sir. I didn't mean to interrupt." He looked like he meant it, if the jump of his Adam's apple and the white showing around his eyes were any indication.

"You have a message for these two?"

He didn't add "bozos," but Mickey felt it was implied.

The uniform, instead of delivering his message, stared at the Captain, a frown furrowing his young brow. "Are you...is she...?"

"Spit it out. Is she what?"

"A...relative, sir. She could be, well, your daughter."

Pryce stared at the uniform long enough to almost wither him where he stood. "Who could be my daugh—" He stopped, the color draining from his lean cheeks.

Mickey felt the internal earthquake that comes when pieces fall into place. It was so obvious, he couldn't believe he'd missed it. The line of the jaw, Pryce's and Luci's straight mouths. Blinded by the legs. And the eccentricity, he told himself as he braced for the sky of his Captain's wrath to fall. Though it was kind of a relief to know that even the Captain hadn't handled one particular Seymour woman as well as he thought he had.

"I MET Lila Seymour the summer before I shipped out for Nam."

Ross and Delaney hadn't asked, but Pryce seemed to need to talk while they waited in the garden for Luci. It couldn't be easy for him to discover in just under one minute that he had a daughter and that someone wanted to kill her. He'd aged twenty years in twenty seconds.

"She'd stalled her car and I stopped to help. It was her battery. I tried to push her with my truck—that's how we jump-started cars back then—but she couldn't get the hang of what I wanted her to do. Hopeless with machines, but with legs like hers, well, she didn't need to be skilled." He stretched his legs out in front, his mind's eye seeing a distant past instead of the azaleas. "I decided to switch places with her. Have her push her car with my truck. Told her to get going about thirty-five and then pull over when I got hers going." A slight, reminiscent grin softened the line of his mouth.

"What happened, sir?"

Because, of course, they all knew something had happened. The Seymour apples didn't fall far from the family tree.

"She was going exactly thirty-five when she hit me." He chuckled. "She'd backed it up so she could be up to speed. Saw her coming in the mirror. Barely had time to brace myself." The smile turned wry. "Should've known then she was trouble and just walked away. But I didn't." He shrugged. "I would've married her before I shipped out. Never understood why she just took off." The lines around his mouth deepened and his fists clenched. "Damn the woman. I could kill her—"

They all heard the door to the patio slide open. Mickey watched his Captain turn to see his daughter for the first time.

She walked toward them in the failing light, gone "gypsy" with some kind of loose wrap skirt and a soft blouse that drooped off her shoulders. She'd tucked a flower behind one ear and carried a tray of sandwiches and drink, despite the elastic wrapped around her left wrist. She didn't look like someone in the sight line of killers as she lowered the tray with enough expertise to give credence to her claim of being a waitress. She looked—

Things he didn't dare think in the presence of his Captain and her father.

"I know you're primed to ask me scores of tiresome questions, but don't until—"

Luci stopped. The silence got long, the gravity of her presence pulling his gaze from the ground in time to see her studying them as intently as they were studying her. As always, her thoughts remained her own behind the calm reflection of her green eyes, but she had to see it, he thought. The likeness was practically neon now that they were together.

Luci thought it was the humidity that was too thick to cut when she came out, but it was now obvious that the humidity was losing, big time, to something else. Mickey looked like he wished he were in a galaxy far, far away. Delaney was trying, without success, to blend into a hibiscus. And the third man?

She turned toward him with an odd reluctance. Much of the tension emanating from the three men seemed to originate from him. Her first thought was that he looked ill. Her second, he looked...like she should know him.

Despite the grayness to his lean cheeks, he had a

strong presence. A man used to giving orders and expecting to have them obeyed. Not someone who could spend too much time in the Seymour zone without developing a twitch. She tried to imagine him in the same room with her aunts, but couldn't. They were incapable of recognizing an order, let alone obeying one. His gaze burned her with its intensity. His hands were clenched as if he wanted to grab her and do—

"What?" she asked, the single word falling like a stone into the weighted silence.

They all looked away, shrugged and mumbled patently false denials, but within seconds they were all staring at her again. She felt like checking to see if she'd grown another head. Instead she crossed her arms over and said, "If you're hungry, maybe you should eat the sandwiches."

"They look good, don't they, Ross?" Delaney asked, his voice too hearty. He clumsily helped himself. Mickey followed suit, in his haste almost tipping over the tray. And why were they both being so careful not to look at the man eating her up with his eyes but without any sexual overtones?

Something was up. They all looked like deer caught in headlights as they stared at their sandwiches like they didn't know what to do with them.

"You put them in your mouths and chew," she prompted. "Or you could tell me what's wrong?"

Each man took a bite, chewing like it hurt. Swallowing dryly. Without speaking, she poured each of them a glass of lemonade and got a round of far too grateful smiles. She turned to Delaney. He was the mediator of the partnership and, as long as Gracie stayed out of sight, could be counted on to be coherent. She arched her brows.

He kind of twitched a couple of times, then produced, "We think someone is trying to kill you."

"So you said." She arched the other brow when he didn't follow this up with anything else.

The source of their discomfort cleared his throat and Delaney rushed to add, "This is the Captain of the Homicide Division, Henry Pryce. Captain." For some reason, introducing her appeared to cause Delaney some pain because his voice got hoarse when he finished with, "This is Luci...Seymour."

Luci took the hand the captain extended, felt it close forcefully, painfully over hers, as if he wanted to hang on to her. She met his gaze, then freed herself because she needed the distance to ease the choking sensation clogging her throat. She sank into her usual, boneless recline on the slider swing. Could it be panic she was experiencing? How could she know? Panic wasn't on the list of accepted Seymour emotions. That didn't matter to her adrenalin gland. The hairs on her arms were so straight they could run as conservatives.

She looked at Mickey. "How can you be so sure I'm the target?"

"Your car just exploded all over the neighborhood," he

pointed out with grim relish. "And then there's the two drive-by shootings—"

"But why? I know I'm annoying—"

"Your—" the Captain cleared the husky out of his voice, then finished, "safety is our first concern. The mother—"

"Mother?" Luci prompted when he stopped.

"Motive. I meant motive."

"Uh huh." He looked so horrified, she added with outward calm, "I always mix up mother and motive." Inside, small tremors of shock quaked through her insides as her mind resisted what her eyes and her heart tried to tell her.

He gave her a far too grateful look. "The motive will become clear when we have the truth. The absolute, honest truth. With no more damn lies and running away."

He stood up, his fists clenched. Luci stood, too, unable —unable or unwilling—to have him towering over her. "Uh huh. What did you say your name is?"

He tried twice before he got out, "Pryce."

"Our captain," Mickey added quickly. "Of detectives."

It was hilarious. Like a bit in a sitcom, but she wasn't laughing. She was, she realized, trying not to burst into tears. She hadn't burst into tears since the day she'd left New Orleans. Crying was another of those un-Seymour things. Her eyes burned with it, but she wasn't about to cry in front of— "Your captain?"

"Of detectives," Delaney said hoarsely.

She let out the breath she'd been holding like a lifeline. "I feel safer already."

Safe. That was a laugh. She was free falling without rope or belay and she hadn't been rock climbing in a couple of years. If only she could see what was at the bottom of the chasm, she'd know...what?

Pryce looked both dazed and gratified. In a mirrored movement, they brushed hair back from their brows, froze and hastily dropped their hands to their sides. For a long, horrified moment he stared at her while she stared at him. She didn't know what to do with her hands. She'd always known what to do with her hands. She'd been born knowing what to do with her hands, but now they just hung there twitching.

Pryce frowned at the sight of the elastic bandage wrapped around her wounded wing. "What happened?"

"I found out I can't fly." How calm I sound, she thought with distant awe. Amazing. Yet disturbing. I should sound different. It wasn't natural. Except it was natural for a Seymour, wasn't it? Maybe I'm having an out-of-Seymour body experience?

"She did a header off an escalator," Mickey interposed, sounding as far away as her Seymour-ness felt.

"It's all in the report we're going to write when we get time," Delaney added with equal haste.

They both looked at Pryce. Since no one was looking at her, it seemed a good time to just leave. Her thoughts were jostling, bouncing, dodging inside her head, with one single disturbing thought at the center that she refused to deal with until she was alone.

Mickey could tell Pryce didn't give a damn about the report. As one, they turned to look at what he did care about and saw her walking toward the house. The seductive side-to-side of her hips stole the furtive cool from the shade provided by the trees and left his throat dry with want. Pryce choked, from a different kind of distress. It was left to Delaney to call, "Luci? Where are you going?"

She stopped, the turn of her head done in graceful slow motion. "I need to feel safe from a safe distance." She stared at them for a long beat, then added, "And you think we're weird."

No one moved until she slid the terrace door closed, then they all exhaled as one. Pryce gave him a look that was fierce, even by his usual standards. "You keep her safe."

Mickey recoiled from the double responsibility of it. "Sir, we don't—"

"Don't what? Protect citizens from bodily harm?"

Delaney leapt figuratively into the breech. "We're homicide—"

"Correct me if I'm wrong," Pryce cut in, "but didn't both your current investigations happen here?" Mickey and Delaney's shoulders sagged. "So, how will staying here in this house interfere with your investigation?"

"We might," Mickey muttered, "need to go somewhere else."

Pryce stepped close, right in his face.

"Anything happens to my daughter, it better happen to you, too."

Mickey waited until Pryce had stalked off in the opposite direction from Luci before saying, "We are so screwed."

"ANY WORD ON MAXWELL?" Dante asked.

"We've turned up a couple more wives. This guy's a regular Casanova with older women, Mr. Dante. And clever in a stupid way. He never lets them get a good picture of him. We've had some wedding photos come in —he's always moved or got something in front of his face."

"I don't see where that matters, Max. I met the man. I know what the bastard looks like."

"I don't think so, Mr. Dante. This guy's got one of those anonymous faces—with a bit of chameleon thrown in. His wives—the number we're turning up is climbing as we speak—can't even agree on how tall he is."

"That's ridiculous! He's—" Dante stopped as the colorless, handsomely vague face of his aunt's cheating husband eluded him. "Son-of-a-bitch, Max. You're right. I have no clue how tall he is." He turned to Max. "We gonna find him?"

"No doubt about it, sir. We're trying to turn up someone who did time in stir with him. We'll get him."

Where was the third Arthur?

Mickey opened his eyes to unfamiliar surroundings and this inscrutable question bouncing inexplicably around inside his aching head.

It was dark, but a tracing of light penetrated from outside. Enough to clue him that he wasn't at home in his own functional apartment. Faintly, from outside, he could hear the insistent beat of rock music. Disoriented, it took him a couple of minutes to trace his route from the Seymour garden and Luci's intransigence, to this room in the Seymour house overseeing the protective detail guarding the Captain's newly discovered daughter.

He pushed back the sheets and swung his feet over the side of the bed, the smooth wood cool against the soles of his feet. He rubbed his aching head, wondering how serious the threat to Luci was, with its mix of the absurd and the serious apparently orchestrated by a couple of octogenarians with a taste for joke glasses? There seemed to be a plethora of elderly mucking about in this case. All except their naked John Doe.

And a dearth of suspects since their prime one had turned up under a bush.

Death was stalking the perimeters of the Seymour house and all he had for witnesses were three crazy old ladies, one presumed ghost, a couple of inarticulate faithful retainers, his uncle's inanimate fiancée, and a partner who was in love with a ghost. With Velma and Luci for contrast.

Whether he needed it or not.

And if all this weren't bad enough, they had to protect the innocent—always assuming they knew who the innocent were—in the midst of a wedding. With the dogs of political patronage nipping at their heels.

Then there were the logistics problems. The department was shorthanded anyway, with sixteen officers under indictment and/or on suspension for various charges ranging from rape to theft to murder. And the problems with their fleet of cars, most of which weren't running because of budget shortfalls. And the ones that were running were driving politicians around so they wouldn't get mugged.

Pryce had only been able to produce one other pair of detectives to watch tonight. They were outside right now. Tomorrow he was hoping to scare up a female officer to relieve some of the pressure on the four men, but he was making no promises—while radiating unspoken threats about their fate if something went wrong.

And there were so many things that could go wrong around the Seymours.

Mickey's thought processes reached this unsatisfactory point when it occurred to him that it was not a good thing for there to be music coming in from outside. His sore muscles protesting, Mickey padded over to the window and heard a very familiar laugh from outside before he could jerk the curtain back.

"No—"

But it was.

Luci.

Dancing directly under a street lamp with some young stud in shorts and a muscle shirt.

LUCI'S AUNTS' aversion to technology extended to air conditioning. The house was cool—thanks to Gracie—but that couldn't come close to six thousand feet above sea level cool. That, humidity-dampened sheets, and thoughts that tended to circle around the question of Mickey's captain and her paternity drove Luci outside where she found the frat boys having another party. She was tired of thinking, tired of wondering if Henry Pryce were her mother's Pooh Bear.

How could she not have realized that finding her father would bring her face-to-face with her mother's lover? There'd been no Immaculate Conception in her case. No comforting fictions to tell herself. She was a "love" child, an outcome of passion.

Her thoughts kept getting caught up in images of Lila and Pryce tangled in sheets. She had to move, to push out thinking, and untie the knotted fragments and figure out what she was going to do. The party seemed like the perfect way to push it all out.

Young firm bodies clutched each other, dancing in the street. Other young bodies sprawled in abandon across the long-suffering lawn in front of their even more long-suffering house. A keg poked out a window, and pizza boxes were stacked four and five deep on the porch.

In other words, it was just what the doctor hadn't ordered.

A couple of slices of pepperoni and a beer later, Luci hooked her bandaged arm over the massive shoulders of someone everyone called Tank, who was large enough to have his own weather system, and started swaying to Roy Orbison's "Mystery Girl." It seemed appropriate on a variety of levels.

Mixed with the smell of beer and pizza, her nose picked up several hundred different plant smells, but magnolia, she decided, was her favorite and it didn't clash with Tank's aftershave which was called, he told her, Mighty Dog.

She felt the disturbance in the force before Mickey tapped Tank on the shoulder—then banged him on the shoulder to get his attention. With a prehistoric grunt, Tank ambled off after a sweet young thing, each step causing minor concussions in the soggy ground.

Without missing a beat, Luci transferred her arms to Mickey's smaller, less rock-like, but infinitely more pleasant shoulders. His aftershave, she was sure, had nothing to do with dogs or other animals. It was, she decided, smiling dreamily up into his frustrated face, probably called Suit.

It was playing with fire to smile at him, but she couldn't seem to give a care. The night, the smells, the sound of the music, the feel of the air were so far out of her time and place that she didn't feel like herself at all. Besides, she was trying not to think about herself. That's why she'd come outside. To become one with the night and forget her troubles and just be a girl with a guy. To pretend she was ordinary, as normal as the next girl.

Mickey spun her in a circle. "Do you think you should be out here dancing when someone wants to kill you?"

"I thought you were in bed."

He could have gotten angry and ground his teeth. His dentist could probably use the money with that new office to pay for, but it was too hot and in this light Luci looked good enough to eat and almost normal. So he grinned and spun her again, liking the feel of her body brushing his and how easily she followed him. "You thought wrong. Aren't you worried about what I might do to you?"

"I don't know how to worry." Her smile dared him to make her.

The air was heavy with moisture and still hot despite the sun's deference to the moon, turning their skin slick and hot as they brushed together. Then apart. The moon brushed soft light across her hair and face, deepening the shadows around her mouth. Making her mouth damn near irresistible.

"Mystery Girl" finished, but Mickey didn't let go, just watched her until another tune filled the flower-scented air. He supported her body with his arms, the slow beat of the music requiring little from him in the way of skill. Holding her gaze with his, he steered their slow steps off the street, inside the gate, and under the canopy of a magnolia tree, where the light from the street barely penetrated.

She looked like she was going to say something. He gave her time. His mother had brought him up to be a gentleman. When she didn't, he bent his head. Her mouth, that sweet, straight mouth, tasted different in the dark. More heat. More spice.

He could have stayed there all night, exploring, tasting, shaping and being shaped, but he went too deep and had to come up for air.

They fell apart, the world rushing into the space with a reminder of all the reasons he shouldn't have done that. The look in her wide eyes the only reason he should have.

"I guess I'm more like my mother than I realized," she said.

"I shouldn't—have done that."

Her hand lightly touched his cheek, the palm moist and soft against his skin, a gentle fire burning in the depths of her eyes. "You were provoked."

She stepped back, then left him, but paused at the

steps to add, "Do you think it's a good idea to hit on your boss's daughter?"

The ground rocked under his feet. "How did you know—"

Her lashes swept down, then up. "I didn't. Not for sure."

She was up the stairs and inside before he could choke. She didn't slam the door behind her, but he still winced. And wondered if he was too old to join the Foreign Legion.

BECAUSE DONALD PUT out the TV, they didn't hear about the explosion until after they picked up a newspaper from a vendor. They read it over breakfast, too discouraged by failure to even think about regrouping until they'd had their coffee and a good long whine.

"Don't care. I don't want to blow her up from a distance anymore, Fern." Donald glared ahead. "I want to do her face-to-face. I want to watch her die in front of my eyes. I want to empty my clip into her even after she's dead. I want to empty several clips into her and then burn her body!"

Fern sighed, trying to shift her broken arm into a more comfortable position. "I suppose that means we head back to Teddy?"

"That's right." Donald subsided into a state of muttering and non-verbal grumbling as he nursed his Café du Monde *café au lait*. From the river, the steamboat hooted derisively. She would be glad, Fern decided as she swatted a mosquito the size of a bee that was trying to crawl inside her cast and feast, to leave this place behind. Focus on Disneyland, she told herself. Only on Disneyland. You'll get there if you believe it, Fern. You'll get there if you have to crawl on your hands and knees, girl.

ARTIE READ about the explosion in the newspaper the hotel brought with his breakfast and his newly shined shoes. It added insult to injury to know the bump on his head and the blood on his shoes hadn't happened in a good cause. It was hard to sound optimistic when he made his daily phone call to Helen. He'd never been able to fool Helen—well, at least not completely.

"You sound like your biorhythms are out of whack," she said. "Are you remembering your bio-vitamins?"

"Wouldn't dare forget them, my dear." Just the sound of her voice in his ear made him miss her like a limb. He didn't get it. He'd loved maybe a hundred women. Loved and left them, and not just for the money. After a while he just got bored with them and had to move on. He didn't much like being married, but he liked having money, and his only real skill was convincing women to marry him and give him their money. Until Reggie handed him a foolproof scam and fate handed him Helen. What was it about her that was so different? If he believed in that yin and yang stuff, which he didn't but Helen did, he'd think maybe it was that.

Helen said they knew each other in a past life or maybe lives. He'd refused to be hypnotized for fear of what he might reveal about this life, but Helen figured he'd been her Troy or her Caesar or maybe her Napoleon. He liked thinking of himself as Napoleon. Bet he had some great shoes in his closet.

"What about your prostate enhancer herbs?" Helen said in his ear. In the background he could hear her counting out someone's change for the stamps they'd just bought while she waited for his answer. If she had a flaw, it was talking about his prostate while at work in the Butt Had Post Office.

"I'm taking it all, honey," he said, "so I can be your love bunny when I get back."

"And when will that be? I miss my love bunny terribly," she said briskly, adding, in the same tone, "that will be thirty-two cents, Reverend."

Artie winced. He was a traditional guy when it came to proper subjects for the ears of a Reverend. "As soon as I get this last bit of business worked out, I'll be home to stay, sweet cheeks. No more business trips for this guy."

Helen's sigh was music to his ears. "I can't wait."

16

Mickey woke the next morning feeling surprisingly chipper for someone who would probably be drawn and quartered when his Captain found out he'd spilled the beans. If it happened, it happened. At least he'd had the best kiss of his life and the best night's sleep in a month. He whistled as he went downstairs, meeting Delaney in the hall.

"Still high on pain medication?"

"Some things are better than drugs, Delaney."

"You aren't hitting on Pryce's daughter, are you?"

"Of course not." He avoided looking at Delaney. "Uh, where is she? I thought we were supposed to be protecting her?"

"She's breakfasting with her aunts in there. And what's this "we" stuff? I'm the only one who's been watching her this morning, while you had a nice little lie in—"

"Well, I had to go pull her in off the street last night, so I figure that makes us even."

"Off the street? Last night?" Delaney frowned. "What was she doing in the street last night?"

"Dancing. The frat had another party. I thought we had some guys watching her?"

"So did I. Guess we were both wrong."

"How quaint. Men who will admit they're wrong."

They both turned quickly to find Luci leaning against the door frame with her arms crossed. Her expression was a puzzle that Mickey wasn't afraid to meet.

No quarter asked, none given.

She didn't say it out loud, but she might as well have. Mickey gave a slight nod, accepting her challenge, his eyes steely with resolve. That other areas got steely with desire, he chose to ignore.

Delaney gave them each an uneasy look, then said, a mite too heartily, "So what's on the schedule for today?"

"I still have a lot of errands to run, but we're going over the guest list this morning for the Sunday garden party. Dull stuff for New Orleans' finest, I'd think."

Mickey looked at Delaney with a sigh. He nodded.

"We probably ought to take a look at it, too."

Luci's answering smile was wicked. "Going to check out my aunts' friends, are you? How deductive. I look forward to seeing you in action." She indicated the room with a sweep of her hand. "Please, feel free to join us."

Mickey paced forward, holding Luci's green-eyed gaze

as he aimed for her instead of the doorway she indicated. It was a harmless game of chicken, a small clash in this private battle of the sexes. But one he was determined to win, would have won, but fate intervened. When he was close enough to smell her perfume, just before she'd have to back down, the doorbell rang.

"You'd better get that," she said. "Just in case it's a mad murderer."

It wasn't the murderer. It was an officer bearing news about the autopsies of the John Doe aka Frosty the Frozen man and Reggie Seymour.

"CAPTAIN MUST HAVE LIT a fire under the coroner's office to get both autopsies so quickly," Mickey said.

"That or promised them his first born—" Delaney broke off, a slight flush staining his face.

Mickey pretended not to notice, then pretense became reality as he scanned the report on their recently thawed John Doe. Delaney worked his way through the one on Reggie Seymour.

Then they exchanged reports. Then they looked at each other in frustration.

"This doesn't help a whole lot," Mickey said. "Both shot through the heart with the same small caliber weapon. Frosty died approximately three to five hours after eating a sandwich and was probably frozen within the last five years because his dental plate wasn't in use earlier than that. Not a real big help."

"Reggie probably as much as five weeks ago. It's been a dry month," mused Delaney. "Got a positive ID from his record. Dental, what's left of his prints are a match. The tattoos and jewelry substantiate the ID." He sighed, giving Mickey a rueful look. "Well, at least we know the how. And half the who."

"But there's still a lot of whys, whens, wheres, the other who—" Unbidden from his memory came, "and that other Arthur."

"What?"

"I don't know," Mickey said. "Just something that's been spinning in my brain. The unaccounted for neighbor. I'll bet the old ladies could tell us something about him. If we can only find a way to get them to tell us."

DANTE LOOKED up as Max slid in the door. Behind him his Persephone was almost finished. He'd miss her when she was gone, but there would be another. There would always be another. He lay down his pencil and leaned back in his chair, stretching.

"I talked to our guys watching the Seymour house." Max hesitated, then said, "It seems the police are watching the house, too."

"What?" Dante straightened, staring at his underling with narrowed eyes.

"Well," Max said. "Maybe, maybe not. I talked to our snitch at the NOPD—seems they think someone is trying to kill Luci Seymour—there's no hint of anything about the money."

Dante frowned. "What's going on, Max?"

"I don't know. But at least the police don't know either."

THE WHITE SQUARE envelope was on the floor, just inside their door, when Fern and Donald got back from lunch.

"What is it?" Donald asked, heading for the beer while Fern studied the envelope.

"Must be some kind of mistake. Name on outside says it's for 'Arthur Miller and date.'"

"Arthur?" Donald looked at Fern. "Open it." There was a short pause, then, impatiently, "Well? What is it?"

"You're not going to believe it. It's an invite to a party Sunday afternoon. At the Seymour's."

Donald stopped, stared at Fern, then grabbed the card. It only took a moment to read the words but Donald had to read them twice—because he couldn't believe his eyes. "Is this some kind of joke, Fern? How'd Artie do it? Get them to invite us to the bash? We don't know them! We're trying to kill one of them!"

"Look, this was inside, too." Fern held out another

scrap of paper. This one took even less time to read. It only had two words in bold black print: Do it.

"It could be a trap," Fern said.

"Could be," Donald said, "or the answer to all our problems. Can't miss face-to-face."

Fern nodded, her thoughts moving on. "I'll need something to wear. Didn't bring a party dress. And a gift."

"A gift?" Donald looked at her like she'd lost it.

"It's a wedding party, Donald. If we don't bring a gift they'll wonder why." She tapped the invite against her chin. "Silver's nice. Or linens. A person can't have too many linens."

"Is your Arthur coming to the party, Miss Theo?" Luci looked up from her list as the two detectives entered.

Mickey pulled out his notebook and flipped it open, wondering if Miss Theo's Arthur was one of the three on his list.

"He's looking forward to it, dear. Since his surgery he can't burp or vomit, but he can eat cake again."

"As long as he can do the important stuff." Luci made a small note on her list, then looked at Miss Weena. "What about your Arthur?"

"He said he was coming before he left," Miss Weena said, taking her admiring gaze off Delaney for a brief instant.

"Did he say where he was going?" Mickey asked.

"He might have," Miss Weena said, inching closer to Delaney and smiling up into his face. "I've never been that good with geology."

Delaney inched away from her. "Is he a geologist?"

"A proctologist. Good with his hands is my Arthur." She stroked Delaney's arm. "Nice suit."

Delaney started to sweat. Mickey wanted to help him, but he felt like he was sinking, too. He didn't mean to look to Luci for help, but he did. She looked startled, then pleased.

"They need to discuss security arrangements for the party, dears. Someone wants me dead."

Miss Theo patted her hand. "Nonsense, dear. You're our Rock of Gibraltar."

"Our Leaning Tower of Pisa," Miss Weena chimed in.

"You don't think our Arthurs want Luci dead?" Miss Hermi asked. "They don't even know her. I'm sure they'd wait until they got to know dear little Luci before wanting to kill her."

Luci looked gratified and gave Mickey a look.

He patted his pockets, found the aspirin bottle and chewed a couple of aspirin, not bothering to track down water. After a time the taste didn't bother so much. Delaney nudged him and Mickey tapped two into Delaney's palm. Only then did he ask, "Is the concept of life and death that hard to assimilate?"

"Not with Miss Gracie here to put it into perspective,"

Luci said, introducing the one topic Mickey wanted to avoid more than any other.

Out of the corner of his eye, he saw Louise enter, blackboard in hand, and approach Miss Theo. She pointed to "excuse me" on her list of pre-written statements, but Mickey didn't have time to see if she could provide the needed distraction.

"I don't think we should talk about Miss Gracie right now—" he began.

Miss Hermi looked coyly at Delaney. "I don't think you feel that way, do you, dear boy?" She sighed. "So nice for her to have a beau after all these years. She hasn't had one since she died."

It was like watching a slow motion accident happening from outside the frame. There was nothing Mickey could do to stop the crash.

Delaney blinked. Twice. Finally he said, "Did you say —died?"

Miss Theo sighed. "Not all beaux are created equal."

"Now let's be fair," Miss Weena said. "We don't know he's the one who shot her." She turned to Delaney to explain, "Gracie didn't see the perpetrator, you know. The cad shot her in the back."

"Edmund's dead now, so it doesn't matter," Miss Theo said with eldest sister finality. She looked at Delaney, who wasn't moving or speaking. "Are you all right, dear?"

Delaney shook his head in slow motion, as if his body and his mind were out of sync. "I think...I must have...misunderstood...dead?" He shook his head again, like a guy shaking off a clean shot to the jaw.

It was time to intervene, Mickey knew, if he could just figure out—

Fate intervened for them. He heard the sound of running footsteps. Out of habit, his hand went to his gun, but he wasn't really worried. Even before the door burst open, he noticed Louise writing Velma's name on her chalkboard.

Velma paused in the doorway, looked around the room, then said with dramatic intensity, "I just can't bear it anymore!"

LUCI HANDED Velma a glass of water, guiding the glass to her mouth to make sure she drank some before saying, "I'm sure that Reggie isn't dating in the afterlife, Miss Velma."

"I wouldn't be so sure," Miss Weena said. "But we could ask Gracie to see if he's oozing around—"

Luci shook her head, but it was too late. The color that had been returning to Delaney's ruddy cheeks faded again.

Velma pushed the glass away and said piteously, "I can't live with Hugo after this. That he would be so cruel—"

She gave a sob that coincided with a choke from Delaney. Mickey had gotten him something stronger than water to drink and almost forced it down his throat. A hair of the dog remedy that took the dazed expression from his eyes and replaced it with bleak, mixed with denial.

"He's not dead," Velma said. "I'd feel it if he were. The psychic connection hasn't been broken. There's been a mistake—"

Mickey looked at Velma. "I don't know if he's dating, Miss Velma, but he is dead. The dental work is consistent—"

"No!" She pushed Luci away and jumped to her feet. "It's wrong! All wrong!"

At her back was the row of family pictures, Luci noticed. Their stern, sensible faces so similar, despite the distance in time and space between them. Luci looked from Velma's face to theirs.

"I think she's right," she said to Mickey. "Something isn't right."

"Do you think?" he asked, groping for the aspirin bottle again.

IF THE SCENE with Velma and the revelation about Gracie weren't enough, Mickey was gloomily standing guard in the hallway, his ears ringing from too much aspirin when Captain Pryce arrived.

"Where's my—Luci?"

Mickey pointed toward the dining room where Delaney had met his Waterloo, before going off to talk to Gracie and see for himself. "They're working on the party preparations." He rubbed his face. "It's going to be a security nightmare, sir. They seem to just randomly invite people. No way to check them out before. And the mayor might be coming!"

"I told you they were connected," Pryce said. "The Chief's got his invite, too, but that's not your biggest problem. You're being watched."

"What? Who? Where?" He edged back the lace curtains and spotted the dark car. "Dante's guys?"

"I'm afraid so. Any idea why?"

"Well—" Mickey realized he was about to tell the Captain about Luci getting grabbed by Dante and stopped himself. It would surely be the last straw. "This just gets worse and worse." He shoved his hands into his hair. "We need that search warrant, sir!"

"I got it—but only for Seymour's room. You'll have to wait until after the party for any more."

Mickey took two frustrated steps away from Pryce. "Did you explain—"

"You don't explain to a judge, Ross. You listen. It's the best I could do—unless you ask the old ladies yourself."

"I don't think they'll let us." And if he tried, he was sure Luci would stop him. Mickey looked at the captain. Too many wild cards in the setup and now their captain was one of them. How good was his judgment going to be now that it was his daughter involved? Mickey took the warrant with a sigh. "Guess it'll have to do."

He turned to leave, but Pryce cleared his throat. Mickey froze, then looked at his captain. "Was there something else, sir?"

"This." He held up an old file with the name Grace Seymour written in aged-looking handwriting on the label. "What's your interest in a forty-year-old murder, Ross? You pursuing a line of investigation you haven't told me about?"

"It's going to be a lovely gazebo, Boudreaux," Luci said. Working together, they'd been able to get the frame in place without the concrete Reggie had been so sure was necessary. Over Boudreaux's shoulder she could see the bougainvillea with yellow Police tape still around it. "Not exactly original, but a workable plan, I will admit."

Boudreaux, not following her train of thought, mumbled a question.

"The body under the gazebo thing. Think about it. You strip the body, remove all identifying clothing and jewelry —except for that touch of squeamishness about the privates it would have worked like a charm for him with Reggie and the bougainvillea—bury him, add a little cement and a gazebo and let nature take its course. In this climate, nature wouldn't take long. Moisture would accelerate decomposition." She waited for him to hammer a board in place, then added, "Reggie would have decomposed faster if it hadn't been such a dry August."

Boudreaux shared his opinion about August, then asked her to hold the next board.

Luci knelt in the dirt and grabbed the board he indicated. "I suppose he was storing the body until you were ready to pour the cement."

Boudreaux indicated a desire to ask her a question.

"Of course. Ask me anything." But when he did, she couldn't quite assimilate it. "You saw someone besides Frosty the dead man in the freezer?"

He nodded and added that he'd seen a different body than the one whose picture was being shown on television.

Luci stared at him for a long moment, then got up and looked at the garden, wondering which flowering shrub this body was buried under. She sighed. Mickey was going to poop a brick when he found out. Probably better not tell him until she knew for sure. She looked at Boudreaux. "Do the aunts know you have a television?"

His alarm turned him almost incoherent.

"Of course I won't tell them! They'd freak and then bury it." The sliding doors to the terrace opened and Luci saw her—her mind wouldn't quite bend around the word yet, so she didn't push it. He looked as uneasy as she felt. Not a feeling she was used to having. "Don't tell anyone, okay? I need to think about this, but first I gotta talk to a man about a gene pool."

Boudreaux patted her hand and mumbled reassurances.

"Is it that obvious?" she asked. "Don't answer that. I don't want to know."

MICKEY AND DELANEY waited until the fingerprint guy was through dusting every surface he could find, then donned rubber gloves and moved in to toss the room.

Delaney didn't talk and Mickey didn't press him. What could he say to him? You'll get over it? How could he say it, let alone believe it when it was obvious that their Captain hadn't gotten over Luci's mother and he wasn't sure he'd get over Luci? The Seymour factor was a great big unknown, even without the ghost factor.

It took them less time to assemble Reggie's meager belongings than it had to dust the room. He hadn't left much behind to tell his tale. Just personal belongings like toothpaste and toothbrush, shampoo and razor, several pairs of barely used shoes and a few papers.

Mickey picked up the bagged papers that he found the most puzzling: the three envelopes addressed to an Art Moon and each of them had a single dollar bill inside.

"This gets worse and worse," he said.

Delaney didn't agree or disagree. He just gave a miserable grunt.

FACE TO FACE WITH HIM, Luci couldn't think of a single thing to say. It was, if not a first, a rare experience in her life. A Seymour might not have a gift for saying the right thing, but they were rarely at a loss for words. The storm of feeling that had robbed her of speech was unfamiliar territory for her.

Her father. The word felt strange in her thoughts as she tried it out. Only now, when he was here to fill it, did she notice the void in her life his absence had left. Or maybe she'd been afraid to notice? With hungry eyes she noted the broad shoulders she'd never been able to rest her head on while she confided her joys or sobbed out her sorrows. The man who hadn't been there to run by her bicycle until she got her balance or to glare at her first date or to tell her what a thingamajig was really called. Luci had a sudden vision of them both bent over a motor while he unfolded the mysteries of internal combustion for her. Felt the pain bite deep for the peculiarly male dad hugs she hadn't gotten. More than anything she wanted to cross the carpet and get her first hug from her very own dad. If only—

With a shock, Luci realized she was afraid. Dying didn't frighten her, but being turned away by this man did. It terrified her.

He looked as uneasy as she felt, and—their images in the full-length mirror to one side caught her attention for an instant—were similar in how they showed it. She fought back an urge to laugh at how they looked with their hands clasped behind their backs, rocking from toes to heels, then back again.

His gaze, more hazel than her green one, met hers in the mirror, humor softening the eyes and the straight mouth that matched hers, only with whiskers.

She found she could breathe again. The fear was there, simmering beneath the surface, but a smile spread across her mouth. Almost in sync, they loosened the death grip they had on their own hands and shook the feeling back into the fingers. Then grinned, bigger this time.

"This is getting scary," Luci said, her voice coming out huskier than she was used to as it squeezed past the fear.

"Yeah." He hesitated, then took the first step toward her, his hand out.

Luci met him halfway, watching with a feeling of awe as her father's strong, brown hand closed over hers and squeezed it. Like a father.

The lump rose so fast in her throat it also came out as a sob, but she managed to squeeze it back down, though not without some wetness around the eyes. She blinked until she could see his hand again, then looked up at him. It wasn't a hug, but it was a place to start.

With only a slight tremor to her voice, Luci asked, "So, you're a cop?"

"Yeah." Was his voice husky, too? She didn't know him well enough to tell. "Do you...have time to sit down and...talk?"

Luci felt that pesky lump trying to make a comeback, but that didn't stop her from saying, "Yeah. I have time."

It was a relief to be alone for a few moments. Mickey looked around the parlor and felt a sudden yearning for a male place. One with swearing and spitting, with men drinking beer and watching football. A place where he could scratch, no matter where he itched, and tell sexist jokes. A place that gloried in male chauvinism and didn't allow women in ever. No way, no how.

He went out into the hall, hoping for some coffee since he beer wasn't an option, and found Luci in the hall an odd look on her face and wearing her grubbing-in-the-garden shorts and tank top. Even dirty, her legs were an inspiration that made him yearn for a male-meets-female place.

She smiled at him, but there was strain in the smile. Mickey wasn't Oprah, but he knew an Oprah moment when he saw one. He hesitated, then decided, what the hell? "Captain find you?"

For the first time since he met her she failed to look at him, instead tracing the pattern carved into the stair railing with her index finger.

"Yeah." She pushed her hair back from her face, leaving a brown streak across her cheek. He caught her hand and made her look at him.

"He scares the hell out of me, too."

Her smile was almost as good a reward as a kiss. It lit up her face, lit up her soul. He'd swear it even lit up her heart. Or maybe it was his? Mickey felt himself tumbling in and didn't care. It was more like flying than falling. He'd always liked flying. It was the landing that he didn't like. This one, he reminded himself, had all the markers of a crash and burn.

"Did he..." He had to clear husky out of his throat before he could continue, "...say what happened?"

"He's a cop," Luci said, sliding to a seat on the stairs, "so what he didn't know, he could deduce."

She propped her elbows on her knees and then rested her chin on her hands. The muggy cool of the hallway put a sheen on her skin and filled the air with her earthy scent, did bad things to his blood supply.

He grabbed a stool and sat down just outside her zone, and brought up a mental picture of his captain in a rage. It helped some.

"After they jumped each other's bones, she did a freeze play on him when he followed up with a marriage proposal. He thought it was because he was shipping out to Nam. She never told him I was in the oven." She sighed. "Don't think mama expected him to come back. When he did, she took me and went west."

She leaned back, resting her elbows on the stairs. The movement stretched her tee shirt across her breasts.

Mickey looked up, studying the carvings that circled the hallway.

"I remember the day we left. We all cried." She ran her hand down the banister. "I hung on to this until she pulled me away. She said we'd visit, but we never did. Now I know why."

"You must have known you had a father," Mickey said. "Why didn't you look him up sooner?"

Luci looked at Mickey, who wasn't looking at her. Dang, he was cute. And when he was kind, he was downright dangerous. He and her father were so far outside her experience she didn't know how to deal with them or the feelings they stirred.

"I mean," he continued, "I understand the men in your life haven't been wonderful, but—"

Luci smiled. Not wonderful? Try a constant, raging embarrassment. But all she said was, "Quite honestly, it just never occurred to me to go looking for him. I know it sounds odd—"

"A little more than that," Mickey put in.

He looked at her then. She felt the jolt of it clear to her grubby toes, which curled.

"Well, we're a little more than odd, I'm afraid. The fact that I didn't have to deal with my father was a source of envy to my cousins. I'd still be blissfully unaware if Lila hadn't called and I hadn't told her about how my neighbor Helen met her husband by hitting him with her Volkswagen." Luci shook her head. Lila had always been a less-than-satisfactory mother, but Luci had come to terms with that a long time ago. "She let slip that's how she met my—him. Suddenly I found myself wondering—"

"Wondering...what?" Mickey asked.

"All the things anyone would. What was he like? Why he got involved with my mother when she almost killed him? Why he never tried to find me? If he's the reason there's this...split in my personality?" That was the biggie for her. She'd always been a Seymour, but not quite—since she seemed to be the only one who'd noticed they weren't like the rest of the world. She wanted to know why she was like them, but not like them. She wanted to find out what it felt like to have a father, to be a daughter.

More than anything, she admitted now, she'd wanted him to want her, the way her mother hadn't. The way her mother never had. In the ways that mattered, Lila never had been a mother. Luckily for Luci, she hadn't needed that much care.

Then, like fate intervening, the invitation to Unabelle's wedding had arrived. It had stirred up her memories of New Orleans, ignited a longing to come back and see if it was as magical as she remembered it. Or so she'd told herself, while the knowledge she had a father who lived there had burned like acid in her brain. Lila had freaked when Luci told her and asked if her father had a name. She'd clammed up, but Luci had been confident of her ability to smoke out her elusive dad. What she hadn't counted on was the body count or the attempts on her life.

Funny that it was what had been the catalyst that brought her father into her orbit. And Mickey.

"And did you?" Mickey asked, breaking into her thoughts right on cue.

Luci gave a kind of half laugh. "I don't know." She shook her head. "I just hope she stays away until he has a chance to cool off. If he ever does."

Mickey's grin started the blood humming through her veins like electricity along a wire. "He has made...threats, but I wonder—"

Luci quit trying not to look at him. There were some things that just couldn't be fought. This was one of them. Her eyes liked looking at him. Her brain liked processing what her eyes saw, and her nerve endings like reacting to what her brain came up with. It was a fact, like her Seymour-ness. "What?"

"I get the feeling he'd do it again if he got the chance." He didn't like admitting it. It was too close to how he felt about Luci. Any chance was better than no chance.

"It wouldn't be...smart," Luci said, her eyes widening with the flickering heat of desire caught.

Mickey stood and pulled her up. He brushed the dirt from her cheek, then used both hands to hold and position her head so that her mouth was an easy target. She didn't object, didn't fight him, just stared at him with that damn, curious Seymour gaze. If there hadn't been so much heat in back of it and if her pulse hadn't been humming like a revved up motor—

"Sometimes you gotta take a chance, even when it's world class stupid," he said.

Her mouth, normally so straight and so infuriating, curved into a smile that turned heat into fire as her arms slid around his neck.

"Well, as long as you're talking world class stupid, not the ordinary kind—"

He kissed her to shut her up and to shut his brain off.

It worked like a charm.

"I HAVE SOMETHING, MR. DANTE."

Dante looked up at Max, surprise a strange expression on his usually expressionless face.

He put down his pen and leaned back in his chair. "What?"

Max hesitated again, unlike him. "You're not going to like it."

"I haven't liked anything since Cloris got involved with that bastard, Max. Spill it. I can take it."

"We've got a name—Maxwell's cellmate in stir."

"And the winner is—"

"Reggie Seymour—"

Dante sucked in but didn't speak, just indicated Max should continue.

"—small-time con artist with more convictions than successes."

"Is he a relative of Luci Seymour?"

"He's the body they just found in their garden, Mr. Dante. A coincidence?"

"I don't think so." Dante frowned. "This makes everything—different. Make sure the boys are packing when we go to the party."

"Yes, Mr. Dante." He started to turn away.

"Oh—and Max?"

"Yes?"

"Get me some mug shots of Maxwell from our man at the NOPD. Make sure everyone's carrying a copy to that party. I have a feeling Artie Maxwell's going to be there. And I don't want him to get away."

"Right, Mr. Dante." This time it was Max that hesitated.

"What is it?"

"How shall I tell them to deliver him?"

"Dead, Max. I have nothing to say to him."

17

I t wasn't easy for Mickey to concentrate on the case with his head and his heart hurting, but he had to try to find a common thread that would pull all the puzzling strings of the case together. Proximity wouldn't help any of them recover from this visit to the Seymour Zone. Now that his ears had stopped ringing, he knocked back some more aspirin and started going through the information Pryce had brought them. Not that any of what he'd brought fit with any of the information they already had.

There was Benny the Book. His file confirmed he worked for Dante, but not where he fit into the mix. He had a feeling Luci knew more about this and the shoe-boxes and why Dante wanted them than she was sharing with him. Someone in this house was gambling, but who? None of the aunts seemed likely to be secret gamblers, but they made more sense than Unabelle, the waster of space his uncle would soon be marrying.

"Damn." He leaned back in his chair and rubbed his eyes. Nothing made any sense! Somewhere, somehow, it had to be about money. With Dante involved, it couldn't be anything else. But how? Where was it?

All paths led to Reggie, but he was such a nowhere kind of guy it didn't help much. Easy to speculate that he was working some kind of scam when he was executed, but difficult to figure out what that scam might be. How had a man who screwed up scams managed to put together something that netted enough money to interest someone like Dante, or his murderer—always assuming that's why he was murdered? And if Reggie had come up with something so successful, how had he managed to do it without leaving any noticeable trace of it except for three dollar bills?

Mickey pulled out the bagged envelopes with the dollar bills. The post marks put one from New York, the other from Idaho, the third from Puerto Rico.

Mickey frowned at the list, managing to produce two rather meager conclusions. First, that this wasn't Reggie's main residence but a stopping over place. He hadn't even left a pair of pajamas here. And second, a scam that netted single dollar bills, if that were the scam, couldn't interest Dante. It had to be something else. Of course, he'd talk to a postal inspector. Mail fraud, no matter how petty, was their bailiwick and might produce a real clue.

Mickey made a note, then looked at the list again. One final question teased his mind. If Reggie didn't live here with the Seymours—

"Then where does he live?" Mickey muttered aloud to the empty room.

"Talking to yourself now, Ross?" Delaney growled from the doorway. He hunched his shoulders and stalked further into the room, gloom riding heavy on his brow. He dropped into the chair across from Mickey, his face daring Mickey to ask about his thwarted love life.

"Just thinking out loud," Mickey said,. The sick dog look in his eyes made Mickey uncomfortable. What do you tell a buddy who's hot for a ghost? At least Mickey's love life involved a living, breathing human being, even if he did sometimes long to make her a ghost. "I—was looking over this list of items you guys found when you searched Reggie's bedroom upstairs."

"And?"

"Well, he's getting mail here, but there's no real sign this was his home base or what was his means of support. No clothes, just personal items you'd leave, say, at a girl-friend's apartment where you sometimes stay over." Mickey flipped open Reggie's police file. "Yet this address is listed on his parole record as his last known. And he gets some of his mail here. If this address is the correct one, and not a smoke screen, where is his stuff? Because it's not here."

"It's probably in Cleveland."

Mickey flipped through the files. "No report from the Cleveland guys yet. I wish—" he stopped.

"What?"

"I wish I knew if it were urgent that we find out where he used to be. But we have no way of knowing if Reggie is connected to the threat against Luci."

"We'll have to assume there's a connection for now," Delaney said, a hint of grimness in his voice. "At least, that's what the Captain said just now."

Mickey shifted. "I'm sorry—"

"Don't be. It wasn't your fault." Delaney gave a half-hearted grin. "At least he isn't talking involuntary retention at a state facility for both of us."

"Oh?" Mickey wasn't sure if that was good or not. A padded cell sounded pretty good right now. Be a relief to spend some time with people who were less crazy than the Seymours.

"Gracie was still with me. He got to meet her."

Mickey looked up from the clutter of paper. "Oh."

"He agrees with our decision to not officially include her in the investigative record. Particularly after she confirmed that the reports of her death haven't been exaggerated."

"Is that the bad news?"

"No. The bad news is, we're not suspended yet."

"I suppose he can't afford to lose anyone else right now," Mickey said glumly. "It's been a bad couple of months for everybody."

"Yeah." Delaney's second attempt at a grin was less strained. "And looking to be a bad couple more unless we can figure this case out. Only way we're getting out of here."

They worked until lunchtime, making notes, occasionally bouncing ideas off each other, but mostly working in silence as they went over the accumulated information.

Finally, Delaney threw down his pencil and leaned back in his chair, stretching. He didn't look at Mickey when he said, "You know we're going to have to talk to Unabelle again. If she's our gambler—" He hesitated. "We'll have to question Eddie, too."

Mickey nodded. "I know. I put it at the top of the list of unpleasant things we're going to have to do. We'll have to pay Dante a visit, too."

"Yeah. Rack up some billable hours for his lawyer."

"I wish we could figure out what the shoeboxes are—"

"Or why Dante wants them?" Delaney frowned. "Obvious answer would be drugs, but Dante's never done the drug route. And if he did change his mind, Unabelle's hardly the logical outlet for that. I mean, she looks like she's on drugs, but—"

"Yeah." Mickey gave a rueful grin as he shoved his hands through his hair, then he frowned. "You found the mail, didn't you? Any thoughts on why Reggie would be getting dollar bills through the mail?"

Delaney was silent for a moment. "I suppose it could

be some kind of scam. But it's a pretty pathetic effort. How far can you get with a dollar a pop?"

"Seems to have gotten Reggie only as far as the bougainvillea," Mickey said.

LUCI NEEDED TO THINK, had needed to since Boudreaux's revelation in the garden that there might be another body, but it was hard with Mickey turning up here and there in the house and her father turning up where Mickey wasn't. The only place she hadn't run into either was the bathroom, so that's where she retreated to, hoping to sort things out in her mind.

Luci closed the lid, settled herself as comfortably as she could and pulled a notebook out of one pocket, a stubby pencil out of another. It was a pity that she and Mickey couldn't have one of those cozy, confiding sleuth-cop relationships so popular in series mysteries. If she only knew what Mickey and Delaney knew—

Of course, being an insider, a Seymour who was in the family but not completely of it, gave her an edge that all the forensic investigation and computer databases in the country couldn't give Mickey. She flipped open her notebook and started writing down questions:

1. Who was the other body in the freezer?

2. Why had Reggie moved in with her aunts?

3. Did her aunts kill both victims? Not likely, but couldn't rule it out.

4. Was someone really trying to kill her? Why?

5. What was she going to do about Mickey Ross?

After the last question she added a notation in parentheses. Was it only his kiss that curled her toes or would just any guy do that to her?

Neatly, but with thick writing because the pencil was getting dull, Luci finished her list with:

6. Where is the body Boudreaux saw?

7. What kind of scam nets dollar bills?

8. Could Reggie have come up with a successful scam? How would that impact the space/time continuum?

9. Could Unabelle be a closet gambling addict?

10. What's wrong with Velma?

11. Am I like my mother? Do I care?

It was a good list of questions. Too bad she didn't have good answers to go with them. A knock at the door interrupted her ruminations. She sighed, stood up, stowed her pencil and notebook, and opened the door.

"I need to go," Unabelle said with no inflection to her voice.

"Sorry." Luci stepped past her, then stopped to ask, "You don't know where a girl could place a bet, do you?"

For just a moment, so quick Luci almost missed it, something flickered in the mud brown of Unabelle's eyes. Then the door closed between them.

"I'M NOT sure the lava lamp was a good idea," Fern said as she tried to fit the wrapping paper around its odd shape. "A toaster—"

"I ain't buying a new gift for someone I don't know!" Donald scowled at her. "Now can we talk about how we're gonna do the bitch?"

Fern gave him a look, then sighed. "Fine. But if I don't get this wrapped, we don't get in the door! Think the bulls won't be suspicious of us coming to a posh party with some crappy gift in torn wrappers? Least we ought to have a box!"

"The pawn shop didn't have no box, Fern. Like I told you—"

The discussion was briefly loud and acrimonious. Until someone in the next room banged on the wall.

DANTE'S AUNT Cloris didn't look like a gangster's relative. She was at the high end of middle age with a bland face, uncertain eyes and a doughy body stuffed unevenly into a girdle. She tended to flutter—her eyelashes, her hands, her voice—when she was distressed, and let the stars and horoscopes rule her life. This was why Dante went to great lengths to keep her from getting upset. It annoyed the hell out of him—made him want to kill somebody, since he couldn't kill her.

"You telling me Arvin didn't tell you anything about his business? Didn't even give you a phone number to call?"

"He called me every night. I didn't need to call him," she said, her voice wavering as she tried to control a sob. "He traveled, didn't have a fixed number."

"Do you know where he called from?" Dante tried to keep the edge out of his voice as he looked at the impassive Max. "We need something, somewhere to start a search."

"He called from a lot of different places. His business took him all over the country. Besides, you just want to kill him—"

"I just want to talk to him. Bring him back to you if I can, so you'll be happy again."

She tried to give him a penetrating look, but her nose was running and tears blurred her eyes. "Duluth," she finally admitted. "He did business in Duluth sometimes. And Salt Lake. And Cleveland. I think he might have worked with someone there."

Dante looked at Max. "What makes you think he had a partner, Cloris?"

"He told me he had a partner."

Dante hid his impatience. If only she'd told him—no sense worrying now. They'd find this partner. If he weren't already lying on a slab in the morgue.

"Did he tell you his name?"

"No."

"Okay. You did the right thing, for both you and Arvin, telling me. If you think of anything else, you just come and tell me, okay?" He patted her hand, giving Max a sharp nod towards the door. "Max and I are going to get things rolling. You just stay here until you feel better. Then I'll take you out to choose a new dress for the party on Sunday. Okay?"

"Okay."

Outside the door, Dante turned to Max. "Didn't the snitch say something about contacting the Cleveland police?"

"That's right. About Reggie Seymour."

"Ten'll get you one Reggie Seymour's the partner."

"You think Arvin Marvin or Artie did Seymour?"

"It does seem obvious, doesn't it?" Dante was quiet for a moment, then said softly, "Find him, Max. And do him. Quick and quiet."

"Yes, Mr. Dante."

"Oh, and find a wedding gift for this party thing. Something nice, Max. Like a toaster or one of those fancy plates. The kind with the gold around the edges."

Dante frowned and Max shifted. "Anything wrong, Mr. Dante?"

"I'm worried about Benny. If the cops are on top of the Seymours—better pick him up. Keep him under wraps until we get the deal locked down.

~

It RAINED EARLY the morning of the party, but as soon as the sun got going it turned the moisture into a fog of steam over the city. Luci's aunts rose late, trailing peacefully downstairs attired in robes, Miss Theo and Miss Hermi in drifting silk and Miss Weena in chiffon, to linger over a breakfast buffet prepared by Louise. The caterers milled around, wondering when they would be able to begin preparations.

Mickey, who was trying to finalize preparations for the security detail during the party, found himself fielding party detail questions instead.

"If we have two roving details—" Delaney, bent over the floor plan of the house, a plan they were using to assign the security teams Pryce had given them.

"Where do you want us to put the tables, sir?" asked one of the caterers.

Mickey, his hands braced on the table, looked up. "I don't know. Why don't you ask the housekeep—"

Delaney cleared his throat, giving a small shake of his head.

Mickey bent his head. "You'll need to talk to the ladies. That's all I can tell you."

The florist came next. Then the bandleader. Then a group of carefully sculpted young men calling themselves the Hepplewhites.

That's when Mickey lost it. "Look I don't know a damn thing about anything. Let me take you to the women with the answers!"

He strode across the hall and shoved open the dining room door. They were all seated around the table, empty plates pushed away, chatting.

"Oh, Mickey, dear!" Miss Hermi turned, her voice comfortable. "Have you had breakfast yet? Louise is about to clear away—"

"No thank you. However, these people all have questions about the party that I can't answer. Do you think—"

Luci stood up, moving around the table, wearing a plaid robe that came down far enough on her legs to be tantalizing without being either too generous or too stingy.

"I recognize the caterers, the florist, and the band, but who," she moved closer to a well-muscled chest and looked up, her eyes lit with admiration, "are you?"

White teeth gleamed when the young man smiled. "We're the Hepplewhites—"

"I hired them for the party," Miss Weena explained, gazing at a pair of well-formed pecs just visible through the deep vee on one young man's shirt.

Luci looked at her aunt. "All right, Miss Weena. Give me five!" Miss Weena obliged. Luci sighed deeply enough to make her robe gap briefly.

Mickey reached for his aspirin, but the bottle was empty.

Luci, subtly buffering her aunts from the worst of the confusion, flitted from room to room. Slowly, almost imperceptibly, the confusion began to resolve into a sort of order. Tables appeared in the garden just off the dining room where the caterers were busy. The smell of breakfast food was replaced by the smell of party food. Flower arrangements began to appear on tables and shelves. The band—brass, not string—set up in the garden inside the newly finished gazebo. Someone took the police tape away from the bougainvillea and set up some chairs over the spot where Reggie had been buried.

Mickey and his men were kept busy issuing ID's to arrivals, making a final security check over the house and going over last minute problems with the teams Pryce had sprung for the occasion.

Half an hour before the scheduled party time, Luci rounded up the aunts and started herding them upstairs to dress.

"Aren't you cutting things a little close?" Mickey asked, the radio in his hand crackling with voices.

"Don't worry! This is the Big Easy. No one will actually come on time."

Mickey watched her hips swish up the stairs out of sight. Then he looked at Delaney. "My uncle will."

It was a good thing Eddie was on time. Since he was the only one who noticed the bride hadn't joined them yet. Pryce was about to order a lock down and search when

Luci descended wearing a black mini skirt, red off-the-shoulder blouse, and cowboy boots.

"Something wrong?"

"Unabelle's not here." Mickey was terse.

"Has anyone checked her room?" Luci looked at each upturned male face as chagrin dawned. She shook her head. "Men!"

FERN GAVE her wispy bun a pat, spritzed it with cheap hair spray, then leaned over to smooth her red lipstick with a bent pinkie. The bright color looked uneasy on her thin mouth, but Fern was happy with the result as she rubbed the edges together, then pursed her mouth.

"Time to go," Donald muttered.

Fern turned as he tugged at the tie around his thin neck. Fern straightened it, then patted his cheek. "You scrub up pretty good, old man."

"You ain't bad yourself." Donald grinned. "You got the invite?"

Fern nodded, picking up the bag that matched her flowing flowered dress.

"Where's the gun?"

"In my cast. Don't forget the gift."

"I won't be forgetting anything." Donald's look was wolfish, eager. "Let's do it."

"Your people in place, Ross?" Pryce looked up from the plan.

Mickey spun around and nodded like a military man. "Yes, sir. We've got good coverage. Thanks for the extra men."

"It's was easy once the governor decided to come." Pryce looked down again, his gaze assessing. "Any last questions? Problems?"

Thousands of both, but none that could be voiced. Mickey looked at Delaney but echoed his, "No sir."

"Right. Let's do it then."

Dante looked up as his aunt came in the room. "Cloris, you look—amazing." He took her hands, kissed both her cheeks and tried not to notice her red-rimmed eyes or the bird nestled in the flowers of her straw hat. At least the dress was perfect. He'd taken her to the best boutique in the city and outfitted her in classic black. If she'd lose the hat...but of course, she wouldn't. Arvin had bought it for her and she was hoping he'd see it, remember what they'd had and come back to her.

She was so deep in denial she couldn't crawl out without a little help from a bullet aimed well-and-true at Marvin's faithless heart.

"Should I wear gloves?" Her body was fluttering with nervousness. "I've never been to a posh party before." She dropped her purse, waiting until Max had retrieved it for her before saying, "Are you sure Marvin will be there, Harvey? I'd much rather stay home—"

"You want to find him, don't you?"

Her lower lip quivered. "Of course I do, but—"

"Then be brave. We won't stay long, I promise." Dante smiled coldly.

"You won't hurt him, will you? I couldn't bear it—"

"Why would I want to hurt him?" He looked past her to Cain and Abel waiting impassively on either side of the door. "You ready?"

Though no unsightly bulges marred the impeccable lines of their identical suits, they both nodded.

"Then let's do it."

New Orleanians learn to second line early. It's easy to do and there are no special steps to learn. One need only to be unselfconscious and have a brass band that can pump out a good Mardi Gras beat. The extras, like sequined umbrellas or a hankie to wave, are second to the joy of forming a line and going where the music leads.

They did the Mambo first. Maybe Miss Weena was saving the Hepplewhites for the grand finale. Or she could have been saving them for herself. The raucous sound of the brass band made radio communication problematical until the second line moved outside. That's why Mickey didn't know until he heard them speaking to Luci that Dante and his entourage had arrived.

"Who let them in?" Mickey hissed into his mike.

"Had to, sir. They had an invitation."

"Did you search them?"

"Head to toe. Nothing."

"Damn!" Mickey paced towards the new arrivals.

"Did you think I wouldn't come?" Dante was saying.

"I never doubted you would." Luci batted her lashes at Dante, then winked at Mickey as Dante bent to kiss her hand. "Let me introduce you to my aunts. They're looking forward to meeting you."

She slid her arm through Dante's and led him toward them.

"Miss Theo? I'd like you to meet Mr. Dante. He's the one I told you about—"

"Mr. Dante!" Miss Theo's face lit up as she turned towards them. "I can't tell you how excited I was when dear little Luci told me you were coming to our party!"

"I'm charmed, Miss Theo—" Dante began suavely.

"Hermi! Weena! Look! He's here! Mr. Dante!"

The remaining two sisters fluttered forward, words bubbling from their mouths like sparkling water, engulfing him in their special form of femininity.

"Trifle long, but I loved your book!" Miss Hermi twittered.

"Dark, definitely a dark story, but droll, too!" Miss Weena patted his arm, her round face tilted up and cut by a wide smile.

"A most interesting book," concluded Miss Theo. "Where did you get the idea for it? Such a large concept! Life. Death. Redemption."

Miss Weena reached up and smoothed the hair above his ear. "It's funny. You don't look Italian."

Mickey bit back his first grin of the day at the look on Dante's face at this reference to Dante's Inferno. The urge quickly left him when he heard a bawdy flourish heralding the imminent appearance of the Hepplewhites. There were only four, but it seemed like more as the undulating pecs and hips cut a swath through the appreciative female crowd. Most of the men fell back with something less than appreciation as the dancers started to shed clothing. Would Luci find this "cool?" Would her eyes be heated like they'd been when he kissed her?

Pryce crossed to join him, his opinion of the Hepple-whites written in large neon across his face. "Where's Luci?"

Mickey looked around, slow at first, then with rising panic.

At that moment, in the mysterious way of the universe, there was a lull in the party sounds and the music as the

Hepplewhites completed their shedding, baring their glory for the pleasure of their interested audience. Before the music and the screams could catch up, Mickey clearly heard the sound of shots in the room directly above them.

18

I t was ridiculously easy for Fern to approach Luci Seymour, the small gun and the cast on her arm concealed in the folds of her loose dress and the lacy shawl she'd picked up in a little dress shop in the Quarter and paid for with one dollar bills.

"Excuse me, miss?"

Luci turned with a friendly smile.

"Is there another ladies' room? The one down here has someone—" She grimaced slightly. With those old aunts of hers, the girl would know all about incontinence.

"Oh, of course. Upstairs—" With a gentle, but firm grip on her arm Luci eased Fern through the crowds and out into the hall. "If you go up here, take a right—"

Fern turned up the edges of her mouth in what she hoped passed for a smile and shoved the concealed gun into the girl's side.

"Could you show me, dear?" The girl's eyes flicked towards the guard, bored of face, rocking on his heels across from them. In a low voice, Fern warned, "Quiet, or he gets it, too!"

The girl gave her a steady look that seemed to test her resolve, so Fern ground the weapon into her ribs a little harder and said louder, "Sorry to be a bother, dear, but at my age, you can't afford to wait too long."

"No, I don't suppose you can." To Fern's consternation, the girl's straight mouth twitched as she turned and padded up the long staircase. Fern was puffing as they reached the top, her heart protesting the fast ascent. Behind her she could hear the opening refrain of the bawdy burlesque.

"The Hepplewhites are starting their act. And you passed them up to shoot me? You really need to work on your priorities."

For just a moment, Fern was tempted. She'd seen their poster in one of the tee shirt shops that littered the Quarter. They were mighty fine. Hard to keep her sights fixed on Mickey Mouse with those pecs in mind.

Luci half-turned, her eyes, a mixture of hope and mischief, inviting Fern to join her. Then the door on the right opened and Donald gestured threateningly.

"What ya waiting for, Fern? Get her in here before someone comes!"

Fern pushed, but Luci didn't budge.

"That's Mickey's bedroom."

"So?"

"Well, it just seems—wrong. Or ironic."

"Just get in there!" Being so exposed in the open hall was making Fern uneasy. Down in the hall below they could hear the sound of voices rising towards them on waves of burlesque beat.

Luci shrugged. "Ironic it is, then."

With a twist that caught Fern by surprise, Luci freed herself and sauntered into the room, not stopping until she reached the four poster bed against the far wall. She smoothed the counterpane and tucked the single pillow on the far side of the bed behind her back. With feigned unconcern, she crossed her legs and arms and looked at them.

"So? What do we do now? I thought I knew my lines for this scene, but you're not at all what I expected. Do you really mean to kill me and why?"

"Course we do!" It wasn't Fern's imagination that Donald sounded defensive.

"You don't look like killers. Is this your first time? Is it just me that you're trying to kill or do you have, like, a quota or something?"

Fern looked at Donald. He looked as bewildered as she felt. This was not following the usual course. The girl was supposed to plead for her life. Ask the usual questions. Not...not... Fern didn't know how to describe what Luci was doing. But somehow it all seemed to fit with the difficulty of killing this girl.

"Quota?" Fern shook her head.

"I'm doing it, aren't I?" Luci gave them a sympathetic look. "My family predisposition is hard to combat. But I will try to play the scene by the prescribed rules. I shouldn't like to die wrong after all's said and done."

"Scene?" Donald shook his head, the gun he held wavering.

"Yeah. The why-are-you-doing-this, you-tell-me-and-I-exclaim-in-shock scene."

"Shut up!" Donald gripped the gun tighter, wiping a hand down the side of his pant leg. "Why we're doing it is none of your never mind," he snarled.

Donald always reacted like that when he doesn't know something, Fern could have told Luci, but she was too bewildered to do so. And too busy fighting the growing conviction that this was going to go wrong, too. That this time they weren't going to be able to get away.

Luci smiled. "Is that a silencer on your gun? I've never seen one before—oops. I'm doing it again, aren't I? But then you didn't quite follow the script either, did you? You're supposed to say it's nothing personal, doll, or something like that, but business is business—"

"Oh, it's personal, doll. 'Bout as personal as it gets—"

"Really? Would you like to talk about it? You seem to have quite a head of steam built up and it might make you feel better to talk about it. And steady your aim. Why don't you sit down—"

Her tone of friendly concern almost had Fern moving towards a nearby chair.

"Shut up!" Donald's voice seemed especially harsh. "I don't like people what gives me trouble and you gives me more trouble than—" He choked a couple of times in his attempt to find a suitable comparison.

"Calm down and just do it, Donald," Fern cautioned. Wouldn't it be just like a man to have a heart attack and leave her to finish the job?

"Let me savor it, Fern!" Donald wiped his beaded forehead with the back of his free hand. "Waited a long time—"

Luci exchanged a worried look with Fern, a look that Fern returned before she realized what she was doing.

"Are you all right? Your color isn't too good—"

"Shut up," Donald snarled again.

Luci looked amused. "Or what? You'll shoot me? I really think I'll do what I want with my last living moments—

When Fern thought things couldn't get any weirder a third voice cut Luci off.

"Well, that was gross," the placid voice said from behind her. "Did you know there's a body—oh, I didn't mean to interrupt."

A chilly wind ruffled the edges of the counterpane and

the curtains at the window. It lifted the straying ends of Fern's and Donald's hair.

"What the hell—"

"This is who has been trying to kill me," Luci put in helpfully.

"They don't look like killers, except for the gun," Gracie said.

"Surprised me, too," Luci said.

"Shut up!" Donald looked right. Fern looked left. There was no one to be seen.

Fern looked at Donald as the voice continued, "I suppose they're the ones who put this body up the chimney?"

Fern froze, her breath constricted as apprehension tightened her chest. Who the hell was talking?

"There's a body up the chimney?" Luci straightened from her pillow and dropped her feet to the floor. "I wonder if its Boudreaux's lost corpse?"

"Did Boudreaux lose a corpse? It's not like him to lose something so large."

Fern looked over her right shoulder, coming nose to nose with Donald doing the same. Continuing their rotation, they turned to face the source of the voice: a female head protruding from the mantle of the fireplace.

She tried to speak, but couldn't manage more than a strangled cry.

Donald sounded worse than her. And the hand holding the gun shook as he pointed it at the head.

"Anyone we know?" inquired Luci from behind them, as if there were no head poking out of solid wood.

"Just a moment." The head faded back into the wood-work just as Donald pulled the trigger. The wood where the head had been splintered twice. "Hmmmm, I don't think so." The voice was hollow and rather distant for the first half of the sentence, but came closer as the head emerged from wood once more.

Donald fired again, this time taking out a bottle of aspirin sitting on the mantel.

"Goodness. The mouth shaped the words placidly as she turned to examine the scars. "I haven't been shot at since I died—"

"No!" The word rose to a shriek. He fired again and again, emptying the chamber, continuing to pull the trigger when bullets no longer spat out of the barrel.

With a howl of rage and fear, Donald threw the gun at the head. Then dropped to the floor—in fetal position. The last thing Fern saw before the red mist enclosed her was Luci stepping close and bending to peer up the chimney. "Dang, there is a body in there. What do you want to bet Mickey will blame it on me?"

"LOT OF PRINTS all over this room," the tech told Mickey.

"I figured there would be. Some of them are mine," Mickey said wearily. "But if we print all the guests and staff, then we can compare for the ones that shouldn't be here."

"If the killer wore gloves—"

"Then we're out of luck. A state we are all too used to."

The tech nodded glumly and resumed his careful dusting of the myriad surfaces in the room. It was much easier for everyone to work now that the aging catatonic killers had been lifted onto stretchers and carried away. The woman, Fern, had finally stopped trying to crawl to Disney World, but it had taken two officers to restrain her until the hypodermic could be inserted into her arm.

The police photographer was lying on his back in the cavity of the chimney taking shots of the dangling corpse while the Coroner's office awaited the signal to pull it out. And in a corner, a tense Captain Pryce sat next to Luci, not touching her, both of them looking uncomfortable, yet pleased.

Mickey rubbed his eyes, trying to push back those nightmarish moments when he'd rushed up the stairs with gun drawn. His careful study of the house's layout had served him well. He'd known what room to kick open the door to, then, while Delaney covered him, dive into with a low flying roll that brought him right to Luci's feet—and in perfect position to see the body up the chimney. Not to mention nose-to-nose with the gibbering Donald. No surprise his rush of relief at seeing Luci safe was complicated by the desire to strangle her for being all right.

"What happened?" he'd snapped, rolling to his feet.

Then she'd pointed at Gracie, still half-in and half-out of the mantle.

"Gracie startled them."

"Startled them." He looked at the couple slumped on the floor.

"I don't usually come through walls," Gracie explained with a gentle air of apology, "but with all the people around—" She started to shrug, but faded from view as the sound of footsteps pounded down the hall.

Luci leaned towards Mickey and said with an air of one giving a confidence, "Maybe we shouldn't mention Gracie."

Mickey looked at Delaney. He was trying not to laugh. Or cry. It was hard to tell because they both began with the same grimace.

Mickey started patting his pockets for his new bottle of aspirin.

"The one called Donald killed it," Luci said from her corner. "You left it on the mantel."

Mickey looked up just in time to see a tech step on a scattered section of tablets and grind them to powder. In the mirror above the dresser he saw his eye give a big twitch, then settle into a small but steady rhythm, in sync with the pounding in his head.

WHO'D HAVE THOUGHT Donald and Fern would lose it so completely, Artie wondered? He had watched them being wheeled out on stretchers from his place with the catering staff and it hadn't been a pretty sight. What had happened to them in that room upstairs? No question the old ladies were trying. He'd come close to offing them himself a time or two, but to reduce that emotionless pair to gibbering idiots? Only upside was they looked too whacked out to rat him out.

Would the cops search the whole place? He had to face it. They'd find the money. He could walk away from it, but —he dabbed at the sweat forming beads on his forehead, he'd worked so hard to get it. It couldn't go wrong now. It just couldn't. He'd worked too long, too hard to make it all happen. He couldn't lose Helen now. He wouldn't. And he wouldn't lose his money, either. Not while there was still a chance to get it. One more chance.

One thing was clear. He'd have to take care of Luci himself. She was the only person who could put him together with Helen and Butt Had.

But how to do it? And how to get out of here before they discovered his other mistake?

A cop approached the restive catering group and said, "We're going to search and print each of you, then you can leave."

Not good, but it could be worse. Much worse. Artie went to the head of line. By the time they matched his prints with his record, he planned to be long gone.

LUCI WAS STARTING to develop a twitch, too. Her father was dying to get into the thick of the investigation, but felt compelled to be paternal. Since he wasn't about to start hugging her in front of the guys, he might as well get on with it.

She turned and said, "If you need to supervise things, I'm fine."

He looked torn between old duty and new. "Well, if you're sure you're all right?"

"Absolutely sure."

His reluctance plain, Pryce joined the group around the fireplace. Idly, Luci noticed Mickey had the best ass in the group, though Delaney's wasn't bad either. Nearly dying sharpened one's appreciation of the finer things of life.

Mickey was in position to see the dead man's face as the techs started to ease it out onto a tarp.

"Damn." Mickey straightened, his face grim.

Delaney's view was still blocked. "What's wrong?"

"We need to get Dante up here. Oh, and Delaney?"

"Yeah?"

"Have someone search them down to their toenails. We'll want their guns for forensics." Mickey rubbed his face again, then turned back to Pryce. "Now can I search this place, sir?"

Pryce looked at Luci. "We'll have no trouble getting a warrant. Be better if you cooperate."

She hesitated, her thoughts on the missing body and

the shoeboxes in the attic that were starting to make more sense, but she nodded. It was time for the chips—and the bodies—to fall where they may. "I'll clear it with the aunts."

"Thanks." Mickey nodded towards the splintered fireplace. "You want to explain why you went off with a stranger when you knew someone was trying to kill you?"

Her mouth twitched. "Hey, I just thought she was an old lady who needed to pee. And none of us were sure—"

"Well, we sure as hell are sure now! Did they say why?"

"No. They said it wasn't any of my business." Mickey gave her an exasperated look that Luci met with a limpid one. "It was a badly played scene from the get-go. I was missing the Hepplewhites and they were missing me—"

"Any idea why they went catatonic without killing you, Luci?" Pryce asked.

"I think they saw a...ghost," Luci said.

He twitched. "Shit."

"No shit," Mickey said morosely.

Mickey's headache was doing better. He'd found some aspirin tablets that had rolled under the bed. The twitch had slowed to intermittent, but everything else was still screwed up. The good news was that Dante wasn't happy either, because it was Max, Dante's assistant, whose body had been taken out of the chimney and was now lying in front of the fireplace with two bullet holes in his back.

Dante looked shaken, angry. "What the hell happened here? And where's my aunt?"

"None of your damn business what happened here," Pryce snapped. "Ross? Send someone to find his aunt."

"Can they take her home?" Dante countered, starting to regain his equilibrium. After all, he was no stranger to the grim reaper.

"Not until she answers some questions," Mickey said, stepping up to Dante, just hoping he'd take a swing.

"She doesn't know anything." Dante looked like he'd like to oblige Mickey.

"Then she doesn't need to worry." Mickey got right in his face. "You, however, should worry."

"I," Dante said, not giving an inch, "want my lawyer."

"Get him out of here," Pryce ordered, shoving a hand through his hair.

"Can I leave then?"

"No. You can wait until your lawyer gets here. Put him outside and watch him."

When a uniform had hustled Dante away, Mickey turned to Pryce. "Look, sir, we can't begin to do a thorough search with all these people around. We gotta clear some space."

"If we get names and addresses, we can let most people leave." Pryce thought for a moment. "I'll go down, pass who I can. Delaney can get statements from anyone I can't personally vouch for. I'll try to free up as many people as I can to help search." In a rare show of emotion, he ruffled his own hair. "What a mess."

"Sir?" Mickey gestured towards the seated Luci. "I'll bet Luci would be a big help clearing people to leave."

Luci shrugged and stood up, her eyes promising future retribution for Mickey as Pryce ushered her out.

Mickey grinned, then turned to his men. "We take this place apart top to bottom. Leave no stone unturned, no cupboard unsearched, no door closed. Got it?"

As soon as Pryce got distracted by the governor Luci slipped away and joined her aunts. Not because she was worried they'd be upset. She was starting to worry they'd done it. There didn't seem to be a lot of other viable suspects that she could see.

The time had come to ask, so she did.

"Kill anyone?" Miss Theo looked thoughtful. "I don't think so, dear. Hermi, Weena, have you killed anyone?"

Hermi smiled. "I'll admit I thought about killing Reggie when he first showed up here. It was bad enough that he was a Seymour without being an ex-con, but he turned out not so bad." She brightened. "And the gazebo turned out lovely."

All eyes turned to Weena. She ruffled indignantly. "What makes you think I'd kill Reggie?"

"Well, you do have a gun, dear," Miss Theo pointed out.

Luci found herself wishing she'd picked up a few aspirin, too.

"So? Doesn't mean I'd kill Reggie with it. Besides, I gave it to Reggie before he left for Cleveland." She stuck her tongue out at her sister, then added, "I must say, I thought it was very tacky of him to show up here with that woman. Can you imagine what Velma would have done if she'd come after all?"

Luci felt her eye twitch. It was an odd sensation, one she'd never felt before. Had finding her father somehow brought her Pryce-ness into ascendancy? She was seeing the world though non-Seymour eyes. And it wasn't pretty.

"Reggie..." She rubbed the twitching spot. "...was at the party?"

Each aunt gave a sigh and a nod. Taking care of them was turning out to be a bigger job than even she had imagined. "With a woman?"

"Well, he was invited." Hermi shrugged.

"Did you talk to him?"

"Well, I was going to tell him how much I liked the gazebo, but then the Hepplewhites came out and—"

"I think I understand." Luci had to smile, though a little ruefully. "It might be better if you don't mention Reggie's specter to Mickey. He has a headache."

"But, Luci dear," Miss Theo protested. "Perhaps the

dear boy would like to ask Reggie who shot him? Wouldn't that be good for his headache?"

"Only if he knows who shot him," Miss Weena pointed out. "I mean, Gracie doesn't know who shot her. And this is Reggie we're talking about. If he hadn't mismanaged his death he wouldn't have turned up under a bush."

"I expect you're right, Miss Weena." Luci was really feeling the strain. Was this how Mickey felt all the time? No wonder he wanted to strangle her. "And it's not like the testimony of a ghost is permissible in a court of law."

"We probably shouldn't mention this to Velma either." Miss Theo glanced towards Velma's house. "They weren't married and Reggie is free to choose a more—accessible companion—now that he's dead, but it's not particularly sensitive of him. She was practically a carbon copy of poor Velma, too."

"Really?" This was interesting, but she couldn't quite put her finger on why. There was something about Velma that kept teasing the edge of her brain. Something...but what?

"Miss Luci?"

The uniformed officer had approached without them noticing.

"Yes?" She felt the beginnings of apprehension tighten her insides. Had they found the missing corpse? Luci looked at her aunts, their aging eyes as tranquil as always.

"Could you come with me?"

Luci gave the uniform a nod, then with a reassuring

look at her aunts she followed him through the thinning party crowd to the front parlor Mickey and Delaney had been using since the discovery of the first body. With a respectful nod, he held the door for her to enter, then closed it quietly behind her.

He'd found the shoeboxes. They were stacked in piles taller than her around the room.

Which is probably why she didn't notice the corpse right away.

19

Artie was shaking as he fumbled some coins into the slot, then sank onto the closest empty bench. With a jerk, the trolley moved forward, the motion barely moving the air around the stuffy interior.

As he waited for his heartbeat to slow, he pulled out a large handkerchief and mopped his damp forehead, then swabbed at the moisture that had collected around his shirt collar. Pity about Harriet. But couldn't be helped. Should have taken her loss on the chin instead of showing up at the party with an attitude.

"Are you all right?"

He couldn't repress a slight flinch as he searched for a face to fit the female voice. He didn't have to look far. In the seat just behind his was an older woman, a plain woman with her graying hair neatly styled beneath a straw hat with a narrow brim decorated with a small bunch of dried flowers. Her clothes were also neat and plain, except for the astrological sign pinned to her lapel. There was a look in her faded eyes that Artie recognized.

He shrugged the slump from his shoulders, his hand moving automatically to his tie. He smiled, using equal parts charm and wan.

"It's the heat, I think. Guess I'm not used to."

"You're from out of town?" A delicate pink touched the pale cheeks.

"From Cleveland. Here on business. But enough about me. Tell me about you—

Like a flower getting needed rain, her smile bloomed on her face.

"You opening a shoe store?" Luci asked from the doorway.

"Come in and shut the door." Mickey watched her comply with his request, then lean against the closed door. She looked good against the stark wooden surface, the crossed ankles and calves hinting at further glories hidden by her party skirt. The shadows that hid her expression made her even harder to read than usual. "I'm sure what's inside will be a big surprise to you."

She stopped by one stack of boxes and lifted the lid to

look at the neat rows of dollar bills. Her brows rose. "Are they all one dollar bills?"

Mickey nodded. "At least now I know what Dante wanted," he said. "Somehow he must have found out about the scam that Reggie and whoever killed him ran and wanted to be cut in."

"Well, well. Reggie, you old dog."

"What do you mean?"

Luci gave a slight laugh. "He cheated fate. A dollar at a time. Finally got his successful scam." Her shoulders rose and fell in a sigh as she fingered the bills, then closed the lid. "And then fate squashed him like a bug."

"It might not have been his scam," Mickey said. "We haven't been able to match any of the prints we've found in the house to his."

Luci seemed to find this interesting. "Really?" She frowned. "But if Reggie wasn't here, how did he wind up under a bush?"

"Unless—"

Luci looked at him. "—the man they thought was Reggie—"

"—wasn't," Mickey finished. "Whoever it is, he was a busy bee at the party." He walked over to a chair and turned it to face Luci, watching her face as the slumped body came into view. Though brief, it was surprise that flickered across her face. "Don't suppose you recognize her?"

Luci was more than surprised. She studied the older woman dressed with a certain dowdy elegance, feeling a distinct sense of deja vu, if only she could figure out why...

"How come you aren't doing the dust and poke thing?"

"Because Crime Scene is still working upstairs. And—" he was almost shuffling his feet, she noticed with amusement. "I didn't notice her right away."

"She looks like she's sleeping." Luci crouched down in front of the body and peered at her face, her sense that she was on the verge of a moment of clarity growing stronger.

"No kidding. I even tried to wake her up. That's when I discovered the bullet hole. Looks like she was plugged right through the heart. Close range, too if the powder burns are any indication."

"My elderly hitters?"

"I don't think so. Different caliber weapon. I'm betting it'll turn out to be the same gun that killed Max, Reggie, and the frozen John Doe. Our geriatric hitters were carrying a silenced 9mm Luger."

Luci looked up at him. "Why didn't we hear these shots? I mean, the music wasn't that loud."

"Killer used pillows to muffle the sound. Found one under her chair with her purse and the one used on Max was tossed behind the bed."

"Really? How very enterprising." She stood up, but continued to stare at the body, straining for that niggling something that was just out of mental reach.

"What?"

Luci looked up and gave a little shake. Mickey didn't like hearing what she could remember. No reason to share what she couldn't. "Odd coincidence we had two killers operating in the same house on the same day. Even for Seymours, I think it's a record."

"What makes you think it is a coincidence?" Mickey stepped closer, risking her volatile proximity so he could monitor her reaction.

"What else could it be?" The honest surprise in her eyes deflected suspicion, but he still felt she knew more than she was telling him.

"It has to be, doesn't it? You just said that my elderly couple didn't do this."

"Just seems like too much of a coincidence. Wondered if you had any ideas?" Her smile was the one that always curled his toes. Made his shoes and his heart feel tight.

"You never like my ideas. They make your head ache."

Mickey shifted impatiently. "That's because—"

He stopped himself from finishing the sentence. Being told her ideas made no sense wouldn't encourage her to share what she knew. And there was no getting away from the fact that her family's pervasive personality played into the whole situation—which gave her an insider's edge that he, unfortunately, needed right now, even if it did make his head ache.

She watched him, her arms crossed, looking at him in a way that told him he'd have to ask nicely. There would be no free flow of information. He didn't mind climbing up, but down—

Luci watched him trying to choke down his pride. Poor guy. It wasn't his fault he didn't know how to navigate the Seymour Zone, but until he was willing to listen, there wasn't much she could tell him that would help.

He gagged a few more times, then managed to choke out, "Anything in particular strike you about all this?"

It was only a small step for her, but a big step for Mickey, so she decided to meet him part way. "I did notice that wedding theme popping up again."

He tried, but failed to control a flinch that also put the twitch back in his right eye. If he didn't do something about all that bottled-up stress he was going to look like Clouseau's Chief Inspector from the Pink Panther movies.

"Wedding...themes?"

"Did you notice her," Luci nodded in the direction of the body, "wedding ring is new? The edges are barely worn."

The twitch got a little worse, but he did go look at the ring. "So it is." He swallowed a few times, then squeezed out, "Anything else?"

The trouble was, so much of what she noticed were feelings, not things that could be seen. Still, she owed it to him to try. "Reggie and Frosty were naked, but Max and this woman are clothed."

"I guess our killer didn't have time to strip these two— what with the party going on around."

Luci gave him an approving smile. "Exactly. He's starting to make mistakes." Playing his sidekick was kind of fun when he didn't whine. It would be interesting to see how long he could take it. She tapped a finger on her chin. "You found the money in the attic, but Dante's guy was in the chimney in your room—"

"Yes." A certain grimness to Mickey's voice alerted her before he got his question out. "How did you know where the money was found?"

Luci gave him her "oops" smile. "I may have run across it when I was in the . . . attic, but I just thought my aunts had developed an aversion to banks. It was a reasonable assumption."

"Uh huh."

She thought he would say more, but he didn't. Instead he opened a file and pulled out a creased picture. "We found this tucked in his pocket. Recognize him?"

Luci took the picture. It was a mug shot, though not a good one, complete with numbers across the bottom. Front and side view.

Luci felt the first tremor of...something. "Who is he?"

Mickey picked up the file. "His name is Arthur Maxwell and he was Reggie's cellmate last time he was in prison."

"Really?" She frowned slightly. "He looks...kind of like my neighbor's new husband. The one she hit with her Volkswagen." The pieces of all her impressions, the faces of the players both dead and alive, spun in her head like snow in one of those globes, with the truth buried some-where in the middle. If she could just get alone to think...

Mickey ground his teeth and snatched the photo back. "This isn't a joke—"

Luci sighed. "I am trying." She lifted the lid on one of the shoeboxes and fingered the bills. "Do you suppose he's given up on trying to get this? He must know you've found it."

"We're keeping it quiet. He might be hoping we wouldn't search the attic." He rubbed his head. "Under normal circumstances, we might not have."

Mickey had the photos of the victims in a stack on the table. She sat down and looked through them, arranging them in order of discovery as her thoughts spun slower and slower.

"Not exactly a rogue's gallery, is it?" Luci murmured. She tapped the photo of the guy found in the freezer. "I wonder how he fits in?"

Mickey sat down next to her. "What do you mean?"

"I'm not sure," Luci admitted. "It's just that, well, this one—"

"Dante's sidekick, Max," Mickey supplied for her.

"Just Max?" When Mickey nodded she continued. "Interesting. He must have been looking for the money, but this woman, Reggie, the hit couple, my aunts and their friends, the—they're all, well, older."

Mickey noticed the stop, the hesitation and the slight emphasis and frowned. What had she meant to say? He stared at her, the innocent widening of her eyes only increasing his suspicion that there was something, possibly several things, she wasn't telling him. He made a mental note to keep an eye on her.

"You don't really fit either," he pointed out.

"No," she said. "I don't seem to, do I?"

She leaned back with an air of decision. "You should have the aunts look at your lady over there."

"Why?"

Her eyes warned him to brace himself.

"I have a feeling she was Reggie's date today."

His whole body twitched. "Reggie is dead."

Luci arched her brows. "Not the faux Reggie."

Mickey sighed. "You're enjoying this, aren't you?"

Luci looked apologetic. "Yes, but I feel conflicted about it."

"Exactly what is it we're doing out here?"

Luci looked at Gracie in surprise. Surely it was obvious.

"We're looking for the missing body, the one Boudreaux saw in the freezer the first time."

She let the beam of the flashlight dance around the darkened garden, then directed it back on the sketch she held. "Boudreaux has marked every area he can remember replanting in the last few months."

"What if he forgot something?"

"I have considered that possibility, but prefer to deal with it only if we strike out. The largest area is over there by the fence. Some kind of bush. Couldn't understand what he called them, but I think that's the best possibility. It's more person- length than the others. Though Miss Hermi managed to stir things up quite a bit this spring. She was in a new broom sort of mood."

"Yes, I noticed that myself. Reggie got her all stirred up. If he hadn't ended up under one of the plants himself, I'd think he had an ulterior motive. You're quite sure there is another body? Couldn't it have been Reggie that Boudreaux saw?"

Luci noticed that Gracie moved, not above the ground, but not really on it either, while Luci had to be careful for the pitfalls of uneven terrain that the fitful glow of flashlight failed to fully illuminate. The moist night was marginally cooler than the day, and the rich smell of earth and flower heavily scented the motionless watchful air.

It's lucky I have no imagination and a working knowledge of the ghostly, Luci told herself wryly, or this feeling I'm being watched might make me uneasy.

"Boudreaux saw this body before Reggie was supposed to have gone to Cleveland." Luci stepped off the path and shone her light against a line of flowering bushes. "I think this is the spot. Apparently Miss Hermi wanted to break up the block of color or something."

She got on her knees and shone the light into the leafy interior of one of the bushes.

"Does the ground look disturbed?" Gracie asked, kneeling beside Luci.

"This is a reclaimed swamp. It probably didn't look disturbed two days after these bushes were transplanted." She leaned back with a sigh, giving Gracie a speculative look as she pondered the right approach for her proposition.

"So? Do you dig now?" Gracie seemed to grow still. "You don't have a shovel. Why don't you have a shovel?" A pause. Then it came. "Why did you invite me along on this little excavation?"

Carefully not looking at Gracie, Luci said, trying to sound casual, "I thought you might be more help than the aunts?"

"Surely Boudreaux would have been a better choice to dig up the garden?"

"I wasn't...actually...planning on...digging up...anything. Disturbing the scene of a crime is a criminal offense, you know."

"How were you planning—" Gracie stopped abruptly. Then, "No. No way. I am not sticking my head into the middle of a corpse—no matter how phantasmal I may be. I already did that once today and it was not fun. Why don't you just have Mickey and Delaney take care of it?"

"There probably isn't a corpse at all. Boudreaux was drunk when he saw this supposed body," Luci coaxed. "I didn't want to bother them until I was sure."

"Bother me, please," Mickey's voice said out of the darkness just before a bright light flashed in Luci's eyes.

Luci looked at Gracie.

"We're busted," Gracie said.

"You don't have to sound so relieved," Luci said. "No one's gonna strip-search you."

Gracie's smile was edged with wicked. "You wish."

20

Artie, disguised as the blind man again, tapped his way down the street past the Seymour house. The dark glasses that covered his eyes allowed him to see one elegantly shod foot in front of the other as he walked. His new shoes, brown for once, needed to be monitored for shine and that something extra that he didn't have a name for but involved how the shoes looked with the rest of him. He still wasn't sure brown was his shoe color, but he'd been caught by the pair. Well and truly caught. It was more than the detailing, though it was very nice. A sweep of leather at the heel, the smooth expanse of brown across the toes. The place to tuck a dollar...

He sighed. And the color had intrigued him, he had to admit. He wasn't sure what Helen would think of them. She'd advised against brown the last time they'd shopped together, but that had been an inferior brown. This one had just a touch of red to it. Ripe and rich, it had been irresistible in artificial light. Now, he was pleased to note, the sun had found richer, deeper browns in the leather. Surely Helen would be as enchanted as he was by the pair.

They also served another purpose. They took his mind off what was happening on the other side of the Seymour's fence where what looked like an army of cops was digging.

What were they looking for? And even more important, had they found his money? There'd been no mention of it in the newspaper story, though the article hadn't been without its worrisome side. Like the fact that the guy he'd shoved up the chimney was Dante's man. Still got cold chills thinking about that close call.

If they hadn't found the money, how was he going to get it past the police and Dante, who had a couple of guys watching the house right across the street from the police? Just when he thought it couldn't get messed up anymore than it already was—

Damn Unabelle. Why did she have to pick right now to get married? Two weeks and he would have been free and clear with more than enough money to keep him and Helen in hog heaven for as long as he lived.

And damn Cloris for being related to Dante. He'd never have gone near her if he'd known! Bad luck the bastard happened to live in New Orleans, too. And Harriet. How the hell had she found him? Too bad she'd been so unexpectedly competent.

At least the old ladies were expectedly incompetent.

They hadn't blinked when they saw Harriet confront him at the party, even though they thought he was dead. Weird, but who was he to look a gift horse in the mouth when he needed one?

Could that be turned to his favor? Because what he really needed was a plan that brought the money to him.

He realized something was dulling the leather of one shoe. He picked up the pace, rounded the corner out of sight of the watchers, then bent down and rubbed a bit of dust from the toe of one shoe. Someone hit him from behind. He felt his face hit the pavement before his brain registered it coming.

Busted, he thought. Then the something started licking his ear.

GRACIE PUT ASIDE her book and stood up, drifting to the window, trailing chilled air in her wake. Luci looked up from the newspaper and her thoughts, relieved to have the thoughts interrupted and even more relieved to have Gracie blunt the muggy warmth of the room.

"Something wrong?"

"It's awfully quiet. Where are the girls?"

Luci smiled at hearing the aunts called "girls."

"They're getting ready for their monthly visit to your grave. Didn't you see the flowers in the entryway?"

Gracie shook her head. "I've been avoiding the hallways since..." She sighed, sending a cold chill into the too warm room. "How's Delaney?"

Luci put the paper down and rose, stretching the kinks from her back, wishing she could so easily rid herself of the kinks in her thoughts. "He's...pretty bummed."

"If only..." Her words sent another chill swirling around the room.

"You weren't dead?"

Gracie nodded. "You're lucky..."

"That I'm not dead?" Luci shook her head. "You couldn't be more wrong." She had to move to stay ahead of thoughts. "I'm beginning to think we Seymours are all born dead." She came up against a wall and had to turn toward Gracie. "Or maybe we're just born afraid." Luci headed toward Gracie until she felt the chill from her presence, then turned and stalked away.

"Um, Luci," Gracie said, amusement threading through the sad in her voice. "You're pacing."

"We don't pace," Luci pointed out, doing her turn at the wall. She was halfway across the room when it hit her. "I am pacing. I'm freaking pacing! I can't believe it! Do you know what this means?"

"That you're not as dead as you thought you were? That you can still change the course of your life? You can still live?"

"Can I?" Luci felt the agitation in her. It was like being possessed by an alien being. "Can I change who knows how many centuries of family conditioning? My brain is hard-wired to do Seymour until I die! To never marry—"

Luci spun around and faced Gracie. "Why is that? Why don't we marry? Why did Lila—who was not designed by nature or nurture to be a mother—leave him, leave me to grow up without him? Why did she do that? Freaking inquiring minds would freaking like to know!"

Luci felt her chest, which had only ever heaved from exercise, heaving with raging emotion. Heaving with...rage. Felt her eyes blur with unfamiliar tears. Felt like, what? She mentally poked the emotion ball and realized what she wanted more than anything was to go fetal and whine. And then find him, her father. She wanted him to hold her and tell her it was going to be all right. Even if it was a lie.

Her mind shifted. So did her body as she stared at Gracie, who lost her cohesion in the storm of emotion coming at her. When she reformed, her eyes were deep and sad. "I've spent a lot of years trying to come up with a good answer to that question."

Luci drew in a trembling breath. "And...did you?"

"Not a good one." She turned and stared out the window.

Luci joined her and saw Delaney talking to another cop in the garden.

"I never meant to hurt him," Gracie said. "I never thought..."

"He'll...probably...get over...you." It seemed cold comfort.

Gracie looked at Luci. "But will I get over him?"

"I'm so sorry, Gracie. So very sorry."

Gracie's gaze sharpened. "Then do something."

"What?"

"Live. Love. Go find Mickey and—"

"And what?" Luci could feel panic replacing agitation.

"Everything you're afraid of." Gracie's gaze bored into her, seeing everything. Luci felt wide open, exposed and raw. "He's in the parlor pulling his hair out. Go to him."

"I can't—"

"Yes, you can. Begin. You don't have to do it all right now, but begin. Before it's too late for you!"

Begin. She could do that. That was just...talking. As if Gracie sensed her capitulation, she smiled. It was like the sun coming out. No wonder Delaney had fallen hard. "I love you, Gracie."

"Get out of here," Gracie said, but Luci could have sworn she blushed. If a ghost could blush.

MICKEY, concentrating on a new stack of papers, didn't hear the door open, wasn't aware of movement until he smelled Luci's perfume tangling in the air around him. It was not unlike her: contrary, mysterious, with an underlying and almost irresistible charm. Mickey hunched his shoulders as she came around and leaned on the back of his chair, tossing a folded newspaper down in front of him.

"If I didn't know you to be the soul of upright, though excitable honesty, Detective Ross," she said, her voice soft and sultry, her lips so close to his ear that he felt her warm breath puff against the side of his face, "I'd accuse you of dissembling with the press."

"Huh?" Concentration scattered, but the will to not react to her remained firm. Without looking at her, Mickey shoved the newspaper aside, tried to focus on the typed words of the report he'd been reading just fine until she came in.

"Why would you deliberately try to live down to the public's low opinion of the NOPD? Is it a plot-in-the-making?"

His chair creaked again as she withdrew, padded around the table and sank with unsettling grace into the chair opposite. Mickey sighed, rubbing his tired eyes in an effort to postpone as long as possible the moment he'd have to face her green enigmatic gaze. It was getting harder and harder to remember all those good sensible reasons not to get involved with her when it felt so damn right just to be in the same room with her.

He was a grown-up. Surely he could control himself and his heart around someone who was so bad for him? At this rate, he'd be doing the late afternoon talk circuit with a label under his name on the screen that read: Love left him for dead. Or something equally humiliating. He felt her gaze and her sympathy, as if she followed his thoughts and was sorry for disrupting his life. He gave in and looked at her, since not looking hadn't helped any.

She sat lightly in the old-fashioned chair, as if she might vanish at any moment. More ghostly than Gracie, like a sleepy cat, her thicket of lashes drooping over her eyes. The eyes, however, were anything but sleepy. Emotions appeared and disappeared like flashing lights on a dark highway, appearing and disappearing too quickly for him to read. But he thought he saw regret go by and it gave him hope.

Maybe, just maybe, he could be the guy to—he realized where he was going and stopped. It was just the challenge, he told himself, wanting what you can't have. It's a guy thing. Everybody says so. He wasn't...in love. Love was for fools, optimists and the pages of novels. Love didn't last. Didn't need a crystal ball to read the odds against anything lasting in this world, and something as breakable as love? Right.

Did he know, Luci wondered, how very readable his thoughts were, how clearly they played out in his too-blue eyes? In the space of five heartbeats, he'd almost talked himself into, and had talked himself out of, doing something about what was simmering between them. Gracie was right. It wouldn't take much to push him over the edge into acting. Her own blood stirred just thinking about what he might do. He was just so dang cute when he was all stirred up. And he was more likely to let down his guard and kiss her. Kissing seemed like a good place to begin.

When he kissed her, she felt Seymour fade and brave creep in. In his arms, maybe she could be brave enough to live the way Gracie urged.

He rubbed the back of his neck and asked on a sigh, "Why don't you just ask me if you want to know something?"

And if I asked you to do what I'm thinking, she wondered, would you do it? Gracie was both right and wrong. Luci did need to begin, but not with the complications from the murder still hanging fire. They both needed their wits about them to sort it all out. If the aunts got hauled off to jail, what would Gracie do?

It was either good logic or a cowardly rationalization.

She leaned forward, resting her elbows on the table, and propped her chin on her hands. "You're still miffed about the extra body thing, aren't you?"

The smooth columns of her arms only partially shielded the dipping curve of her tee shirt that exposed the shadowy slope of her breasts.

Mickey swallowed dryly. "Miffed?" He shook his head. "The 'extra body thing' could get you charged with evidence tampering—"

"I had no intention of tampering with anything. The drunken hallucinations of Boudreaux are hardly evidence, and since you haven't found another body—"

"We haven't found one yet." They had found an interesting variety of appliances, everything from the "I'm falling and I can't get up" gizmo to an early model of an electric toothbrush. The "I'm falling and I can't get up" gizmo still worked, to everyone's surprise but the aunts, who had ordered it removed from their property. The aunts must be tough to shop for at Christmas, he decided.

"You dug up most of the garden, Mickey." She leaned back again. "Not that I'm complaining. Miss Hermi's wildly excited about embarking on a new round of landscaping. It seems her—exposure—to the male physique has inspired her. She wants a fountain—complete with a statue of David—"

"I'll bet Delaney would appreciate your input in the garden—"

"Do you really think so?" She rebuked him with her eyes.

His fingers closed in fists. He looked down, saw the fists and deliberately straightened his fingers. He rifled a few papers. Picked up a pencil and made a mark on a page that didn't need a mark.

"Besides. Gracie's fulfilling that function. I haven't seen her so animated since—" She stopped.

And he had to look up. Just in time to catch the full force of her smile. The lashes lifted just enough to give her eyes a sultry depth full of invitation that had the edges of his mouth curling before he was hardly aware of it. The ground beneath him shifted off center. The room grew unaccountably warm around him as she held his gaze.

"Actually," she said, her voice dropping to a husky,

confidential level, "I've never seen her animated. But Miss Weena assures me she used to be before she died."

The smile got lost in the painful thump around his temples. He threw down his pencil and grabbed the bottle of aspirin. "What do you want?" It was almost a wail.

"Information. If we pooled our resources—"

"You don't have resources—"

"Not true."

"Oh?" He arched his brows as he looked at her. It was a mistake. Caught once more in the full force of her velvet-fisted gaze, coherence shattered like broken glass. And somewhere deep inside, in the place where honest thought meets honest emotion, he acknowledged that Luci Seymour did far more than drive him angry. But before honest thought could get out of hand he started a rear guard action with anger. "Damn it, Luci—"

"I'm half- Seymour." She marked each point with a raised finger. "I've played a sleuth on the stage. I have friends who are in law enforcement. And my aunt was a security guard—"

She shrugged, leaned back and crossed her arms as if daring him to question her credentials. The movement rumpled the edge of her tee shirt, revealing more of her smooth, curving flesh. He forced his gaze away and chewed harder on his tablets, then remembered he had a glass of water and downed that. Used the surge of lust to fuel his anger as he groped for the pencil again. Work.

330 PAULINE BAIRD JONES

Work would be his salvation from this unaccountable, bewildering temptation. His fingers closed over cool wood.

"Those aren't credentials! Those are—" He didn't even know what to call them.

"Face it. You need my inside information if you're going to crack this case." Luci's voice was a siren call to pleasure with its sweetly offered entreaty to reason. "Be fair—"

The pencil snapped in two. "Fair?" This time he didn't try not to wail. He pushed his chair back, half-turning away from her. Was it fair for her to have this effect on him when he'd done nothing, nothing to provoke it?

The room was too close, too warm, too full of her scent and her uncomfortable gaze. Too full of her. With her lean, graceful body and her slumberous eyes. He leaped up, tugging at his tie.

"You're leaving?" She straightened in her chair, giving him a heady view of the long, smooth angle of her neck and the fragile tracings of her shoulders and collar bone that naturally directed his gaze down—

"I need some air—and I've got to talk to Delaney about —something." He strode to the door, jerking at his tie and then ripping the top button from its mooring to allow air into his painfully constricted lungs.

He didn't slam the door behind him. But only because he lost his grip on it too soon.

Luci looked at the closed door, her shoulders rising and falling in a sigh that fell somewhere between relieved and regretful. Gracie would be disappointed in her. She was disappointed in herself. She'd tried to be brave, to be bold. Instead she'd tripped over Seymour and fallen flat on her face.

She picked up a folder, using it to fan away the heat Mickey had sent coursing through her body. "How's a girl supposed to know what to do? Do I take advice from a ghost? Listen to my heart? Or just give in and follow the Seymour imperatives?"

She dropped the file, leaning on the table while her fingers beat a reflective tattoo against the table. Her hand brushed against the discarded file. The tapping slowed, stopped. A distraction was good right now. She ran her finger along the edge and glanced towards the door. Surely he wouldn't have left her alone with this stuff if he hadn't meant for her to look at it.

He wants my help, she decided, but he can't bring himself to ask for it because of the other stuff. The lust stuff. She smiled slowly, then shook herself. Concentrate, girl. With another glance towards the door, she picked up a file. Nothing terrible happened, so she opened it.

And still the day proceeded on its usual course.

She started to read.

"Interesting." So Reggie had collected his bucks through some kind of a chain letter. She read the chain letter, once, then again, this time focusing on the list of names and addresses at the bottom. The letter directed the receiver to send one dollar bill to each of the twenty names on the bottom of the letter, then remove the top name and add their name to the bottom and send it out to a bunch of their friends. After a few weeks, they'd receive dollars in the mail.

She'd done something similar with panties in high school. Not a pleasant memory. There were a lot of people out there with very strange taste in underwear. It had pretty much cured her of chain letters.

Artie's offering reaffirmed that conviction. What he'd failed to tell the people receiving the letter was that all twenty names were AKAs for Reggie. Mickey had also found phone books from cities across the country. Enterprising, Luci concluded, with a take small enough to operate under the radar of the Postal Police. Who was going to complain when they lost a couple of bucks on a scam they should have been too smart to fall for in the first place?

Mickey had plenty of the chain letters, boxes of them, so she pocketed one to study later and picked up the next file.

This belonged to Arthur Maxwell, who had been masquerading as Reggie. Luci studied his picture, then found the dead woman, Harriet's picture. The snow in her head turned to a blizzard, but despite the debris of too much input, she had a feeling that the shadowy Truth would soon emerge from the drift. Or was she suffering from a massive attack of hubris? Only time would tell which.

In another file were pictures taken at the party. The one of Dante and his aunt caught her eye. Luci frowned, the whirling snow dipping to let her get a peek at an interesting piece of the puzzle. She closed the file, her tapping fingers keeping time with her thoughts. Mickey and friends had a plan in the works, but would it take into account the Seymour Factor? Even as she asked the question, she knew the answer was a big negative. Mickey was working overtime to factor them all out. It had become his primary goal in life.

"I wonder—"

The door opened and Pryce walked in. Though they had tacitly acknowledged their familial connection, she wasn't yet comfortable calling him anything fatherly out loud or in her mind. Not yet. Maybe not ever. It felt so weird, like a pair of shoes that should have been the right size, but didn't quite fit. Or maybe she was the one who didn't fit?

His preoccupied frown gave her time to distance herself from the files before he noticed her. The worry in his eyes deepened. His gaze did a quick survey of the room, then, reluctantly it seemed, returned to her.

"I thought Ross was here." He seemed like he wanted to say more. When he didn't, Luci pushed her chair back and stood up.

"He went outside to talk to Delaney." She refrained from looking at the pile of folders. Perhaps she refrained too much.

"Oh." His gaze narrowed. He looked at the files, then at her.

Luci tried to hold her innocent look, but she'd never tried to face down a father.

"Been doing some reading, have you?"

It was lucky for her he hadn't been around when she was a teenager, she decided. The thought was followed by regret. It would have been nice to have someone around who cared what she did. She tilted her chin against the regret and the question. "No one said I couldn't."

A smile flickered on his face as he gathered up the files, his expression unreadable. His long fingers, so like hers, hesitated over the last one, then he asked, his voice stilted, "Would... you—"

The door popped open and Luci's aunts flowed in like a babbling brook, engulfing Luci in their midst. Gentle, but irresistible, they pulled Luci toward the door.

"...need your help, dear... "

"...wedding plans to finish..."

"...cement to buy..."

He made an involuntary movement towards her and her heart jumped with hope, then fell when he stopped and let the aunts take her away.

Did he regret her coming into his life now, she wondered, looking back at him as her aunts dragged her out the door? Was he sorry she'd found him? She couldn't read his face any better than she could read her own heart. All she knew was that after years of going men-less, she had two of them seriously upsetting the paradigm of her existence.

Out in the hall, her aunts talked fast and avoided making eye contact, but their babble faltered, then faded into the slight sounds of clearing throats and shuffling feet. Shuffling feet? What was going on with them?

Luci opened her mouth to ask, but Miss Theo forestalled her by handing her a sheaf of papers.

"We knew you wouldn't mind doing these few things for us, dear girl. For the wedding." Her smile was too bright, too anxious to be real.

Luci looked at the "few things" that went on for at least four pages. "This should keep me busy," she said, looking up just in time to see three sets of parchment pale cheeks turn pink. This was getting curiouser and curiouser.

DELANEY SAT in the rubble of the garden on a bench, a droop to his broad shoulders that could have been exhaustion, discouragement or both.

"I take it you still haven't found anything?" Mickey handed him one of the glasses of water he'd gotten from the still speechless Louise. Judging by the glare in her eyes, they were lucky she was speechless.

The misery in Delaney's eyes as he emptied the glass in one long gulp made Mickey shift uncomfortably. And to wonder if his eyes were acquiring the same emotion.

Attraction to the Seymour women, dead or alive, was an exercise in masochism.

"There's not a body here." Delaney rubbed his unshaven chin. "I don't know what Boudreaux saw that night. Or where it is. But it ain't here."

"Captain arrived with our relief. We get four hours off, then he wants us back at headquarters. He wants us in position to move if either Dante or the perp makes a move. And to go over everything again. He thinks we're missing something."

Delaney nodded morosely. Mickey sank down next to him, stretched his legs out and stared down into the empty glass—an appropriate metaphor for their case. "How can we have so much data and still not know anything?"

"Yeah, I thought we'd really gotten a break when the Virginia Beach PD linked Harriet Maxwell to our frozen John Doe. Course they still might come up with a connection between her hiring a private dick to find her missing husband, and her and the private dick ending up here as corpses." Delaney stretched before asking, "Anything more come in on PI Munn?"

Mickey shook his head. "Not yet. Herman Munn wasn't a high profile snoop. Most of his clientele appeared to have been middle-aged women with wandering husbands. Maxwell's file only had minimal info in it. His secretary thinks he had most of it with him. Now that we know his name, we're doing a check of local hotels, etc. See if we can scare up some luggage. At least we have a date to look around. Munn definitely flew to New Orleans a month and a half ago. Coroner thinks Munn was frozen at least two weeks. Possibly more."

"Seymour's been dead at least a month," Delaney said. "If Seymour killed him, that would place time of death shortly after he got here. But it's more likely he was killed by Maxwell." Delaney sighed. "We know Munn was tracking Arthur Maxwell for Harriet Maxwell, but not why he got killed."

"The VBPD says Munn wasn't an upstanding member of the community. What if he somehow got onto the scam and wanted to be cut in—or to be paid off for not tipping off Harriet?" Mickey yawned so hard he almost fell off the bench.

Delaney caught his yawn. "Let's get out of here. I'm too hammered to think straight."

"Yeah." It would be a relief to get away from the house, from the Seymours and even from Luci.

As the two men walked towards the house, Delaney asked, "Everything in place here?"

Mickey nodded. "We've put the money back where we found it."

"Captain Pryce is blanketing the neighborhood with middle-aged and elderly appearing officers," Delaney said. "The news the case is solved has already showed up in the newspaper and should be on the twelve o'clock newscasts. We make a very visual withdrawal—"

"And wait for the fly," Mickey finished. "Pryce really think he'll fall for it?"

Delaney shrugged. "He's a pretty cool customer. He's already managed to kill two people under the noses of a house full of cops. And damn near killed Luci, too. Even if he isn't buying our withdrawal, I think he'll go for it. He has to be feeling pretty well invincible. That's his weakness —and our strength."

"Yeah. If only the Seymour ladies—" Mickey stopped, sighed.

"Yeah. If only."

MEETING SARAH WAS a piece of luck, Artie decided. What better place to hide and watch the Seymour house than from the respectable neighborhood itself and only a couple of blocks away? It didn't get much better than that. Any closer and Sarah would have known him. But his luck had always been good.

Except for that one time, when he'd met Reggie. Artie frowned—but jail was far behind him. And it had turned out for the good. Who'd have thought dumb old Reggie would come up with such a good scam? Old idiot didn't have a clue how to really cash in on it, of course. A pity his vision was so...limited. He'd miss old Reg. A little. While he was living his life of wealth and ease in Butt Had with

Helen with all the shoes in his closet he could need or want.

Of course, there was still Dante to deal with. He wouldn't be as easily duped as the police. And killing his man had raised the stakes. He'd seen Artie under his disguise, which the police hadn't.

"Look." Sarah pulled him out of his plotting as she pointed to the television. "They've caught the couple that killed those people at that party."

"That's not far from here, is it?" Artie asked, caressing the back of her neck and smiling with practiced charm.

"Too close for comfort." Sarah shuddered. "Not that I know them—except by reputation. Frankly, from what I've heard about the Seymours I'm not surprised bodies are turning up all over!"

Only somewhat aware of her burbling, Artie listened to the report. Did they think he'd fall for something so blatant as that? It was insulting.

Good thing he already had a plan to get his money and finish off Luci. Now all he had to do was think of some way to get Dante off his ass. Well, he'd always been lucky, in an unlucky sort of way. Dante wouldn't be bought off, so maybe he could be drawn off...maybe with Cloris's help?

21

Mickey looked up as Delaney came back balancing two cups of hot coffee and four doughnuts. Another doughnut protruded from his mouth. All around them was the comforting clatter, chatter and ringing phones of other detectives following other leads in other homicides.

He didn't like admitting it, but he missed the quiet, phoneless, nearly people-less Seymour house. Of course, it didn't help that he could feel Caroline's glare boring a hole in his back. One date and he was in the dog house. Women were so unfair.! Mickey gave a half-twitch, half-shrug to shake it off. It didn't work, but lucky for him, he saw her grab her purse and head out with her partner. Until now he wouldn't be relieved there'd been yet another homicide added to their yearly tally, but he needed the hostility break.

"Any movement yet?" Mickey asked Delaney. Ever since they'd driven away from the Seymour's he'd had the feeling they were in the calm before the storm. He'd been a cop too long not to know when serious shit was about to hit the fan. He'd like the chance to duck when it did.

"Nada." Delaney put one cup and one doughnut in front of Mickey. "You know, he could have decided to cut his losses and booked on out of here."

"He didn't," Mickey said. "If he was gonna leave, he'd have done it before he started offing people. He's in too deep to stop now."

Delaney nodded, studying the circle of fried dough like it held the answers to all the questions if he could just learn to speak doughnut. Mickey had never found any answers in food, up to and including tea leaves. Just got heartburn and a few extra pounds.

Mickey looked at the file, then tossed it aside with a snort of disgust. They'd exhausted their leads and themselves. It was a waiting game now, with the ball in Arthur Maxwell's court. Mickey hated waiting games and the noise he'd missed while doing time at the Seymour's was now giving his headache a chance to do a return show. He dug out his mega bottle of aspirin and tossed back two, then two more. He'd get over it, he told himself. He'd been orbiting the Seymour planet for nearly five days. That long in what amounted to a loony bin would leave its mark, but he had to admit, if only to himself, that the real problem was distance from Luci.

Would the people they'd left as watchers know how to deal with her? How to keep her safe from Maxwell and herself? And, like a rat following a maze, his thoughts went back to the big why. Why did Maxwell want her dead? Mickey pulled the chain letter out of the file and studied it, but none of the addresses were in Wyoming, let alone Butt Had. That didn't mean Maxwell had never been to Butt Had, of course. Be stupid of him to leave a trail to his home base.

"I'm going to fax Maxwell's mug shot to Butt Had. The connection has to be there. Luci said she doesn't travel much." Something teased at the edges of his mind. Something Luci had said. Problem was, she'd said too much and he was too tired to recall half of it, let alone sort out the important stuff. Always supposing she'd said anything important. "Should have thought of it sooner."

"We're both tired." Delaney looked up, shaking off his blues long enough to say, "Send it to the local Post Office, too. Whole town passes through the PO. Then go lie down. I'll wake you in an hour."

IT WAS Artie's knowledge of the old ladies' habits that formed the basis of his plan. It took some heavy thinking and some careful circuits through the neighborhood before he located the cemetery he'd escorted them to a couple of months ago. He walked down the rows until he found the Seymour crypt. He was early, so he scored some flowers off another grave and sat down out of sight of the street.

There were too many people looking for him. He had to finish this and get out of town. Max had made sure Artie knew Dante was gunning for him, just in case he hadn't figured it out. If Cloris could get Dante to call off the dogs long enough for him to get clear...he could soothe her down, spin her a tale, promise her what she wanted to hear and then disappear.

It was risky. He didn't know how much power Cloris had, but he had to try. If he'd just left her, not taken the money, would Dante be looking so hard? He was so close, so very close.

"Such a lovely day," he heard Miss Weena say in that breathless way of hers. He peered around the crypt and saw, with satisfaction, that all three of the old ladies were walking into his trap. All he had to do was close the door.

MICKEY DIDN'T GET to lie down. He faxed the mug shot and was heading down the hall to the lounge when Delaney intercepted him, his face grim. Cold fear started a slow creep through his body.

"The old ladies took a walk this afternoon and haven't been seen since. Louise got worried and gave a note to one of our watchers."

Mickey cursed and rubbed his face in hopes it would clear his head and not just his vision. "Well, we wanted Maxwell to make his move. He smelled the trap and decided to have the money come to him."

Delaney looked frustrated. "We should have told them what we were planning. Warned them—"

Not to tell them had been the captain's decision. He'd be sweating this one out, big time, Mickey decided, but they'd all be in the hot seat if the old ladies got hurt.

Fear quit creeping and started a stampede. "We should go over there—"

Delaney shook his head. "Captain wants us to stay here for now and keep working."

"APB?" Mickey asked, following him down the hall.

"Being treated as a kidnapping." Delaney dropped into his chair. "Be interesting to see how Maxwell makes contact, since there's no phone."

"Did he say how Luci was taking it?" Mickey asked.

"She's not home yet. Old ladies sent her out to run some errands—"

"What? Is she—"

"With a uniform," Delaney said, a faint grin lightening his expression. "She'll be back soon. I understand it was a long list."

～

DANTE KNEW the police were tailing him, but he wasn't worried. They could follow him home if they wanted to waste their time and the taxpayers' money. He missed Max but was too annoyed about Artie smoking him to do anything about it. He brooded all the way to his Garden District mansion. He'd do something about Artie when he found him. And Luci, who he was sure had set him up. It made the trip seem fast, despite the rush hour traffic slowing everything to a crawl.

When the limo swept around the curving drive in front of his house, he saw Cloris peering out the window, watching for him. It was enough out of character to stir up a mild interest.

Inside, she waited until the butler had taken his brief-case and handed him a drink before pulling him into the parlor and shutting the door. She was wringing her hands like a heroine in a melodrama and there was wildness to her eyes that sharpened his suspicions to a needlepoint.

"What's going on?" He stopped her from turning away from him. "What's happened?"

"He called me."

This was just what he wanted to hear. Dante let her go and smiled. "Really? And what did he say?"

"He wants to meet—"

Dante grabbed her again. "Where?"

"Promise you won't hurt him!"

"Of course." The promise came easy. He could work out a story later.

"I mean it. He wants to come back to me. He misses me." Pink flushed her cheeks. Dante wasn't surprised she couldn't look at him. He could hardly look at her. Did she believe him? Did it matter? Not really, he decided. He smiled more and patted her shoulder. "Of course he does. He was a fool to leave you." He hesitated. "Did he mention your money?"

The pink turned red in her sallow cheeks. "He's giving it all back. He only meant to borrow it until a deal came through for him."

Sure he did. It was going to be a pleasure popping the bastard.

"What time is the meet?" Dante asked.

"At eleven tomorrow night," she said. "In the Metairie cemetery. It was his idea," she added, as if she expected Dante to object. "And I'm going."

Dante gave a mental snort. It was a perfect meeting place. He made a mental note to put Cain and Abel on alert. They could quit watching the Seymour house, which was, of course, what Maxwell wanted. Get them in place at the cemetery well before Maxwell would be watching. Might as well let Maxwell have a clear field to move the money. When it was over, he'd tell them where he took it. He'd tell them everything before he died. When they were through, Cloris would pull the trigger herself.

22

The sound of a big truck accelerating away brought Mickey out of a sleep plagued with nightmares of being tortured on the rack. When he opened his eyes, he realized why. He'd fallen asleep in a chair. Now it felt like a drill was boring its way up his spine to the base of his head. When the Captain had sent them back to the Seymour house, he'd picked the chair for its discomfort factor, hoping it would keep him awake. He'd over-estimated the chair and under-estimated how tired he was.

Inch by painful inch, Mickey straightened out his spine, then took a breather before trying to stand. He heard a snore and discovered Delaney sprawled on a Victorian sofa across from him, his head bent at an angle that would soon make him wish he'd never been born. Another gentle snore issued from his slack jaw. Mickey rubbed his face and discovered a deep sleep crease running the length of one side that would probably take all day to fade.

"Delaney." When Delaney didn't move, Mickey kicked him, then wished he hadn't moved, let alone kicked.

"Huh?" With some snorts and groans, Delaney came awake, revealing an interesting paisley pattern adorning one whole side of his face from the pillow he'd been resting on.

It was going to be a long day.

When they'd sorted themselves out, shaved bristling jaw lines and tried without success to rub away the creases, they joined Luci in the dining room.

She was sitting in Miss Theo's place at the head of the table with an almost queenly aura about her. So might Queen Elizabeth had looked when she summoned her advisors to plan for war. It didn't matter that she was wearing shorts and a tank top in deference to the muggy warmth of the room. Her eyes, so like their captain's, followed him as he sat down on one side of her.

"What?" Mickey asked, as his instincts went from dormant to full alert. "What's happened?"

Her gaze pinned him in his chair, her search for words playing out in her eyes. "I got a note from Arthur Maxwell this morning."

Mickey straightened, looked at Delaney, then back at Luci. "Let's see it—"

Luci shook her head, the movement sharp and regal.

"What?" Mickey almost shouted the single word as rage did a quick crawl up his throat.

"What's going on, Luci?" Delaney cut in.

Luci leaned back in the chair, her hands relaxed against the carved wood. "We need to agree on a few things first."

Mickey choked twice before he gritted out, "The only thing we're going to agree on— "

"If you don't, then I'll handle it myself. He says no cops. By talking to you I put my aunts at risk."

"Really?" Mickey leaned back. "You'll handle it yourself?" Luci nodded, her eyes calm in the face of his glare. "You may have the note, but we have the money— "

The gentle shake of her head, the apology that softened the determination in her eyes, were the first warnings that she controlled the board.

"I'm afraid you don't," she said. "I took the liberty of moving it while you were asleep."

"How— " then he remembered the truck that woke him earlier.

She pushed back her chair and stood up, looking first at Delaney, then at Mickey, showing them her resolve. "I would be grateful for your assistance, but only on my terms. They're my aunts and we're going to do this my way."

It was, Mickey realized, probably the most frustrating moment of his existence. And there were a lot to choose from, most of them revolving around her in some way. An earthquake, at least an eight on the Richter scale, shook him from the inside out. His fingers curled as he visualized them around her neck—

"I'm sorry," she said, her sudden smile a mixed package of sorry and entreaty, "but I've thought this through. This is the best way."

"Why can't you trust us to do our job?" he burst out.

"I do trust you." She looked down, one hand tracing a pattern in the lacy tablecloth. After a long moment, she looked up, her gaze slamming into his. "It's you who can't trust, Mickey. I may not see the world the way you do, but that doesn't make me an idiot. Or wrong. Will you, can you, trust me?"

Mickey stared at her, his thoughts churning with protests, with defenses, with reasons why he couldn't...

Except for one small thing. He did. He did trust her. It was insane. It was madness. But looking at her, looking into her calm and steady gaze, he found he did trust her. Of course, it was far worse than that. Like a wave breaking over his bachelor head, he realized that the reason he trusted her was because the worst had happened.

He loved her.

He'd done the unthinkable. He'd fallen for a Seymour woman.

He looked away, took a steadying breath and sat back down, more worried about Luci and Delaney finding out his awful secret than about being right.

"Sure. Fine." What did it matter anyway? If she got him killed, it would be a mercy. "I'm in."

He felt Delaney looking at him as he, too, sat down. Mickey kept his gaze fixed on the tablecloth and after a pause heard him say, "Okay. I'm in, too." The chair creaked a protest, then subsided. "What's the plan? What do you want us to do?"

MICKEY HAD THOUGHT the Seymour house was quiet before, but he discovered it was worse without the old ladies. It had lost its heart and its soul. It didn't help that Louise glared at him and ran her fingernail down her chalkboard every time she saw him. And the seconds of the old grandfather clocked ticked away the time like a Chinese water torture. It was a day with too much time to reflect on the insanity of his promise to trust Luci's plan and his feelings for her, neither of which inspired hope, joy or optimism. That she'd also extracted a promise to keep their bargain from Pryce also upped the temperature in his personal hell. Mickey felt singed after a short session with his captain.

Delaney looked as shaken when their captain's gimlet gaze had lighted on him, but he had also stood firm, then sought out Gracie to cool off. He was sitting in the corner with her, the heat of his passion and her cooling draft almost creating their own weather system.

At least Delaney knew where he stood with his lady. The only thing that kept him from assuming the coyote position in front of Luci was his dissipating pride and the fact that he still couldn't bend from his night in the chair. Besides, what girl wanted to be proposed to by a guy with a sleep crevasse running like a scar from hair to chin line?

Luci sighed as Mickey paced by her for the hundredth time in a quarter hour. If he kept up the pace he'd be through to China before it was time to go. Maybe she shouldn't have told him about the note until closer to the hour. Though it seemed like more was bothering him than the Plan. He kept throwing brooding glances her way, like a sleep-creased Heathcliff. What was going on inside his cute head?

She felt like her brain was playing ping-pong. There were too many things to think about. Pryce, her aunts, Mickey, Delaney and Gracie, and, of course, her Plan. If it didn't work and she survived, Mickey would never let her hear the end of it. It seemed that coming here and discovering her past had triggered more than her capacity to pace. She didn't know she had pride until it was on the line. The grandfather clock announced the noon hour, making her jump. Too many more hours. Would it work? She jumped up, but Mickey was using all available pacing space, so she slipped out and found an empty room. She was still there, pacing its ancient and rather ugly rug, when Gracie drifted in.

"The house seems so empty without them," she said,

surrounding Luci in a layer of cool as she settled onto a nearby couch. "Do you think they are all right?"

"He has to keep them alive until the meeting, but I'll bet he's feeling the strain. I just hope he can keep it together."

"He's spent time with them," Gracie pointed out. "Surely he has some immunity."

"But how much? From what I can tell, he mostly came and went. Now he's doing serious time in the Seymour Zone."

Gracie chuckled. "I wondered why you weren't worried about how long it would take. Trying to soften him first, I see." She hesitated, then added, "I thought that maybe..."

Luci looked up in surprise. "What?"

"Well, he does seem to want you dead. Doesn't that worry you?"

Luci shrugged. "Why should I worry with you here to put death into perspective for me?"

"Don't!" Gracie's cohesion wavered like a rock dropped into a pool. "Don't let someone take your life without a fight!"

It was, Luci realized, so much easier when you didn't care. When people didn't have the power to touch your heart, to delight or hurt you. Maybe that was the secret, the true curse of the Seymours: this inability to feel anything deeply, the failure to live fully. Life, she was only now beginning to realize, was meant to be lived courageously, to be faced bravely. There was no virtue in merely surviving and even less virtue in spending your life observing the ones who were living. In being so afraid, you never got started with life.

The Seymour Zone was a dead zone and she was moving out.

If Maxwell did succeed in killing her at least she'd know she went out having lived more in the last few days than in her whole life. She just hoped Maxwell wasn't counting his chickens before they hatched. The Seymours may not be great at living, but when they put their minds to it, things happened. Amazing things. Scary things. And when five Seymour women put their minds to something, look out.

ARTIE HAD a twitch in his right eye. He hadn't always had a twitch. This was the first time it had happened to him. He wasn't sure when it started, but he did know it wasn't long after he grabbed the old ladies. He knew they were kind of loony, but this was beyond loony. If he didn't need them to get the money, he'd have held a pillow over their faces just to shut them up.

Listening to them was like the damn chalk on Louise's blackboard, only without the pauses. Their voices rose, they fell, they blended. One sister would start a sentence, another would pick it up and the last would finish it, then start a new one. Their ideas flowed together and away, shifting from one thing to another with no rhyme or reason for the change.

It was a torturous form of insanity. If he hadn't had Helen, the idea of Helen to cling to, he'd have popped them all, then put the gun to his own head.

Maybe he should just pop them? Once she was there, what could they do? She'd hand over the money hoping the old broads were all right. And then he'd pop her because she was sure to recognize him. Then all he had to do was take the money and head home.

Home. Closest he'd had to a home was his cell in stir. Been his most permanent address until Helen. He'd even hung a few pictures and bought a plant to brighten their cell. Course Reggie'd watered the life out of it. Guy was poison. A loser with a capital "L." But in a nice way. If he hadn't threatened to tell Helen...

It was his first kill. Munn was easier. He'd heard it was that way. First blood was always hardest. He didn't expect Luci to be hard. Or the old ladies. He checked his chamber. Six bullets. Two to spare.

Through the closed door he could hear their voices, still rising and falling without a break. His eye twitched so much he could hardly see to unlock the door. It swung open. Three round buns atop three tiny faces swiveled away as they turned to look at him. Finally, mercifully they fell silent.

He could have cried with relief. All he had to do to keep it quiet was pull the trigger three times.

23

The clock hit half after ten o'clock when Dante held the door open for Cloris, then slid into the black limo after her. She sat in the corner, clutching her purse like it was a life line. Her face was in shadow, but she'd been quiet and jumpy all day. He felt a little bad about deceiving her, but she'd have to understand. He was just trying to protect her. And get his money back.

Abel was at the wheel, Cain riding shotgun as they pulled into the desultory flow of traffic. On the main drag it was still busy, more so on the freeway. New Orleans never completely went to sleep and good thing, too, since he did most of his business after dark. When they got to the cemetery the gates were ajar, as if they were expected. Dante smiled. This was going to be so easy—

Something cold pressed against his temple as the car passed between the gates. Something like a...gun?

"What the— " he began.

"Did you think I didn't know what you were planning?" Cloris said, not sounding like herself at all.

He mouthed a string of swear words, while taking care not to move. There was nothing unsteady about the way she held the weapon. Abel wouldn't lower the window between them until they got to the rendezvous point, so he'd have to talk her out of this himself.

"He's not worth it, Cloris." He turned his eyeballs her way, trying to pierce the darkness to gauge her attitude. No sign of tears, plenty of grim determination. Damn.

"You think I don't know that? I raised you. Remember? Who taught you to run numbers? How to shoot straight? Wasn't your working mama. I was your stay-at-home aunt."

"Oh, yeah." He had forgotten, but now he was remembering a lot of things. "So what are you going to do?"

"I'm going to take care of him myself. And to make sure you and your boys stay out of it," she said as he felt something land in his lap, "put these on."

Remaining still, Dante felt around, then held up something metal and cold.

"What the hell?" He had to look at her, even if she shot him between the eyes. "Where you been shopping?"

Headlights flashed in the darkness. The window between the front and back rolled down. Cain turned to speak and found himself nose to nose with a gun.

With an efficiency that did him proud and made him want to kill her, Cloris disarmed them, tossing their guns and the car keys into the dark grass. Then she wove the bondage handcuffs, with its long chain and multiple bracelets, through the steering wheel, around the open window frames and the men, leaving them thoroughly trussed to the car and each other.

"Don't do this, Cloris," he warned her. "I make a bad enemy."

"Put a sock in it, young man," she told him, then reached in and flashed the headlights at the car that had flashed them. "I can still whup your ass and don't you forget it!"

The car pulled alongside and a door opened. When the overhead light came on he saw— double...no, triple...no, quadruple?—before the door closed Cloris inside and pulled away.

"What the—? Hey! Come back! Damn! Did you have to leave the window down?" He slapped at the mosquito. Then another. Then he just flailed as every mosquito in a mile radius scented fresh blood and buzzed in for the feast.

FOLLOWING the instructions in the latest note from Maxwell, Luci took a circuitous route to City Park and the so-called Dueling Oaks, where the exchange of aunts-for-dollars was supposed to take place. She'd studied the map long enough to know he was trying to confuse her with all the twists and turns, discounting the fact that twists and turns de-confused a Seymour. A more direct route would have left her feeling hopelessly lost.

Is there such a word as de-confused? She drove past Storyland Playland, then turned right on Victory Drive. Not in the real world, but in the Seymour Zone, no question, she decided.

There were streetlights, but not close together, so she was glad that the headlights of Delaney's car cut two tunnels of light into a road lined with moss-draped oaks. As directed, she stopped the car where it intersected the circular road that ran in front of the art museum and killed the motor, but not the headlights.

It was a cheerful, friendly spot in daylight, but the night left deep, sinister shadows where accomplices, or even the ghosts of fallen duelists, could lie in wait.

One thing for sure, she was feeling alive right now. Almost too alive for comfort. Like Data on his first outing with his emotion chip. Or Spock when he got zapped by the joy flower. On the upside, her senses were stretched out and at full alert, sorting through the night sounds like a high-octane computer.

"He's late," she murmured, noting the time.

"He's probably watching to make sure you're alone," Mickey's voice was soft, but full of reassurance to her ears.

"Good thing you guys have friends in black," she said.

"There's a car directly across from you, Luci." This from Delaney.

As if it had heard him, its headlights came on, nearly

blinding her. She put a hand up to shield her eyes, opened the door and scrambled out, her footsteps sounding loud in the silence as she stepped on gravel.

A door creaked on the other car, illuminating the interior too fast for her to count heads or even see heads. He was too far away. Someone got out and stepped up to the edge of the headlights.

"You got my money?" Arthur Maxwell called.

"You got my aunts?" she countered, careful to stay out of the light, too.

MICKEY, dressed in the latest in SWAT gear, lifted his night vision goggles and peered around the tree trunk he was using for cover. Luci was a shadowy figure on the other side of Delaney's car. Across from her he could see the headlights of Maxwell's car, but he was lost in the shadow behind the light.

"Can you see the old ladies yet?" he whispered into his mike.

"Not yet. Had to take off the goggles because of the light."

Mickey stepped back into cover and put his goggles back on, scanning the shadows. Something, a flicker of movement, caught his eye, but when he looked that direction, there was nothing. "We the only ones out here?"

"That was the deal," Delaney said. "Why?"

"Guess I saw a cat or something moving."

"Let's try to keep our focus on the human predator? Captain's gonna fry our asses if we blow this."

Mickey gave a soft snort. "He's gonna fry us anyway. We should have told him—"

"Too late now."

"Could you two shut up?" Luci's voice was soft and insistent. "I'm trying to hear what the bozo is saying." Then like stereo, he heard her in the earpiece and for real call out, "I'm not showing you a single bill until I see my aunts are all right!"

"Okay, okay." Maxwell sounded grumpy and frustrated, like someone whose nerves had been stretched raw by too much time in the Seymour Zone. Mickey grinned. Luci had called it right. He was almost at the end of his tether. "Get in the car and drive toward me. I'll drive toward you. Stop at Dreyfous."

Luci got in the car. Just before she fired the engine, Mickey heard her murmur, "I was hoping you'd do that…"

Then the whine of the engine drowned her out. Mickey frowned. She had told them everything, hadn't she? Of course she had. She'd said he could trust her. Trust involved full disclosure.

He realized she was driving away from him and pulled down his goggles. Keeping low, he followed. He didn't have to cross the road. Maybe that's what Luci had meant. That's it. Had to be. And the twitch between his shoulder blades was just…a twitch.

LUCI STOPPED the car when only the width of the side road separated her car from Maxwell's. She shut off the motor, then her headlights, when he shut off his.

He got out.

She got out.

"Give me the money," he snarled, the white of his eyes showing all around the irises, even in the half-light from the streetlight.

"Give me my aunts."

"Happy to." His gave a twitchy grimace, then turned and yanked open the rear door of the car. "Get outta the car."

Luci heard a familiar and most welcome twittering precede the first aunt's egress. The twitch got worse when she extended a hand for assistance. She noticed, trying not to grin, that he helped her. He growled while he did it, but he helped them all out.

Miss Hermi caught sight of Luci. "Dear little Luci, Reggie kidnapped us! Can you imagine?"

Miss Weena just wriggled her excitement and pleasure, while Miss Theo gave the fake Reggie a glare that had him shuffling his feet until he remembered he had the gun.

"Just stop it!" He turned to Luci, his shoulder and his eye twitching. "They're fine. Now show me the money!"

"How do I know you won't kill us as soon as you have it?" Luci asked.

"You don't!" he snarled, then had to wipe a bit of foam from his chin.

"An honest, if intimidating response." Well, faint heart never won anything. She lifted the whistle she'd hung around her neck and blew it hard.

The sound blasted through the microphone with painful intensity. Mickey cursed and pulled it out of his ear.

Delaney did, too. He knew, because he heard a tiny cursing from the dangling piece.

Artie cursed, jumped and looked wildly around. "What are you doing?"

Luci looked surprised. "Summoning your money."

"It ain't in the car?"

Luci tapped her temple. "Think about it for a minute—"

Her words were lost in the roar of a truck. It almost, Mickey thought with awe, sounded like a...dump truck. Red taillights appeared in the dark tunnel of Dreyfous Drive. The roar got louder and the lights moved closer and closer until Mickey could see that it was indeed a dump truck.

Luci stepped toward it, using the whistle and her hands to guide it toward them.

"Who's...driving?" Then he realized he was missing his cue. He shoved the ear piece back in. He almost had to shout to be heard over the roar. "He's distracted, Delaney. Can you get the old ladies?"

"Yeah, sure." He sounded as dazed as Mickey felt.

Mickey crouched and moved around to the back of the car Luci had been driving. He could see Maxwell shouting something. Luci indicated she couldn't hear him, then gave a final, long blast of the whistle. He saw Delaney reach the old ladies, but none of them seemed able to move as the rear of the truck began to tilt up.

24

Maxwell jumped forward and grabbed Luci, shoving the gun into her side as the contents of the truck rushed toward the point of no return.

"Nobody move!" he shouted, but what was in the truck wasn't listening or intimidated by his firepower.

Mickey had only time to curse himself before the contents shifted, then rushed out of the swinging gate and over the top. "What...?"

Bills. Dollar bills. Hundreds of thousands of them. All of Artie's ill-gotten gains roared toward him like the wrath of God. One minute he was shouting at Luci, then they were gone.

It seemed to take forever for the bills to stop coming, but as soon as it slowed, Mickey and Delaney leaped on the pile and began digging. Mickey saw a hand pop out of the mass. A woman's hand. He had crawled forward and started to grab it when the bills under him shifted, then Maxwell erupted from the mass, knocking him onto his back.

He still had the gun, pointed it right at Mickey and started to pull the trigger. Mickey heard Delaney yell, saw Maxwell turn toward him. Mickey knew he yelled "No!" but he didn't hear it, just felt it erupt from his mouth as the gun flashed once, then again. He saw Delaney drop out of sight and the gun swivel back toward him, but before he could fire again, a new voice spoke out of the dark.

"How many people are you going to kill Maxwell?"

Mickey saw Maxwell falter and started to move, but Maxwell snarled at him, "Don't move! I'll shoot." With his free hand, he rubbed the sweat from his face. "Who's there?"

"You know who it is, Maxwell, or whatever your real name is." Mickey saw a woman, also dressed in SWAT gear, step into the light. He heard the creak of the dump truck door and another figure climbing down from the cab. And other figures, all in black, moving into a circle around them.

"H-Helen?" Artie swallowed, the sound loud and dry in the silence. "What-what are you doing here?"

"Well, if the wanted poster the police sent hadn't done it, the phone call from Luci would have. Do you have shit for brains?"

"W-What do you mean?"

"Did you really think I wouldn't find out about your other wives?"

Maxwell staggered off the money pile, pulling Luci with him, pointed the gun at Mickey and snarled, "Get back, cop!" Then he faced Helen. "Love bear, honey, they meant nothing to me— "

"Nothing?" One of the dark, waiting figures stepped forward.

"C-Cloris?" He tugged at his collar. "Is...Dante with you?"

"What, you think I can't deal with a little weasel like you all by myself?" Cloris demanded. She looked at Luci. "By the way, thanks for those handcuffs."

"Handcuffs?" Mickey looked at Luci. If he hadn't been frantic with worry about Delaney, he'd be laughing at the way Maxwell cowered in front of the two women.

"I got them in this little bondage shop in the Quarter," Luci said.

"Shut up!" Maxwell's whole body was twitching now. "Everyone just shut up. I need to think."

"You've only got four bullets left," Luci pointed out.

"Well, I can just beat the old ladies to death," he snarled back at her. "Can finish you," he said, pointing the gun at Cloris, "the cop and you." He gave a Luci a shake. "And still have one left over."

"But that doesn't take into account the others," Luci said.

"Others?"

Mickey sensed Maxwell's will faltering and tensed.

"All those wives you left. They're not happy with you."

More dark figures moved in like Heralds of Doom. Maxwell couldn't keep them all covered. There had to be, Mickey looked around amazed, at least twenty of them. They pushed past him. He tried to back up, but they were behind him, too. He let go of Luci.

"I'll shoot!"

"Go ahead, Arthur. Use up more bullets," Helen said. "You can't escape the judgment of the stars."

The circle closed in, hiding him from sight. He could hear Maxwell's howls of pain as he and Luci scrambled over the pile of money to where Delaney lay, surrounded by aunts.

Miss Hermi cradled his head in her lap while Miss Weena ripped lengths of what looked like her petticoat into pieces. Miss Theo had her hands pressed against his wound, pressing with all her fragile strength. She looked up.

"Hurry."

Mickey tossed Luci his cell phone. "Dial 911. Tell them we have an officer down."

He dropped to his knees and added his hands and strength to Miss Theo's trying to stem the tide of red flowing onto the ground. He looked at Luci kneeling beside him, then nodded toward the circle of ladies. It was quieter now. Just some moans from the center of the mob. "What was that all about?"

"Old men for counsel, pissed off women for war."

"What?"

Luci shrugged. "It's a quote I heard somewhere."

Mickey looked at the now silent women. "Sounds more like a prophecy."

In the distance, they heard the wail of the ambulance siren.

"Hang on, buddy. Hang on."

THE AREA in front of the museum looked like a police parking lot. Or a K-mart blue light frenzy, Luci decided. Someone had taken the aunts home. The wives had been divvied up between cops and were giving statements. Those not taking statements were shoveling dollar bills into boxes. The ambulance carrying Delaney had pulled out some time ago, but Mickey hadn't moved from the spot where it had been. She'd urged him to ride with him, but the attendants had closed the doors and sped away, as if they knew his time was running out.

Another ambulance had arrived and left carrying a bruised, bloodied and bowed Arthur Maxwell. Two cops and a multitude of dirty looks had accompanied him. Luci suspected he'd pick up a few more bruises on the trip.

Luci had retreated to the cab of the dump truck. It was quiet there, nothing to interrupt her guilt trip. So this was Life. This was living. This pain. This guilt that twisted her insides, ripping and tearing in its rampage. She'd planned for injury to self but not to Delaney, who she'd blackmailed into following her plan. Delaney, who'd been trying to save her life.

It was so unfair! So bloody unfair!

The air around her was thick from heat and humidity and her chest hurt with the effort of breathing, only she was cold, too. Shuddering with it. She wrapped her arms around her middle, but it didn't help. The chill burrowed deeper, turning over more and more furrows of pain and guilt. Something wet splashed on her hands and she realized she was crying.

She wasn't very good at it, so it hurt, like someone was stabbing her in the chest. She wanted to go to Mickey. Be held by him, but he hated her. Hated her for what she'd done. For her wonderful plan. She wanted her father, but he probably hated her, too. Then she saw him getting out of a car, his face grim and cut with deep lines. Mickey started toward him, "the" question on his face. When Pryce shook his head, Mickey reeled back, then turned and stalked into the dark.

Tears blurred the rest. Luci sagged back. "If this is living, let me die now, God," she whispered, "Let it be me instead of Delaney. I'm useless. No good to anyone."

But God didn't strike her down. He probably figured it was more punishment to let her live, she thought dully.

"Luci?"

Luci opened her eyes, saw the blurred figure of her

father standing there. She rubbed her eyes clear. "I'm so sorry. I'm so..."

"Oh baby..." It seemed like a miracle when he opened his arms to her. She slid in and his arms closed her in. He was warm and strong and for the first time in her life she felt safe.

"Oh, Daddy, do you think he'll ever forgive me?"

He patted her back. It was amazing. A dad pat. A real, honest-to-goodness dad pat. It was better than chocolate and almost better than Mickey's kisses.

"I think you'll find that men in love will forgive almost anything, baby." His voice got so low, she almost didn't hear him add, "Almost...anything."

25

Luci found the days both too short and too long, but the nights were pure hell. She'd close her eyes and see Delaney fall. See Mickey's face as he turned and walked out of her life. It seemed a heavy price to pay for setting her face against family tradition. The only bright spot was her dad, and her aunts seemed determined to mess that up. He'd show up at the door and they'd circle her like wagons until she finally put her foot down.

"What is with you? Do you think I don't know he's my father? Because I do! And I'd like to spend some time with him!"

They looked at her with pale sad eyes and heaved heart-wrenching sighs. Since her heart was wrenched because of Delaney, it wasn't too pleasant.

"Don't you like him? What?"

Miss Weena and Miss Hermi nudged Miss Theo who cleared her throat, hemmed and hawed a bit and finally said, "We don't want to lose you again, dear girl."

Luci sank onto the stairs and looked at them in shock. "That's what this is all about?" They bobbed their buns. "But...why would you lose me?"

"He seems to get what he wants," Miss Weena muttered. "Even when he shouldn't."

"He didn't get Lila," Luci pointed out, "and he didn't even know about me."

"He did get Lila or there wouldn't have been a you," Miss Hermi said with a blush. "And she's afraid he'd get her again or she wouldn't have moved to California and taken you away from us."

"Oh, my dears," Luci said, trying not to laugh, "don't you get it? I'm more likely to stay if my dad and I are friends. You should be encouraging him, not discouraging him. If anything takes me away, it'll be my responsibilities back in Butt Had."

"I don't think anyone should live in a place called Butt Had," Miss Hermi said. "It sounds like an insult."

"Why don't you invite your father over for dinner?" Miss Theo suggested. She'd always been a fast study.

MICKEY'S WORLD didn't come to an end the night Delaney died, but it did slow to a crawl through a dark tunnel that seemed like it would never end. He went to work. He put on his dress blues and went to his funeral. Through a fog of guilt, he saw Luci look at him, but he couldn't make himself walk to her, so he turned and walked away again.

It wasn't her fault Delaney was dead. He wanted to tell her that, but then he'd have to admit whose fault it really was. His. Only his. He let himself get distracted and a good man, his best friend in the world, was dead. Gone.

It wasn't real.

It was too real.

He couldn't deal with it, so he dealt with it by getting busy and moving so fast he didn't have time to think or feel. But he couldn't move fast enough to get away from Eddie's wedding.

He stood next to him holding the ring while Miss Weena strewed her rose petals for the bride in a puce dress he couldn't have described later if his life depended on it. He shook Eddie's hand and kissed the bride's lifeless cheek, then followed them out into the bright, hot sun. He blinked, like a mole emerging after a long winter and felt the first flicker of warmth in his body, a twinge like blood returning to a limb that had been asleep. It hurt. But it was better than being numb.

Almost relieved, he pelted Eddie with rice, then stood there, feeling the sun warm his face as the crowd fanned out for cars and the drive to the reception at the Seymour House. After the reception, Eddie and Unabelle were heading over to Mississippi and the gambling boats. She'd promised not to bet on the Saints anymore if he'd teach her to play poker.

He felt Luci watching him and turned to her.

She looked beautiful and so...sad. He'd never seen her that sad.

He cleared his throat, felt the bitter regret slough away. "It wasn't your fault."

Tears started in her eyes. She drew a shaky breath and said, "It wasn't your fault either."

"Yeah, well—"

She touched him, stopping his breath and starting his heart pounding. "Delaney doesn't blame you."

"Right." Like he didn't know that. Delaney wasn't feeling anything anymore. He rubbed his face. "You going to the reception?"

"Are you?"

"I guess." He sighed. "I'll need to look in. For a few minutes. Still not in a party mood, but want to see Eddie in the gazebo." He managed a grin and held out his hand. "Go with me?"

Luci smiled and he realized just how much he'd missed her. Her smile. Her insanity. Her... essence. His other half. The crazy part.

Like him, she still bore the bruising of Delaney's death. There were new lines around her eyes and mouth. But beyond that, there was something different about her. Something vivid. As if she'd waked from a long sleep, too.

She took his hand and they turned together.

"I'm sorry," he said.

"I know." She squeezed his hand and he knew it was going to be all right.

They didn't talk on the drive, but he noticed Luci kept biting back a smile, as if she had a secret.

"What?" he asked as he helped her out of the car. Her dress, virginal white and more bride-like than Unabelle's, fell around her calves like foamy waves against a beach. Like a phoenix from the ashes of his grief, he felt love rise up and almost choke him. He wanted to grab her, tell he loved her, make her stay and not ever leave him, but it wasn't his decision to make. She had to choose to abandon family tradition, take that step into the unknown. He had no idea if she could or even would.

She shook her head, like she'd heard his thoughts, and his heart plunged in his chest until she said, "Wait until we get inside. Then you'll see."

"See what?"

But she just shook her head again and pulled him up the walk. Inside he could hear the Hepplewhites bawdy intro.

"Oh, no. Not beefcake. Not today."

"Trust me," she said, taking the resistance out of his sails. "Just...trust me."

Her fingers meshed with his. A perfect fit. Did she realize it? Her eyes glowed a yes, but how good was he at reading her eyes? He let her pull him up the steps and in the door.

It was a madhouse inside. Wall-to-wall important people. Mickey almost recoiled. There was a surge and counter-surge in progress. The women were trying to get into the drawing room to see the Hepplewhites, while the men were trying to get out before they saw the Hepple-whites. Laughing, Luci pulled him between the two forces until they got to the stairs. Like a child, Luci sank down and peered through the banister.

"Look."

Mickey sat down below her and saw Miss Weena at the front of a bunny hop line that extended back into the dining room.

"What?" He wanted to get her alone, not watch Miss Weena shake her aging booty.

"Wait for it." Her hand gripped his, as if he might fall if she let go.

Miss Weena led her line toward the drawing room, her fluting voice coming in tiny pants over the noise. "Much nicer when it's not frozen..."

"Well, I'm glad I didn't miss that—" he began. Then he saw it. Or rather, saw him. Them. Felt a cold chill run around the over-heated room.

Gracie.

And Delaney.

At the end of Miss Weena's line.

Luci's hand gripping his kept him grounded while his thoughts spun off-center. How could it be? For a long moment, he wondered if he was having a heart attack, but his vision cleared when Delaney gave him that old, familiar, shit-eating grin and called out, "Not cracking up on me, are you?"

Then he and Gracie broke free from the line and he spun her in a circle, both of them laughing as they rose out of the crowd and up through the ceiling. Mickey wanted to call him back. As if he had, Delaney's head reappeared. "We'll talk later, bubba. You got some business to take care of."

Then he was gone. But not gone. It took him three tries before he managed, "Did anyone else...see..."

"No, that was just for us." Luci sighed. "They're both so happy, Mickey. Gracie keeps talking about the 'little life.' And every night they sneak over to Boudreaux's to watch the romance channel and smell popcorn."

"Why...why didn't you tell me?"

"I didn't think you'd believe me. Or even talk to me." She seemed too interested in the carvings on the banister. "And we don't have a phone..."

"I'm sorry," Mickey said again.

Her smile lit up his heart as she slid across the stairs and leaned against the wall, stretching her legs out with a sigh. "I know it's not the same, but it's something, isn't it?"

Mickey slid up next to her. "Yeah, it's something. I don't

think he would have gotten over her. I've heard the Seymour women are hard to get over."

Luci felt her heart speed up, then try to crawl out her throat at the sheer pleasure of being smiled at by him. He'd been so distant for so long, she'd been sure he'd never come back. Now he was here, just inches away and she couldn't breathe from the look in his eyes. Everything around them slowed and got fuzzy around the edges, like an old romantic movie. The music wasn't quite right, but that didn't matter, because everything else was right. The guy. The moment. The smell of cake. It didn't get much better, she decided with a sigh.

"So, does this mean the Seymour women are making a new family tradition?"

"I don't know about the other Seymour women," Luci said, throwing her heart over this fence and hoping he'd catch it, "but this one intends to." Would he understand what she was trying to say?

He smiled and her toes curled up in her shoes. "I'm glad to hear it." He hesitated, then said, "Been thinking of making a few changes myself. Giving up the bachelor digs, maybe find something with room for two?"

"What a couple of cowards," Delaney said from above them.

They looked up to find Delaney and Gracie watching from the upper floor.

"I can see I'm going to have very little privacy from now on," Mickey said.

"Just tell her you love her and kiss the girl! An Affair to Remember is coming on in a few minutes," he urged. "Gracie wants to find out if she can still cry."

"This is the nineties, Delaney," Gracie pointed out. "Luci could ask him."

"Well, I hope someone does something..." he broke off as Mickey pulled Luci up and headed for the front door. "Where you going?"

Mickey looked back. "Outside! There's a magnolia tree that's perfect for a proposal."

"Mickey." Luci dug in her heels. "There's something I need to tell you before..."

"What?" She saw the dread form in his eyes.

"What I really do in Butt Had."

"Oh?"

"I'm not a waitress. Or a dancer. Or an actress."

"You're not?"

"Well, only sort of. You see, I own half of a Dud ranch."

"A...what?"

She grinned. "Was just making sure you were paying attention. Actually, it's a dude ranch, with all the 'e's' intact. As half-proprietor, I do all those things. And something else."

She was so serious, Mickey felt the first pang of fear. "What?"

"I'm the sheriff." She gave him a worried look. "I guess being a cop kind of runs in the family."

Mickey shook his head. "A sheriff?"

"I have a badge and gun and a uniform and everything. Except deputies. It's a small town."

"How are they managing without you?" Mickey linked hands with her and pulled her close.

"The highway patrol's covering for me.

"Well, they'll have to keep on covering for you after I get you under that tree." Mickey put his cheek against hers and inhaled as deep as his lungs would let him. "But if you can't give it up, I hear the NOPD is looking for a few good cops."

"It'll be something to do until the babies come," Luci whispered. "I figure if I'm gonna break tradition, I oughta go whole hog and just blow it outta the water."

"Ross!" he heard his Captain and Luci's father bellow.

They jumped apart.

"Dad!"

"Sir!"

"Going somewhere with my daughter, Ross?"

Mickey looked at her and smiled. "Just as far as the magnolia to propose."

Pryce looked at Luci. She beamed. "How do you feel about being a grandfather, Dad? Think you can handle it?"

He blinked a couple of times, then said, "Give it my best shot, baby."

He stepped back. Mickey opened the door for Luci to go through, but she stopped in her tracks like someone had shot her.

"Lila!"

Mickey had a feeling he should know that name.

"Lila!" Pryce went for his gun.

Lila. *Uh oh.* He grabbed Pryce's arm. "Getting strip-searched is a bitch, sir."

Pryce gave a low growl.

"I'd hate to have to visit you in prison, Daddy." Luci grabbed his other arm.

He gave a big sigh. "Oh, all right. She can live."

Lila, an older version of Luci, only with a softer jaw, stepped into the hall. "Pooh Bear? Is that you?"

As Mickey pulled Luci past her mother he looked back and saw Pryce straighten his tie, a dazed look replacing the murder in his eyes. He looked at Luci, who grinned, shrugged and said, "Where's that tree, Ross?"

THANKS FOR COMING ALONG on this slightly ridiculous, unexpectedly dangerous adventure.

When humor and mayhem collide, anything can happen — and that's half the fun.

One More Invitation

If you enjoyed the mix of **romance, suspense, and a healthy dose of humor,** you're exactly the kind of reader I love writing for.

I write stories where:

danger is real

attraction is inconvenient

and laughter sometimes sneaks in at the worst possible moment

If you'd like to step into another adventure, I'd love to invite you through one more door.

ANOTHER DOOR in Time

Not every adventure fits neatly into a category — and some of the most fun ones start when things go just a little sideways.

When you join my email list, you'll receive **Another Door in Time** — an exclusive short story created just for readers who enjoy action, adventure, romance... and the occasional surprise.

It's a complete standalone story.

It's not connected to this book.

And it's my way of saying thank you for reading.

Step through Another Door in Time here:

Get Another Door in Time

What to expect from me

I write action-packed adventures with romance at the heart of them — sometimes serious, sometimes playful, and always driven by characters who don't quit when things get complicated.

A final note

Thanks again for reading. I hope this story made you

smile — and I hope I'll see you again in another adventure.

If you enjoyed the humor in this story, you might also enjoy **The Spy Who Kissed Me**, another standalone romantic suspense with a playful twist.

The Spy Who Kissed Me

ALSO BY PAULINE BAIRD JONES

Romantic Suspense

Lonesome Lawmen Series:

The Last Enemy

Byte Me

Missing You

Lonesome Mama (Bonus short story)

(The *Lonesome Lawmen* is also available as a digital bundle)

Do Wah Diddy Die

The Spy Who Kissed Me

*Perilously Fun Fiction Bundle (*includes *The Spy Who Kissed Me* and *Do Wah Diddy Die.* Bonus: *Do Wah Diddy Delete Short Story Collection)*

Dangerous Dance

Dangerous Duet

Science Fiction Romance/Paranormal

Project Enterprise: The Cyborg Chronicles

Cyborg's Revenge: The Cyborg Chronicles Book 1

Cosmic Boom: The Cyborg Chronicles Book 2

CabeX: The Cyborg Chronicles Book 3

AzumC: The Cyborg Chronicles Book 4

MircoP: The Cyborg Chronicles Book 5

ScytheQ: The Cyborg Chronicles 6

OmnitronW: The Cyborg Chronicles 7

Open With Care (Christmas collection that includes, "Riding For Christmas" and "Up on the House Top"

Specters in the Storm: A paranormal/steampunk/science fiction romance novella

Out of Time Series:

Out of Time

Just in Time

Telling Time

Out of Time Series (Three Book Bundle)

An Uneasy Future

(A science fiction romance mystery series set in future New Orleans)

Core Punch (1.0)

Sucker Punch (2.0)

One Two Punch: An Uneasy Future Bundle

Short Story Collections

Project Enterprise: The Short Stories

Do Wah Diddy Delete

Let's Fall in Love

Take a Chance on Me

The Real Dragon and other short stories

Nonfiction

Guiding Lights: A Tribute to Earth's Lighthouses

Let's Get Lost in New Orleans (You'll Like It)

Penning Pulse-Pounders: A Spirited Guide to Writing Your Own Suspense Novel

The Author's Odyssey: Humorous & Real-world Insights from a 25-year Journey in Publishing

ABOUT THE AUTHOR

Award-winning author Pauline Baird Jones writes *perilously fun fiction*—from romantic suspense to space opera, time travel and more. With 40+ books, a flair for humor, and a love of adventure, she creates heroines braver than they realize and heroes brave enough to love them. If you crave thrilling plots, smart laughs, and happy endings, you're in the right place!

To find out more about Pauline or her books:
http://paulinebjones.com